Beautiful One

by

Mary Cope

Beautiful One

Cover Art by *The Wild Rose Press, Inc.*

The Wild Rose Press, Inc.
PO Box 708
Adams Basin, NY 14410-0708
Visit us at www.thewildrosepress.com

Publishing History
First Edition, 2023
Trade Paperback ISBN 978-1-5092-5175-9
Digital ISBN 978-1-5092-5176-6

Previously Published 2014 with Astraea Press
Published in the United States of America

I rushed out to the parking lot. Relief washed over me when I saw Aidan's truck still there. The windows were shut, so I stood on my tiptoes and peeked inside. I wasn't able to see anything and reached for the door. It was locked. My eyes scanned the parking lot. Finally, my eyes found his. He maneuvered his way through the cars. He was coming toward me with such a vengeance I wasn't sure what was going to happen. Within seconds I was trapped between Aidan and his truck.

Aidan narrowed his eyes at me and yelled, "What was that, Liz? I've been begging you… begging you to sing with me, and you sing with him? I am so mad at you!" He cursed under his breath, and, with a clenched fist, slammed his hand against his truck.

"I tried to step to the side, fearing for my safety, but with each step I took, Aidan closed the distance between us.

I stared into his furious eyes and finally was able to speak. "I had no idea that was going to happen. What else was I supposed to do?"

"I glanced down at his tendons bulging on his forearms. He bent down and brought his face to mine."

"Is there something going on with you two?" His penetrating eyes were fixed on mine. "Answer me." His tone was ominous as he placed his hands on my arms and began to squeeze.

Praise

"I loved this book. It took me back to my own high school experience, the characters were very real as were the scenarios. The main character was the ugly duckling that became a swan but was so humble and like able."

"There are themes of love and there were very clever insinuations of sexual situations which I actually felt were more impactful than heavily descriptive situations because it went with the innocence of the character."

Dedication

Chris and Sarah,
You two are my greatest accomplishment.
I love you, Mom

Chapter One

The faint sounds of a guitar drifted through the walls of my bathroom as I savored the last of the hot water before it became lukewarm. Stepping away from the spray, I turned the shower knob and watched the droplets trickle down the drain. Inhaling a deep breath my mind focused on one thing. *Aidan Mitchell.*

Hearing Mason's band practicing meant he would be here. I was ninety-nine percent sure Aidan wouldn't blow off their practice. He knew how serious my brother was about the band, but he also had been avoiding me for days.

The past week had been awful. I was determined to talk to him. All I wanted was a few answers. My emotions had run the gamut from confusion, frustration, regret, and sadness… sadness consumed me most of all, at night usually, and I was exhausted from it. But at this moment all I felt was anger. Anger was good. It was certainly better than pain.

As I rushed down the hallway, the floorboards creaked beneath my feet and the walls began to vibrate with the beat of Derek pounding on the drums. When I entered my room the music was deafening, but today I didn't mind. I untwisted the blue and white polka dot towel from my head and tossed it to the floor.

The deep conditioner I used helped my fingers glide through my long damp curls. If I was going to confront

Aidan, I wanted to look my best. No Frizzy Lizzie for me. That nickname, coupled with my big butt, had tormented me, growing up in a beach town surrounded by beautiful people. I had longed to look like a typical California girl: tall, blond, perfect. But, with dark hair and bordering on five feet three inches, that was never going to be me.

After I blow-dried and flat-ironed my hair, I took off my purple robe and draped it over my desk chair. I slipped on a pair of jeans... yes, slipped them on. I didn't have to tug, pull, or jiggle my butt to get in my pants anymore. When I easily pushed the button through the top of my jeans, it still made me smile. I couldn't even count how many times I had to lie on my bed and suck in my stomach so I could zip up a pair of pants. Every time I slipped them on, I never took it for granted. I had worked my butt off... literally. I put on my bra and a green sweater before I pulled on my boots.

I rushed downstairs to the door that led to the garage. Thinking about confronting Aidan and having to stare into those piercing blue eyes started to intimidate me. But this was my chance. I knew he was a few feet behind the door, and I needed to deal with him. Before I completely lost my nerve, I inhaled a deep breath and exhaled then pushed open the door.

The stream of sunlight coming in through the open garage door blinded me for a moment. With squinted eyes, I made a beeline to the old brown sofa in the corner. My heart was beating so fast it almost seemed in tempo with Derek pounding the drums. I scooted over our yellow Labrador, Maggie, and wedged myself between her and the arm of the couch. Finally, I looked up to focus my attention on Aidan.

He didn't show.

I sunk my head back into the cushions, exhaling a deep, long sigh, trying to rid the tension from my body. The guys were practicing their newest song. Indie Alternative was their style, and they called themselves Random Plan. I glanced at Mason and could tell he was angry. I mouthed the word "*Aidan?*"

Mason just shook his head.

"Derek!" The tone in my brother's voice made me sit up straight. "Derek!" Mason snapped again.

Finally, Derek stopped and silenced his cymbals.

"What?" He lifted the front of his black t-shirt to wipe the sweat from his forehead, exposing his six pack. His brown eyes bored into Mason's. "Hey! Just 'cuz you're ticked off at the pretty boy, don't take it out on me."

Derek reached back and grabbed a water from an old bookcase that held a few water bottles, electrical cords, an old CD player, and a collection of CDs. "Hey, Kyle, ya want one?"

Kyle nodded and Derek tossed one across the garage to where he stood behind the keyboard.

"Mason?"

"Yeah, I'll take one… Sorry, Derek."

Derek gave Mason a head nod and tossed him a bottle. He took a sip while Derek chugged his down.

"Okay, start again." Mason commanded. Derek picked up his sticks and began tapping.

I leaned my head back, closed my eyes and listened to the music. Funny, I'd come into the garage so fearless it almost made me laugh. Who would have thought the once overweight Elizabeth Ryan would stand up to the likes of Aidan Mitchell? I smiled to myself, allowing my mind to drift back to the time when I'd found it hard to even look at him…

I would think coming into a new school as a senior would be difficult but not for a good-looking guy like Aidan. Mason had already formed a friendship with Aidan. They'd met in history class and become fast friends after they discovered they each had a love for music. Soon after, they put together their band. Mason was the lead vocalist and played rhythm guitar. Aidan played the bass guitar and sang backup. Their band had generated a healthy buzz, and word spread quickly about them. The guys were pleasantly surprised when they'd auditioned for a local restaurant venue and were asked to return every other Sunday night to perform.

It was a few weeks into our senior year when I first set eyes on Aidan. I sat in the lunchroom during our morning break with my best friend, Melissa. It was hard not to notice him. He was surrounded by a bunch of girls desperate to get his attention. With his back toward us, at first all I could see was his blond, slicked- back hair. Eventually he turned around, causing a few golden strands to fall against his forehead. He swept the wisps away with one hand, calling attention to his blue eyes. He wore black jeans and a black and grey striped t-shirt that hugged his firm chest. Looking at his attractive face and toned body, I could understand why word about him traveled so quickly. I continued to stare, envious of the cute girls who circled him.

Melissa didn't even bother to turn around. She only had eyes for my brother, Mason. She and Mason were the *it* couple of the school, and they adored each other. Melissa was the typical beach girl: tall, long, blond hair, and beautiful blue eyes. I would have thought, with her beauty, she would be conceited, but she wasn't. Melissa was spunky and fun. She brought out the best in me and was loyal to the core. If anyone commented about my weight, Melissa was always there to defend me. If guys came on to her, and they did, she would put them in line. Basically, she didn't take anyone's crap.

My friend group dwindled to non-existent until Melissa came along. Girls would act like they were my best friend, but I would soon find out they were more interested in my brother than me. It was Mason who saw through the myriad of girls who would traipse through our front door. You would think I'd get a clue, but I was so desperate for friendship I was happy with the scraps they tossed me.

The funny thing was, I could see why girls used me. My brother was cute. Mason's deep green eyes were surrounded by thick, brown hair that was usually a multi directional mess. On top of that, he sang. Yep. The girls liked my brother. But Melissa, she loved me like no other friend ever had and never gave me reason to doubt her.

Aidan soon joined Mason and they headed our way. A few of the girls had left, but several decided to stick around. At that point, Melissa had heard Mason's voice and turned toward him just as he sat next to her.

"How's my pretty lady?" he crooned.

Melissa giggled, then Mason kissed her on the lips. A few girls gave her a dirty look.

Clearly jealous my brother was off the market, they then focused their attention toward Aidan, expanding his group from three to five. Aidan stood next to the table, flirting with a couple of beach beauties, and I continued to stare. Just about the time I thought to myself, *Look away, you idiot,* Aidan caught my eye. I felt myself blush and looked away. Turning my body toward Melissa, I was desperate to make conversation with her, but she and Mason were engaged in a big ol' make out kiss.

Needing a distraction from the blue of his eyes, I picked up my notebook and flipped through the pages. The next thing I knew, Aidan was standing next to me. My heart pounded. Thankfully half my fat body was hidden under the table.

"Ahem." Aidan cleared his throat.

When I looked up, his eyes were fixed on mine. I stifled a gasp when he gave me a crooked smile and leaned down to my ear.

"So, I finally get to meet Mason's twin. Elizabeth, right?"

The smoldering way he said my name sent a thrill down my spine. I felt my cheeks redden, then I corrected him with a barely audible, "Liz."

"Well, it's nice to meet you… Liz. I'm Aidan. He smiled and flicked his head to the side to remove a few stray hairs in his eyes. It didn't work. They just fell back where they were before.

That wasn't what I was expecting. He seemed kind of nice. I gathered my courage, looked up at Aidan, and answered, "Nice to meet you too."

He smiled at me and glanced at what I was eating. He returned his attention to one of the skinny girls and continued to flirt.

I looked down at my cinnamon roll, covered in frosting.

That was the day I decided I was done being the fat girl.

Chapter Two

The buzz of my alarm clock woke me for the second time. Glancing at the glowing red numbers, I felt a pang of unwelcome sympathy for myself. I curled my legs under me before I reached up and hit the snooze. The excuses came in waves... like they always did.

Why even get out of bed? Every time you've tried to lose weight you fail, you'll never do it. Just go back to sleep.

The moonlit sky shed faint light through my bedroom window. My arm stretched out from under my warm blanket and pushed the alarm button down before it could go off for a third time. The urge to roll over and go back to sleep was tempting, but I was either going to do this or not. Painfully aware time was ticking, I made my decision.

Pushing my blanket aside, I reached up and turned on my bedside lamp. When my eyes adjusted from the transition from dark to light, I surveyed the clothes that littered my carpet. My eyes zeroed in on grey sweatpants, and I pulled them on. Within seconds, my oversized sleep shirt was off and tossed on the bed. Rifling through my underwear drawer I grabbed my lime green sports bra and a pair of white socks. The newness of the bra caused a bit of difficulty when I stretched it over my head, securing my girls in place. I sat back down and pulled up my white socks. On my way into the closet

I grabbed my grey hoodie that was slung over my desk chair.

It wasn't hard to spot my bright pink sneakers. My mom had bought them for me a few months back hoping to motivate me, but, sad to say, they had never seen the light of day. The doorjamb of my closet gave me support while I toed each foot through a snug sneaker and loosely tied the laces.

Finally, I grabbed my cell phone and a hairband from the top of my white dresser. My fingers snagged through my thick, wavy hair and I bound it back into a ponytail. I walked past Mason's room down the stairs.

Maggie woke up from her overstuffed bed in the corner of the family room, wagged her tail, sniffed my sneakers, and started jumping around.

"Sit." I bent down and ran my hands the length of Maggie's soft fur. "Good girl." I gave her snout a succession of quick kisses before I clipped on her leash, and we headed out the front door.

****

Living on the coast was great, but the morning air was usually overcast and foggy. This morning was no different. I embraced the thick, moist air, allowing it to fill my lungs. I turned on my music, put in the earbuds, and walked toward the creek bed that led to the ocean. This was going to be my routine.

Maggie tugged on her leash, guiding me through our tree lined neighborhood. When we approached Mrs. Chapman's yellow house, I pulled Maggie back and made her sit. The pink and white rosebushes that lined the side fence needed to be trimmed, and the grass was overgrown, but the home was still as charming as ever. Bracing myself against a streetlamp, I stretched out my legs. My eyes focused on the *Sold* sign in the front yard.

The house had been vacant since she died. Those last few months of her life had been difficult for me, but I had wanted to be there for her, no matter how much the pain of losing someone hurt. Every free moment I had, I found myself at her bedside, looking into her wise, blue eyes that never seemed to lose their sparkle. When she was tired but still wanted my company, I would read to her, love stories usually, but her favorite was when I used to sing. I couldn't even count the number of times she'd made me sing her favorite song, "The Way We Were," from the movie that always made me cry.

When the end of her life had been near and she hadn't been able talk to me anymore, I sang her favorite song through tears of pain and said my final goodbye. A few days later, her hospice nurse told me she had passed, and I knew I would never sing that song again. I walked away, wiped a tear from my eye and wondered who had purchased the home that held such bittersweet memories for me. I hoped they would love it the way that I did.

The fog was beginning to lift as I rounded the dirt trail and headed toward the ocean. The warmth of the rising sun felt good against my back. Inhaling a deep breath, I surveyed the shimmering blue Pacific in the far-off distance. Dana Point, what a beautiful place to grow up and live, but finally, I made the decision… I wanted a life.

The music that blasted through my phone spurred me on, taking me from a stroll to a fast-paced walk and finally a light jog. After about thirty minutes, I was panting as much as Maggie and decided it was time to head back. "That's enough for today, girl. We'll go farther tomorrow." I gave Maggie a few face rubs, and we headed home.

When I opened the front door, I was immediately hit with the aroma of coffee brewing. That meant my mom was up. She would never admit it, but I knew Mom was embarrassed I was overweight. How could she not be? When my mom had been younger, she'd been striking. Even now, at forty-four, Mom still turned heads with her shoulder length light brown hair and hazel eyes.

There was no doubt my mother was proud of my brother and me. We did well in school, had impeccable manners, and both sang and played with the band at church. But the bottom line was I was heavy, and Mason was not. Mom had never had a weight problem, so she couldn't relate to me. I knew when she saw me sweaty in workout clothes, she'd be ecstatic.

My mom entered the kitchen and glanced down at my bright pink sneakers.

Wide eyed, her face lit up. "Morning, sweetie, where were you?"

"I went for a walk with Maggie." I took a long drink of my water.

Immediately, Mom started in, "Oh, sweetie, I think that's great! Are you trying to lose weight? How far did you walk?"

"I went up the creek bed for a bit."

"Well… you know you should start out slow. You don't want to overdo, because then you might not keep it up. Do you want me to make you some oatmeal? You should eat something to get your metabolism moving."

My mom was just trying to be nice. I knew she was excited for me and hopeful to say the least, but I was already tired, and my day had just started. All I wanted was to drink my water and get ready for school. I answered her with a simple "No thanks, Mom" and headed toward the stairs.

"Why do you have to be like that, Elizabeth? I'm just trying to be helpful."

The tone in my voice may have sounded disrespectful, but I didn't mean it. I guess I was having a hard time looking at my thin mother while I was sweating from the exercise I hated doing.

"I'm sorry, Mom. I just need to get ready for school."

My mom gave me a nod, and I climbed the stairs. Sometimes she could be so temperamental. Maybe it was a mother-daughter thing, who knows? I wished she could be more even-keeled like my dad. Not that I didn't love my mom any less, I just found it easier to relate to my dad. Perhaps because he struggled with weight too.

People always said how much my dad and I resembled each other. I always took it as a compliment because my dad was an attractive man, but other than our eye color being the same light shade of green, I didn't see it.

I hopped in the shower, checked the time, and was already out when I heard Mason's alarm clock ringing. Since Mason and I shared the bathroom, I was always first up, first in, and he followed behind. Mason and I each had our own cars, but because our school schedules both finished at lunch, we usually drove together.

My brother and I have always been close. I'm not sure if it was because it had been just the two of us growing up, or maybe it was a twin thing. But I knew he always had my back, and I loved him for it.

"I'll drive today, Liz," Mason yelled. A few minutes later he lightly knocked on my door and peeked his head in. Munching on a granola bar, he mumbled, "Ya ready?"

"Yep, let's go." I grabbed my green sweater from the closet and followed Mason out the door.

When we reached his black sedan, he clicked his automatic door locks, and I got inside. I had never asked Mason about Aidan. Now that I had seen him, I was so curious. I wanted information. I turned on the radio, and, when I settled back in my seat, I decided to start in on my quest to find out more about him.

"What's Aidan like?" I fixed my gaze out the side window and watched the scenery blur by.

"Aidan? He seems like a good guy. He's liked. Especially by the ladies." Mason smirked.

"Does he have any brothers or sisters?" I lowered the volume on the radio. "What about his parents? Have you met them?"

"I don't know. Usually we just talk about music. Why so many questions? You're starting to sound like Mom." Mason chuckled.

"I don't know… just curious I guess." I turned the radio back up and looked out the window. I realized Mason wasn't going to be much help. I guess I'd have to find out more about Aidan on my own.

****

On my way to first period, I found myself scanning the halls looking for Aidan. No luck, but I smiled when I saw Melissa fast approaching me.

"Hey, Liz." She paused, giving me that I-want-to-tell-you- something smile. "I know you hate when I bring this up, but Mason and I were talking about you last night. He wants you to sing with the guys' band. Mason said he doesn't want to bug you about it anymore, but you know me, I'm relentless." Melissa batted her big blue eyes at me.

"We've been over this so many times." I rolled my eyes. "Singing for a bunch of church kids is one thing... but getting up in front of a restaurant full of strangers — no way."

"You've got so much talent, I wish you'd just..." But before Melissa could continue to badger me, the bell rang.

"I hate to be late. I'll see you later." I took off running then my stomach growled. For a second, I wished I had eaten the oatmeal my mom had offered me.

Melissa laughed and yelled, "I'm not giving up, Liz!"

"You never do," I hollered back. I heard faint laughter as I entered my calculus class.

****

My day was pretty uneventful until I was walking to Mason's car. I noticed a few girls standing around a silver truck. Leaning against it, looking model-perfect, was Aidan. I rushed to the car and quickly got inside. Thankful for the tinted windows, I was able to stare across the parking lot and watch Aidan interact with his fan club. I couldn't hear what they were saying but one of the girls kept giggling and touching his arm. *Oh, brother.*

The other girl was desperately trying to get his attention. I was pretty sure she was out of luck. Aidan seemed set on the handsy one. The next thing I knew, Aidan gave Miss Touchy Feely a sexy smile and motioned for her to get into his truck. Left alone, the dejected girl walked away. I was surprised when Aidan walked over to her. He motioned to his truck, but the girl shook her head. Aidan shrugged his shoulders and smiled. The girl smiled back and waved before he hopped into his truck and started it up. I craned my neck to watch them as they left the parking lot. The last thing I saw was Aidan and his pretty passenger laughing when they drove away.

****

Each day blended into the next as I continued my workout routine. I was surprised I was starting to enjoy it. Sort of…

Feeling energized and slightly proud of myself for losing my first ten pounds so quickly, I decided to take Maggie out for a late afternoon run. When I rounded the corner, my mom was pulling into the driveway.

"Hey, Mom," I huffed.

"Hi, sweetie, perfect timing. Can you help me with the groceries?"

"Sure." I dropped Maggie's leash and grabbed a couple bags.

My mom pulled a couple of bags from the mall out from the back seat of her SUV. When she opened the front door, she yelled upstairs for Mason to come down and get the rest of the groceries. I heard him holler, "Okay." I placed the bags on the kitchen island and started to unload them.

When my mom entered the kitchen, she held a bag up from my favorite store. "I bought you a present, two actually." She grinned. My mom loved to shop. Not so much for herself, but if she had an occasion to shop for someone, she loved it. I guess I had become that occasion. "Well… come see!" My mother's eyes were bright with excitement.

I opened the bag and pulled out a teal chiffon top with a small keyhole opening in the front.

"Mom! Thank you, it's adorable." I held it up in front of me as Mason walked in juggling three bags of groceries.

"Good color, Liz," Mason said, placing the bags on the island.

"Mom picked it out." I smiled, glancing at the tag that had an *L* on it instead of an *XL*.

"This too, sweetie." Mom tossed me the small brown bag.

I pulled out what looked like a keychain with a pump attached to it. I read the tag because I had no idea what it was.

"Pepper spray?" I questioned. That got Mason's attention. He immediately came to my side and held out his hand so he could inspect the safety device. "Mom, what am I supposed to do with this?"

"Clip it to Maggie's leash... you never know."

"Cool... c'mere, Maggie."

Maggie came bounding over to Mason. She still had the leash attached to her neck, so Mason unhooked her and clipped the spray to it. He handed the leash back to me. "You're all set, Liz... for all those bad guys hangin' out in the bushes waiting to attack." Mason smiled at my mom, and then we both laughed.

"You two..." She smirked.

****

Melissa and I sat on the couch with Maggie snuggled between us. The crisp October breeze drifted through the open garage door with the scent of fall in the air. Mason was chatting with Kyle next to the keyboard. Kyle's brown eyes widened when he grasped what Mason was trying to get across to him. He started to tap the keys while Mason hummed along to their newest collaboration.

Kyle and Mason had been friends since grade school. He was kind of like a second brother to me. His family was over-the- top wealthy, but they never flaunted it. I think that's why I liked him so much. He was kindhearted and sweet, which made his average looks more attractive. Derek was the complete opposite of Kyle. Kyle's shoulder-length dark brown hair was such a contrast to Derek's spiky blond. Kind of like their personalities. Kyle was more of an introvert, like me, and Derek... he was as outgoing as Melissa.

Mason and Kyle continued to look over the pages of their spiral binder. Derek exhaled in boredom and then started to lightly tap on the drums, which surprised me. I couldn't believe he could lightly do anything, with Derek it was all or nothing.

Aidan had his cell phone out and was texting. When he finished, he slipped his phone in his front pocket and casually walked over to us. I felt the heat rise to my cheeks when he sat next to me on the arm of the couch. Maggie's head popped up. She glanced at Aidan and crawled over my body to get to him. We both laughed. Melissa chuckled and got up to go see Mason.

Aidan bent forward and stroked Maggie's soft face. "I love dogs," he murmured, then Maggie began to nuzzle into his touch.

"Do you have a dog?" Unable to make eye contact, I continued to pet Maggie's soft coat. Aidan didn't answer right away. I looked up at him waiting for a response.

"No. I always wanted one. But, my mom wasn't into it. She said it was too much work." He shrugged.

"Did you ever have any animals?" "Nope, we

moved around too much."

Aidan got up and glanced over his shoulder. The guys were getting back in their positions to play.

"That's sad," I whispered.

"Yeah, it sucked…" He gave me a brief smile and picked up his bass as the guys began to play.

****

Melissa and the guys were still in the garage. My fingers mindlessly glided across the keys of the piano in our living room. I had my own practicing to do, but I was glad I'd stayed in the garage for as long as I had. That was the longest conversation I'd ever had with Aidan. Even though I only said a few words. At least it was more than *Hi*.

I was lost in the sweet sounds of the piano while I belted out the last chorus of "Desert Song." When I finished, I opened my eyes to Aidan standing next to the piano. His gaze was so intense I felt butterflies in my stomach.

"Liz, your voice is incredible. Mason always said you could sing, but I had no idea you were so good. That was amazing. Seriously."

I couldn't help but blush when Aidan slid in next to me and his arm briefly touched mine sending a chill down my spine.

"Thanks, Aidan," I murmured.

"With your voice, you totally should sing with the band. It'd be awesome!"

"No, it's just not my thing." I began plinking the keys. Aidan grabbed my hand, his blue eyes focused on mine. "I'm serious. You're great. Why won't you think about it?"

His attention was so focused on me. It was like he

couldn't understand why I wouldn't jump at the chance.

I swallowed, trying to find my voice, and finally answered, "I'm busy at school with a bunch of AP classes, and I sing with the band at church. So, I don't have the time." There. That sounded convincing. There was no way I was going tell Aidan I was too scared to put myself out there. It was hard enough singing at church.

Aidan let go of my hand and shook his head in frustration. "What a waste, that's too bad." He rubbed his hands on his knees, cracked his knuckles, gave me a smirk, and began playing chopsticks. It made me giggle. Then he stopped tapping the keys and moved closer toward me, "I've been wanting to ask you something. I know you're smart and I suck at calculus. I'm having a hard time with the formulas, and my grades are starting to slip. Would you be willing to help me out? My dad would pay you… what do you think?"

My heads was spinning — *What do I think? I'm freakin' out. That's what I think!* I was able to hold it together enough to say, "Sure, I can do that."

"Okay, great. Let me have your number."

I rattled off my number, and Aidan programmed it in his phone.

He texted me the word *thanks*. A slow smile spread across his face, then he slid out from the piano bench and walked toward the front door. "I'll text you."

When the door closed, I sat there for a minute, staring at my cell phone then added him to my contact list.

Did that actually happen?

When realization set in, I jumped up from the piano bench and ran to the front window to make sure his truck was gone. Certain that he had left, I made my way to the door that led into the garage and peeked my head inside.

"Melissa... you're not gonna believe this!"

Chapter Three

Several days had passed since I gave Aidan my cell number. I kept picking up my phone, trying to will the text to come through. While shredding carrots on the third night of anxiously waiting, my cell phone vibrated from my back pocket. The air left my lungs when I saw his name flash across the small screen.

Aidan: *Hey Liz, Does twice a week work for you?*
Me: *Sure.*

Twice a week!

Aidan: *How about Mon & Thurs? I'll work it out so I'm off on those days.*
Me: *Sounds good. Where do you work?*

Aidan's Instagram wasn't set to private, so I had already stalked him. I knew where he worked, but he didn't know I knew that.

Aidan: *I'm a valet at a ritzy hotel.*
Me: *Do you like it?*
Aidan: *The tips are good. Does 8 work for you?*
Me: *Sure.* Aidan: *Ok, bye.*

The thought of Aidan coming over in a few days was

getting to me.

How am I going to tutor him? I can hardly look at him he's so cute. What was I thinking? Why did I say yes?

"Liz… Liz!"

I looked up from what I was doing and then back at the cutting board covered in carrots.

"That's more than enough," Mom said.

"Oops, sorry." I added half of the carrots to the salad and put the rest in a plastic bag.

My mom finished getting the meal on the table. Mason put out the plates while my dad grabbed the milk. I placed a small chicken breast on my plate, followed by a large portion of salad with low-cal dressing.

Mom glanced over my plate, "How much weight have you lost now, Liz?"

I rattled off, "Fifteen pounds."

Dad eyed me with a loving smile. "I'm proud of you, sweetie. Maybe I should join you," he said and patted his belly.

"Thanks, Dad." I giggled.

Mom chimed in with a grin, "It's almost time to go shopping again!"

"Oh, Mom."

When I sat down I noticed Mason wasn't being his usual, upbeat self. "Hey, Mase? Are you okay?" I whispered.

"Just tired." Mason pushed his food around his plate.

"I have some news." All eyes focused on me. "Umm, I got a job. Well, sort of." I took a sip of my water before I continued. "I'm going to tutor Aidan Mitchell."

Mason's head snapped my way, but he didn't say

anything. "He seems like a sweet boy." Mom seemed pleased with the idea.

"I don't know him that well," I confessed. *But I'm sure hoping to.* I felt myself smile at the thought.

Mason was quiet for a few minutes and then excused himself from the table.

****

Maggie and I began our walk at a brisk pace, spurred on by the fact it was Saturday, and I had lost another three pounds.

Weight loss today. Eighteen pounds! Yes!

I stood next to my usual streetlamp, braced myself, and began to stretch. When I saw a moving van in front of Mrs. Chapman's house, it tugged at my heart a little bit, but I was so curious I stopped stretching and walked down the street to get a better look. I strategically placed myself behind a large tree so I was able to observe my new neighbors without being seen.

The first thing that caught my eye was a baby grand piano. I had always wanted one. Playing the baby grand at church was awesome. My upright at home paled in comparison. They also unloaded a couple of electric guitars and a beautiful acoustic one. From what I could see, the furniture was nice too. Off to the side of the moving van were a few dirt bikes and a sleek black motorcycle. In the garage was a bunch of camping equipment, and a red jeep.

These people liked to have fun.

A couple of boys came bounding out of the front door, pushing each other, and laughing. An attractive older woman followed, her long dark hair was pulled up in a ponytail. I heard myself gasp when I watched what walked out of the door next. This guy was attractive…

seriously attractive. His shoulder-length hair was a deep brown tousled mess, but it worked for him, in a good way. I was too far away to make out his eye-color, but his body. *Yikes!* The form-fitted grey shirt he was wearing left nothing for the imagination. His sleeves were pushed up, and tattoos were peeking out on his left forearm. This guy was a hottie.

In stealth mode, I continued to watch the activity of my much-too-good-looking neighbor. I assumed these were his brothers and his mom. The boys started to roughhouse with their older brother, and it was obvious he adored them.

Maggie was starting to get antsy, so I began my jog to the creek bed. So unlike me, but determined to get a better look, I crossed the street and slowly jogged passed the house. We made eye contact. He flashed me a dimpled smile, and I smiled back. My heart rate picked up, as did my pace.

Light grey.

The most beautiful eye color I had ever seen.

****

Mason still seemed out of sorts while we drove to church for practice. I couldn't take his sullen demeanor another minute. "What's up, Mason? You haven't been yourself lately. Why won't you talk to me?" I could tell Mason was considering what he wanted to say.

Finally, he took a deep breath and told me what had been bothering him. "I think something's going on with Melissa and Aidan."

I felt sick to my stomach, then I choked out the words, "What? No way. Melissa would never cheat on you... never!"

Mason's neck tensed, and his profile became ridged

while he began to share the emotional rollercoaster he had been on for the past few weeks. "I thought she'd never cheat on me, but I don't know anymore. I haven't said anything to her. I feel like every girl falls at Aidan's feet. I just didn't think my girl would be one of them."

Speechless for a minute, my mind was racing. "What makes you think something's going on?"

We were stopped at a red light when Mason's sad, green eyes met mine. "It's little things I've noticed. Like the two of them at school walking around together. And at band practice, the way I see them looking at each other. Melissa and I have been together since freshman year. Maybe she's over it."

"No, Mason, I'm sure nothing's going on. Melissa loves you.

I think you're being paranoid."

We drove in silence the rest of the way to church. I could tell Mason was feeling overwhelmed when we pulled into the parking lot.

"Mason, you know Melissa. She isn't like that."

"Look, we're here, let's talk about this later." Mason grabbed his guitar and headed inside.

****

I was seated at the baby grand looking over my sheet music while Jake and Matt were chatting on the opposite side of the stage.

Jake had finished up a bag of chips, wiped his hands on his jeans, and picked up his bass. We always joked about how he could eat anything and not gain weight. He was on the gangly side and didn't compare to Matt in the looks' department. Jake was average- looking with his brown hair and eyes to match, but his fun personality easily brought him from a six to an eight.

Matt, our drummer, was more on the stocky side, not overweight, but if he didn't work out he could be. Matt had brown hair he usually shaved just because he didn't want to deal with it. His face was attractive with expressive blue eyes that made him a favorite with the college girls. A solid nine, easy.

The guys were always joking around and laughing. Today was no different, except Mason was just going through the motions. I knew he was still upset, but covered it with a fake smile. The guys didn't pick up on it, but I did.

After about twenty minutes, I noticed Lance's plump silhouette in the back of the church. He caught my eye and smiled at me as he moved from the shadows. The way his dark brown hair surrounded his round face and kind smile was heartwarming. Everyone adored Lance, but no one as much as we did, his team.

Lance approached the stage and stood silent for a few minutes. His dark brown eyes focused from me to the guys goofing around. When the guys saw Lance, they stopped their joking and gave him their full attention. The shift in the room was immediate, from light-hearted to tense. Lance made eye contact with each of us. Finally, he said the words we knew were coming but dreaded to hear.

"They've found my replacement."

Unable to control my emotions, my eyes pooled with tears.

The rest of the guys were stunned as they stared back at Lance.

Lance leaving us was no surprise. Seattle was his wife's hometown, and he had promised her eventually he'd take her back home. We all hated to see him go, but the right job had come up, and he couldn't pass it up. Knowing didn't make it any easier, but Lance was determined to take care of us until the bitter end. He'd said he wouldn't leave us until a replacement was found and now the time had come. To soften the blow, Lance went on to tell us what he knew about our new bandleader.

"You all know I wanted to lead our church in a new direction, bringing in a younger crowd. Well, I can see this guy being able to pull it off." Lance walked up the three steps to the stage and pulled up a chair. "Let me first say, he's a go-getter. He's twenty-one, attends UC Irvine, and has the enthusiasm and commitment to lead this church exactly where we want it to go. He was the lead singer at his former church, plays piano and guitar, and is familiar with everything from stage lighting to working the soundboard. There's something about him. Just wait until I introduce you. You'll see."

For the first time since Lance shared his news, a small smile crossed his face.

I wiped away a stray tear, then Mason blurted out, "So when do we get to meet him?"

"He has to take care of a few things. It'll be anywhere from six to eight weeks. I'm not starting in Seattle until after Christmas, so I'll be here until then. I just wanted you four to be the first to know."

Finally, I found my voice. "What's his name?" Lance answered with confidence. "Spencer Hayes."

****

Mason was silent on our walk to the car. "Can today get any worse?"

"Everything's gonna be okay. Lance seems excited about this guy. And whatever you think is going on with

Melissa and Aidan, I still think you're imagining it." *At least I hope so.* "I start tutoring Aidan Monday, I'll see if I can find out anything."

"Don't say a word!" Mason snapped. "Let me handle this.

Don't make me sorry I said anything to you."

"Okay, okay," I muttered. But I knew I wasn't letting it go. I was going to keep my eyes open until I figured this out.

****

The vibration of the blaring music was below us. Melissa and I laughed when we heard Mason yell at Derek. Even though Derek was a few years older than Mason, he could be so immature. Derek loved his drums. He always referred to them as *The Ultimate Chick Magnet.* More often than not, he'd get carried away during his drum riffs, and Mason would have to constantly reel him in so the tempo of the song wasn't lost.

I shook my head and finished flat-ironing my hair. "Poor Derek." I giggled.

Melissa and I were sharing the mirror, getting ready for their show. While I watched her apply her second coat of mascara, I thought about tonight. This was going to give me the perfect opportunity to watch Melissa and Aidan together. I was determined to see if Mason's fears were accurate.

"You should just leave your hair. I love your long curls. It looks so good when you just let it dry." Melissa put the mascara down and grabbed my pale pink lipstick.

"I know you like it…but, I don't know… I guess I still think of myself as Frizzy Lizzie."

"Let it go already. Your hair is awesome!" Melissa

smiled at me while gliding the sheer color across her full lips.

I pulled on a pair of my jeans.

"Lizzie!" Melissa squealed, "Your jeans are falling off you!" Melissa and I both stared at each other and she was grinning ear to ear. "That's it! It's time for a shopping spree!"

"Not yet, Melissa," I pleaded. "I want to lose a few more pounds."

I could tell Melissa was disappointed. She loved to shop. Like my mom did. But then again, if I resembled either of them, I'd like to shop, too.

"How about if we go for my eighteenth birthday? It's in a few weeks."

Melissa thought about what I said for a minute and then seemed pleased with the idea.

"Okay, but at least put a belt on. I'll go grab one from your mom."

Watching Melissa scurry out of my room, I couldn't help but feel a slight tinge of pain. If anything was going on with her and Aidan, it was going to devastate my brother and me.

****

The venue the guys played at was a restaurant off Pacific Coast Highway. It had an outside patio and bar. The inside had an eclectic feel to it with a small, wooden stage and dance floor. It was a favorite spot with the locals, and since Random Plan had joined, their line up business had increased. Melissa and I maneuvered through the crowd and made our way to a small, round table near the stage. Mason was in a corner talking to Derek. No doubt trying to calm him down. He was always so amped-up before a show. Aidan and Kyle were chatting with a few girls off to the side of the stage.

"Can you believe how packed this place is?" Melissa said, glancing around the crowded venue.

"I know. The guys are starting to make a name for themselves. There's way more people here than last time." My heart swelled with pride, watching more people file into the crowded dance area.

"Ya know, Lizzie, you could be part of that." Melissa waved her outstretched hand and motioned to the stage.

I shook my head and rolled my eyes.

"I wish I had your talent. I'd be up there in a heartbeat. Why is this so different from singing at church?"

"It just is. I feel safe at church. Probably because I've grown up there. I don't know. This would be hard for me." I turned away from her harsh gaze and focused on the shimmering bottles that graced the back of the bar.

Melissa rubbed my arm. "I'm sorry, Liz. I always forget how shy you can be. You're just so good. You know I'm your biggest fan."

"Thanks." I gave her a warm smile. "Maybe one day."

The atmosphere surrounding the small stage was becoming electric with anticipation. Derek strutted across the stage first. He was wearing his customary cargo shorts and a black t-shirt that hugged his muscular chest. As usual, his colorful tatted arms were exposed. His spiky blond hair glistened under the lights, and his expressive brown eyes were wild with excitement. He gave the crowd a fist pump and took a seat behind his beloved drums. Derek ate it up when a few of the regulars called out his name and cheered.

Kyle walked to his keyboard in a more subdued fashion. His warm brown eyes matched his gentle heart. He was wearing a plaid button-down shirt with the sleeves pushed up and dark jeans. Next up was Aidan, looking all California-surfer-boy in ripped jeans and a powder-blue t-shirt. His blond hair was slicked back, emphasizing his bright blue eyes. He walked flirtatiously to his mic, and a few girls squealed with excitement. He gave them his signature smile and picked up his bass.

The crowd erupted while Mason casually walked front and center. He removed his striped hoodie and tossed it to the side of the stage. A few of the college regulars wolf-whistled as he untucked his grey t-shirt. His gaze scanned the enthusiastic audience, and he smiled while he adjusted the mic. He was completely confident and relaxed. Part of me envied that about him... I wished I wasn't so shy. My brother began to strum his guitar, and the rest of the guys followed suit. The adoring crowd continued to applaud while Mason began to sing.

Melissa's elbows were on the table, then she leaned in, focusing her attention on Mason. She glanced my way and moved in closer. "I never get tired of listening to him. Or looking at him." She smiled.

Mason's suspicions confused me. I just didn't see it. Watching the guys continue their set, I decided to broach the subject.

"What do you think of Aidan? Do you think he's a good guy?"

"How should I know? I barely talk to him. Besides, you'll find out soon enough. Isn't he coming over tomorrow?" Melissa countered.

"I was just wondering what you thought of him. I

mean, just look at him."

"He's cute, but he doesn't come close to my Mason. Just look at my man up there." Melissa's eyes followed Mason around the stage, and she gave me a devilish smile.

I just shook my head and smiled at her. *Mason's gotta have this wrong.*

When their final set ended, the crowd roared in unrestrained delight. The guys took their bows and began milling around the small stage. Melissa left me alone at the table while she met Mason off to the side of the stage. She whispered something in his ear and kissed him on the lips. Mason stared lovingly in her eyes, and, for the first time in days, I saw him relax as he embraced her.

Derek wiped the sweat from his brow and chugged a bottle of water then he and Kyle started to pack up their gear.

Aidan sauntered over to a group of girls beckoning for him. A cute brunette took out her cell phone, and they exchanged numbers. Aidan raised an eyebrow and gave the girl a sexy smirk. He hopped back on stage and grabbed his guitar. He stopped for a moment and looked at Melissa and Mason. They were huddled in the corner locked in a passionate kiss. He ran a hand through his hair and then glanced my way. He caught my eye and motioned for me to come over. I felt my nerves getting the best of me as I made my way to the stage.

"Hey, Aidan, that was a good show," I stammered.

Aidan lips were pursed then morphed into a wicked smile." Well, it could be better."

"What do you mean? You guys were great!" I hated how I was gushing. *Idiot.*

Aidan hopped off the stage and leaned in close. His

eyes bore into mine. "I think you know exactly what I mean."

I swallowed and stared at him. I felt the heat spread across my face, and my heartbeat quickened.

"One day you're gonna get your butt up here, Liz."

His proximity, his piercing blue eyes, his smile — it was too much. I took a step back and tripped over a chair, but Aidan grabbed my arm before I hit the floor.

"Are you okay?" Aidan seemed amused at my less-than- graceful fall.

"Yes, I'm fine." I quickly removed myself from his firm grip. "I've gotta go, Aidan. I'll see you tomorrow." I dashed back to the table, grabbed my purse, and waved at Melissa and Mason before I walked toward the exit sign.

"See ya." Aidan chuckled.

I could sense he was smirking at me as I walked out the door.

Chapter Four

My nerves got the best of me during dinner, and I hardly ate a thing. I still had a few more hours to kill before Aidan would be over, so to rid my body from some pent-up energy, I clipped Maggie to her leash and dashed out the front door. I braced myself against the streetlamp across the street from Mrs. Chapman's house and stretched my legs, hoping to get another glimpse of my smokin' hot neighbor, but no luck. The jeep was gone, and it seemed like the house was closed up tight. When I noticed the rosebushes were cut back, it made me smile. Mrs. Chapman would have liked that.

Maggie pulled me forward as we headed up the street toward the creek bed. I picked up the pace when one of my favorite running songs blasted through my phone. We continued to weave our way through kids on bikes and skateboarders until finally, we did it. Maggie and I were standing in the sand looking over the blue Pacific. The beach was so peaceful this time of year. The tourists were gone. The lifeguard stations were closed, and the beach was deserted. I reveled in the fact we were the only ones on the sand for miles. Lost in my thoughts, I allowed my mind to daydream about Aidan.

Can we be friends? Will he want to be friends with someone like me? I hope I can be myself when he comes over. But… more than anything, I hope I don't make a fool of myself.

****

When Maggie and I walked in the door, I unclipped her leash, hung it in the hall closet, and climbed the stairs two at a time. Entering my bathroom, I stripped out of my sweaty workout gear, grabbed a new razor, pulled back the blue-and-white, daisy-covered shower curtain and stepped inside. The steam from the hot water filled the room. I propped my leg up on the side of the tub and slathered it with shaving cream. The razor glided across my now-defined calf muscle, removing the stubble, leaving a smooth patch of skin in its wake. The scent of lavender calmed me while the steady stream of water ran down my back. I breathed in the moist air and gave myself a pep talk.

I can do this. I'm smart. He's coming here because he needs my help. I'm getting paid for this. Don't be an idiot. This was my mantra.

I finished blow-drying my hair and checked the clock for the umpteenth time. My heart was racing, knowing Aidan would be here any minute. I wiped my sweaty palms on my jeans and giggled when they slipped past my hips. It was still hard to believe my once-tight jeans were now huge. After I pulled them back up, I grabbed a belt. At least I was wearing a new shirt, courtesy of my mom's closet. The deep shade of green was in contrast with my fair skin, and I knew it was a good color for me.

I rolled Mason's computer chair next to mine then heard Maggie bark. Seconds later the doorbell rang. My heart started to beat faster while heading down the stairs. Taking one last deep breath, I exhaled as I opened the door.

Aidan was casually dressed, wearing worn-out jeans

and a grey V-neck sweater. His black backpack was slung over his shoulder. He gave me a smile then walked through the door.

"Hey, Liz."

"Hi, Aidan. We can study in my room," I stammered and motioned to the stairs.

When we entered my room, Aidan didn't seem like his confident self. He seemed... nervous. He paced around my small bedroom, picking up my knick-knacks and putting them down. When he saw a few framed photographs on my bookcase, he leaned forward and grabbed one. It was a picture of me at the piano. He examined it, then his eyes went from the photograph to me.

"Nice picture."

"Thanks. Um, do you want to get started? We can share my desk." I nervously took a seat while Aidan pulled his calculus book from his backpack.

Aidan sat next to me, brushed back his hair with one hand, and exhaled. "Okay. Let's do this."

We sat side by side with Aidan's book between us. As we reviewed a chapter covering differential equations, I found I was in my element. Having had spent my first two years of high school tutoring in the math lab, I knew I had a knack for this, and when I saw Aidan grasp the concept, I was rewarded with his beautiful smile.

Aidan hunched over his paper, elbow bent, and rested his forehead on his hand. With a furrowed brow he whined. "Help me out, Liz, I'm not sure about this one."

Aidan moved the book from between us and pulled my chair closer to his. Our arms touched briefly, and I quickly moved mine away. Aidan gave me a smirk and shook his head.

"I don't bite, Liz. Well, unless you want me to." His lip curved up into a flirty smile.

"Let's just work on getting the solution." I rolled my eyes. "Yes, ma'am." Aidan grinned.

It was almost ten-thirty by the time we finished. Aidan stood up, rolled his chair out of the way, and plopped down on my bed.

"Ugh. I'm done." He bellowed then stretched his arms above his head.

I rolled my chair around to face him. Aidan hugged my pillow while he braced himself up on his elbow. I smiled. *Lucky pillow*.

"Where are you applying to school?" "Mason and I are going to Saddleback."

"What? Why are you two going to a community college?" "Because there's two of us." I shrugged. "My parents can't afford to send us both to college. Mason and I are going to get our associate degrees and then transfer somewhere."

"Wow, I'm shocked. I thought you'd be headed off to some Ivy League school straight outta high school."

"Oh stop it." I giggled. "What about you. Where are you applying?"

"Either San Diego State or UC Santa Barbara." Aidan smiled.

Arching an eyebrow, I gave him a smirk, "Oh, the party schools."

"Nope, I just gotta stay near the beach, baby."

A slow smile spread across his face that made my heart beat a little faster.

"Aren't you in a bunch of AP classes?"

"Yessss." Embarrassment caused my answer to drag out.

"I took AP English last year, and it about killed me. How many are you taking?

"Three." I felt myself blush.

"What? You're crazy. That's so much extra work. Why would you do that?"

"I like the challenge. I guess it's fun for me."

"Fun? You have got to get out more." He chuckled. "My dad would love it if I were more like you. The only time he talks to me is when he's bustin' my butt to crack down on the books. That's why he's paying you to tutor me. He wants me to follow in his footsteps."

"And that is?" "Engineering."

"And what do you want?"

"I have no idea… but I can tell you one thing, it's not engineering."

"What about your mom? Does she push you like your dad does?"

"They're divorced." Aidan was quiet for a moment, then his demeanor changed. "Besides, she doesn't care what I do." Aidan got up, tossed the pillow near my headboard, and gathered his things. "I'd better take off." He slung his backpack over his shoulder. "I'll see ya at school."

"Oh… okay."

I stood. Then he walked out my door. I shut off my light and peered through the window. Seconds later, he got in his truck and sped away.

Hugging the lucky pillow, I replayed the evening in my head. Everything had seemed to go well until I asked about his mom. What was that about? She doesn't care what he does? How sad. I picked up my cell, considering if I should text him or not. He texted me.

Aidan: *Thanks for tonight.*
Me: *No problem.*
Aidan: *Night*
Me: *Night*

That was unexpected and nice…

The last moments before I felt myself drift into sleep were of calculus formulas and Aidan.

****

After our tutoring session, things at school began to change between Aidan and me. When I walked by him, he made a point to say hello, causing glares from his entourage. One day he sat with me during morning break and, after his calculus class, he couldn't wait to tell me he had actually paid attention. I found myself looking forward to the times when I *wasn't* in class and for me… that was crazy.

****

Panting, Melissa choked out, "I'm dying. One hundred and eighteen stairs! I'm not doing that again! I'll sit up here and wait for you." Melissa took a seat on a stone bench at the top of the stairs at Lantern Bay Park.

"Okay, I'll be right back." I took off down the long stairway to the sidewalk below.

At the halfway point, I heard Melissa shout, "You go, girl!"

I smiled, pumped my fist in the air, and continued my descent.

When I reached the bottom, I noticed a group of skateboarders flipping their boards in hopes to stick the landing. As soon as they eyed me, I braced myself, ready to hear the taunting words I had heard so many times before.

The fat girl was always invisible, unless she walked by a group of teenagers. She became the unwanted center of attention. I avoided eye contact, but what I heard shocked me. This group of unruly adolescent boys wolf-whistled at me. Stunned, I climbed the stairs, and when I reached the top, Melissa handed me a bottle of water.

"I can't believe you did that, Liz! Down and back twice, that's four-hundred and seventy-two stairs!"

"I can't believe it either."

"Did you hear that group of guys whistle at me? Nothing like that has ever happened to me before." I felt myself getting emotional.

"I think you'd better get used to it." She gave me a heartfelt smile. "C'mon, let's go sit down."

Melissa and I sat in silence and gazed over the view of the Pacific Ocean. We could see all Doheny State Beach, Dana Point Harbor, and beyond. It was beautiful.

"We can't stay too much longer. Aidan will be coming over soon. And… oh wait! I didn't tell you what happened today. I walked by Aidan, and he was talking with stuck-up Cassie. When I passed them, I heard him say he had to go, and he caught up with me and walked me to my class! Can you believe that? I wish I could have seen Cassie's face. You remember I told you how mean she was to me in grade school?"

Usually news like this would have Melissa jumping up and down. But she was quiet.

"Melissa… what's wrong?

After a few minutes of silence, our eyes locked. "Aidan tried to kiss me."

"What?" My stomach dropped. I had completely put

the thought of anything between Aidan and Melissa behind me. "When? Does Mason know?"

"Are you crazy?" Melissa was wide-eyed. "I can't tell Mason. He'd beat the crap out of Aidan if he knew. I didn't even want to tell you, but I thought it'd help you get over this." Melissa flailed her hand at me. "This infatuation you have with him."

"How'd it... what... happened?

"To be honest, I don't know. Aidan and I have a few classes near each other, so we would hang out before the bell rang. Ya know, just talking." Melissa glanced toward the harbor and then back to me. "When the guys would get together to practice, he kept checking me out, but I just blew it off. Knowing how Aidan is, I didn't think anything of it." Melissa hesitated and swallowed. "Sunday, just before the guys played, Aidan and I got to the restaurant at the same time. We were hanging out in the parking lot, just talking. He got close to me, leaned forward, and tried to kiss me. I pushed him, and he backed off. He tried to pass it off, like he was joking, but I knew if I would have gone for it, he would have too."

After a few minutes of silence, I cleared my throat, finally able to speak. "I can't believe it. How could he do that to Mason?" The protective sister side of me took over as denial turned to anger. "I'm sorry, Liz, I should have told you sooner. But honestly,

I just wanted to forget about it. Promise me you won't tell Mason. The band is doing so well... I don't want to cause any problems. Besides, I handled it. Aidan hasn't tried anything since that night. In fact, he avoids me now."

"I won't say anything. I promise. I can't believe I've been such an idiot." Feeling a slight chill in the air, I zipped up my hoodie.

"You were just caught up in his spell. Now maybe you'll move past it." Melissa rubbed my back.

"I'm glad you told me. I guess we'd better go"

Melissa and I got up and headed down the stairs as the sun began to set over the ocean.

****

I'm not sure if it was from the workout at the park or Melissa's impromptu confession, but I was desperate for a shower. While the water ran down my back, I thought about Aidan.

An hour ago, I was so happy. Things between Aidan and me were starting to change. I was hoping for friendship... maybe more... but now? How can he do that to Mason? Who does that to a friend? Isn't that written in the bro code?

Melissa was right... I had been falling under his spell. What was I thinking? Guys like Aidan don't change. They go after what they want at any cost. Well, there'd be no more of that for me... I'm done.

I felt a sense of empowerment as I prepared for Aidan's arrival. Instead of my usual ritual of blow-drying and flat-ironing my hair, I decided to let it dry naturally. Instead of borrowing a cute top from my mom, I opted for yoga pants and a plain white t- shirt.

No makeup, no mantra. I was moving on.

****

Mason and the guys were in the garage working on a new song. Usually I would be down in the garage watching them practice, but tonight I decided to skip it and text Aidan.

Me: *Come upstairs when you guys are done.*

Aidan: *Ten more minutes.*

I sat at my desk, singing to myself while finishing up my AP English homework. Aidan peeked his head through the door and it silenced me.

"Whoa, you're good." Aidan smiled and pushed the door open then stepped inside.

I spun around in my chair as Aidan dropped his backpack on the bed.

"Thanks. Are you ready to start?" I stood up and rolled my chair to the side.

Aidan grabbed his book and took a step toward me. "Something's different." He gazed at me with curious eyes.

"Oh, it's just my hair. I didn't blow dry it." I shrugged.

Aidan cocked his head to the side before he took another step forward. He reached out and touched a ringlet of my hair. "It's beautiful," he whispered.

I felt a flush spread across my face then took a step backward, breaking eye contact.

"Thanks. Let's get started. I'll go get a chair from Mason's room." I forced myself to dismiss any romantic thoughts of Aidan as I walked down the hallway.

Chapter Five

"C'mon, girl, c'mon." I coaxed Maggie up the last few steps of the stairs, and as soon we made it to the top of Lantern Bay Park, we both sprawled out on the cool grass. The smell was earthy and alive. The late November air was crisp and felt good against my heated body. I gave Maggie a few kisses then crawled to my knees.

When I stood to my feet, my heart leapt then my eyes zeroed in on my neighbor. I hadn't seen him since move-in day. I started to think maybe his parents had bought Mrs. Chapman's place as a summerhouse. But... here he was looking all bad-boy sexy in a brown leather jacket with his head buried in a college textbook.

Smart and sexy. What a combo.

Taking a few steps back, my thoughts shifted into fantasy mode. I imagined introducing myself to my nameless neighbor, striking up an amazing conversation with him, and ending up on some awesome date. Maggie's tug of the leash pulled me back into reality and away from my much-too-good-looking neighbor.

Making our way toward the stairs, a large part of me wished I could be that type of girl, outgoing and flirty, but that just wasn't me. I glanced over my shoulder to get one last look. He noticed me... *Is that a nod? At me?* I didn't know what to do. I felt my face flush then turned and took a few steps down the stairs. I realized that I just wasn't that girl, and, *that girl,* was never going to be me.

****

The guys were finishing up their band practice as Maggie and I walked up the driveway. I was headed for the front door when I heard Aidan call my name. Several weeks had passed since I'd made my decision to move on from him. It seemed the further I tried to pull away the more he worked to bring us close.

I stopped a few steps before the front door as Aidan rounded the corner from inside of the garage. His soft hair blew back in the breeze, and his blue eyes glimmered in the last rays of the setting sun.

"Hi, Aidan." I unhooked Maggie's leash and tossed it on the front porch. Aidan crouched down to give Maggie some attention.

"Hey, Liz." Aidan rose to his feet.

My heart quickened when his eyes followed the length of my body.

He reached in his back pocket, fished out his wallet, and pulled out a check. "Here ya go. I forgot to pay you last week."

I still felt funny taking money for tutoring, and Aidan knew it.

"Take it, Liz. It's my dad's money not mine." Aidan placed the check in my hand but didn't let go. Our eyes locked for a few seconds before I backed away, and he dropped his hand from mine. "It's the least he could do for me."

Aidan hadn't spoke about his home life since our first tutoring night in my room. His tone sounded pained, so I decided to question him about it. "What do you mean?"

"My dad's getting married again." "Again?"

"Yep. Third time's the charm, he says, but knowing my dad, he'll end up screwing things up. He always does.

"Do you like her?"

"Natalie? She's alright." He shrugged. "I've learned not to get attached. So, I guess it doesn't matter."

Aidan's cell phone chimed, and I watched him read the text. "I gotta take off." Aidan went back in the garage to pick up his bass.

Kyle and Mason were sitting on the couch while Derek was standing in front of them, arms flailing, in the middle of some elaborate story. Mason was laughing hard, and Kyle just shook his head.

I made my way toward Aidan's truck and he called out, "I'll see ya guys later." When he hopped inside he gave me a ghost of a smile. "Bye, Liz."

"Bye."

Watching him drive away, I felt my heart thaw a little.

****

The weeks leading up to our eighteenth birthday were busy. Most of my time was occupied with singing rehearsals, working out, and planning mine and Mason's birthday party. Melissa was ecstatic at the idea, such an extrovert. She loved a party. I, on the other hand, did not. The thought of being the center of attention was unsettling. Even the shopping outing with Mom and Melissa was difficult for me.

"Oh, Lizzie! Just come out and let us see how it looks on you!" Melissa summoned from outside the dressing room door.

"Yes, sweetie, let us see too." Mom chimed in.

Reluctantly, I opened the door. Simultaneously, they both gasped. Bouncing on her heels, Melissa let out a shriek. My mom was awestruck with tears welling in her eyes.

"Elizabeth, you look absolutely beautiful." I could feel myself blushing while I fiddled with the hem of the dress. Melissa took a step toward me and pushed me in front of the three-way mirror.

"Lizzie, look at yourself. Look at your waist. Turn around and check out your butt. It looks amazing!" Melissa gave me a swat.

I'd hit the twenty-pound goal over a month ago, but our shopping day had had to be postponed. That is why, as of today, I was at The Mission Viejo Mall in front of a three-way mirror, thirty-two pounds lighter.

Staring at my reflection, it took me a moment to process what I saw before me. My once doughy middle was now tight and shapely. Where Melissa was slender and leggy, I was petite and well… voluptuous. My legs were toned, and Melissa was right, my butt looked amazing.

Our birthday was in December, so all the holiday dresses were out. I was wearing a fitted black cutout dress, size four. The front of the dress was modest with a scoop neck and long tight- fitting sleeves. The back was cut low with a cutout crisscross design showcasing my fair skin. I was stunned at my silhouette. Melissa and Mom were beaming with joy.

"Look no farther, Liz! That's the dress. It's perfect!" Melissa said with certainty.

My mom was so taken aback with my new appearance we ended up leaving the mall with three pairs of jeans, two sweaters, four t-shirts, my black party dress, and a pair of black satin pumps with four-inch heels. It was the first time in my life I'd ever enjoyed shopping.

****

After our shopping spree, I felt exhilarated. Melissa and I laughed as we clamored up the stairs. Mason heard us and opened his door. He popped his head out and smiled. Melissa ran past him giggling, then he came bounding behind us with Aidan at his heels. Mason attacked Melissa, and they both fell on my bed laughing. I tossed my bags on the floor and sat on the edge of my bed, smiling at the display of affection between the two of them. Aidan had a goofy grin on his face as he plopped in my computer chair.

Mason pulled Melissa in close and kissed her on the top of her head while she nestled in next to him. "Did you get anything today?" he asked her.

Melissa smiled up at Mason while batting her eyelashes. "Yep. But you can't see my dress until the party."

He groaned and kissed her on the lips.

"Liz got a bunch of new stuff. And an amazing dress!" Melissa started chanting "Fashion show… fashion show…"

The guys joined in Melissa's plea until I stood up and grabbed one of the bags. They all cheered when I pulled out my black party dress.

"I'm just showing it to you guys. I'm not putting it on." They each let out a whiny "Aww…"

I smirked and held the dress in front of me. When I turned it around to show the back, Aidan let out a slow sexy whistle, and Melissa clapped.

Mason raised an eyebrow. "Whoa, Liz, that's pretty… sexy."

Melissa elbowed Mason in the stomach and a burst

of air left his lungs.

"Do you think it's too much?"

Aidan looked the dress up and down and smiled "Don't listen to your brother. You're gonna look hot."

Mason grabbed a pillow and chucked it at Aidan.

Aidan caught the pillow before it smacked him in the face and laughed. "Hey now, I'm just speakin' the truth."

I glanced at Aidan, and he winked at me. I felt my face redden as I picked up the rest of my bags and tossed everything in the closet.

"Hey, we're gonna go get some fish tacos in the harbor. Do you girls wanna come?" Aidan was looking at me when he asked. Melissa and Mason got up and straightened out my bed.

I glanced over at Melissa eyeing me. Before she could say anything, I heard myself answer with an enthusiastic "Yes!"

****

The night air was chilly. There was no room on the inside of the small establishment, so Melissa and I grabbed a wooden picnic table outside.

Aidan leaned toward me. "What are you having, Liz?" I reached in my pocket to grab some cash.

Aidan shook his head. "No, no I got this. What would you like?"

I could see Melissa's eyes widen in my peripheral vision, but I didn't look at her.

"Um… two grilled fish tacos and an iced tea, please." Aidan nodded his head.

After Mason took Melissa's order, they went inside to purchase our food.

"What was that?" Melissa scooted in close and

nudged me. "This almost seems like a date. What's been going on in those tutoring sessions?" She raised a speculative eyebrow.

"Nothing's been going on. He's been sweet to me, that's all." I glanced over my shoulder to make sure they weren't coming back yet. "You even said how he seems different. People can change... can't they?" My confession made her frown.

"Yes, he seems... better... but, after... ya know... the almost kiss... I still don't trust him. I'm worried about you. I don't want you falling for him. I just don't want you getting hurt." Melissa scooted over while the guys sat down with our food.

The attempted kiss... she had to bring it up. Suddenly, I'm not hungry anymore.

Nibbling on my half-eaten taco, my eyes drifted from the conversation of our table and focused on two boys who looked familiar. The small one kept jumping around, weaving in and out of the patio tables, and the older one was leaning against a wall, texting. I was wracking my brain trying to place them. As soon as I saw their older brother, it hit me. Unable to tear my eyes away, I watched as he furrowed his brow at the younger one.

His voice was raised, so it was easy to hear him when he said, "Hey, buddy, people are eating here. You know better. Come on, let's go."

He handed the young boy a brown bag bearing the restaurant's name then glanced up and caught my eye. It seemed as if he was trying to place me. He motioned to the older boy they were leaving and glanced over his shoulder. He caught my eye and smiled before he stepped off the sidewalk and walked toward the parking lot.

"Liz… Liz!" Mason snapped. "What?"

"Are you gonna eat that?" He pointed to my remaining uneaten taco. I shook my head. Mason reached across the table and wolfed it down.

My eyes lingered on my neighbor as he maneuvered his way through the small parking lot.

Aidan leaned in next to me. "Do you know that guy?" "Sorta."

"What do you mean, sorta?" Aidan asked. "I've never met him, but he's my neighbor."

"Hmm… seems like he'd like to know you." Aidan kept his assessing eyes focused on my neighbor as he watched him get into his jeep.

Mason hopped up from the table and began picking up our plates. "You guys want to walk around?" He threw out our trash and wrapped his arms around Melissa.

"Sure, why not?" Aidan stood, answering for both of us.

Melissa and Mason led the way with Aidan and me trailing behind.

I wrapped my arms around myself as we strolled through the harbor. Aidan took off his black hoodie and held it open for me.

"No, it's okay. I'm not cold."

At that precise moment, a gust of wind blew through the harbor, causing goose bumps to rise on my exposed forearms. He chuckled and placed his jacket around me. I slipped my arms through his much-too-big hoodie and pushed up the sleeves. Aidan's jacket smelled of him, a mixture of body wash or cologne. Whatever it was, the fresh scent had me inhaling deeply.

"Better?" he asked. I nodded while Aidan vigorously rubbed my arms. He stuffed his hands in his front pockets, and when we turned around, Melissa and Mason were way ahead of us. Aidan looked down at me with a smile that had my heart racing. "C'mon." He nodded toward the harbor. "Looks like we're on our own."

We walked around not saying much of anything but it wasn't awkward. Aidan caught my eye and a slow smile spread across his face.

"What?" I asked.

"Well… I want to say something, but I'm not sure if I should."

We kept walking, but curiosity got the best of me. I turned my gaze to his. "What?"

Smiling crookedly, Aidan hesitated before he blurted out what he wanted to say. "You've lost so much weight you look like a different person." Aidan stopped. "Did that sound as bad as I thought it did?"

"Don't worry about it… I know I look different. It's still hard for me when I see myself sometimes." My eyes narrowed. "I have something to confess too…"

"Oh?" Aidan moved in close, but I took a step back.

"Do you remember when we first met? In the lunchroom?"

Aidan closed his eyes for a minute and then opened them. "Sort of…"

"You were hanging out with a bunch of girls, then you introduced yourself to me? Do you remember now?"

He still looked lost, like nothing was jarring his memory.

"I was eating a giant cinnamon roll." I raised an eyebrow at him.

Finally, recognition washed over his face. "Yes!"

"Well, that was the day I decided to get serious and lose my weight." Aidan's eyes softened.

"Crap, Liz. What did I say? Was I a jerk?"

I dropped my head down, remembering how emotionally painful the day had been for me. Feeling like an idiot for having brought it up, I gazed over the boats in the harbor.

"No, Aidan, you were fine. You didn't say anything. I just remember it being the day I started." I lied but I didn't want him to feel bad. I wasn't even sure why I'd brought it up.

Aidan reached out for my hand, and his face softened. "If I did say something and you're not telling me… I'm sorry."

"You didn't, so don't worry. Okay?"

Aidan nodded, and I pulled his hand toward the boats that lined the harbor. "Which one would you want?"

Aidan's bright eyes glided over the marina. "That one." He let go of my hand and pointed to the largest yacht within our eyesight.

"It figures you'd want a yacht, and the biggest one out there." I smiled as a stray lock of my hair blew in front of my face.

Aidan removed it and placed it behind my ear. Our eyes locked, and my heart started to pound as Aidan leaned in close. Melissa's words echoed in my head.

"I don't want you to get hurt. I don't want you falling for him. I'm worried about you."

The one and only thought that caused me to break eye contact and step back was that he had tried to kiss Melissa.

"I should probably text Mason. It's getting kinda late, and… you must be freezing."

Aidan seemed embarrassed.

I pulled my cell from my pocket and began texting as I walked away.

Chapter Six

Our birthday party was going to be next week. Kyle's parents owned a beautiful home on Beach Road and had offered to let us use it for our celebration. Melissa and I were making all the arrangements. Because of Mason's popularity and his band, I was certain a lot of people would be there. In anticipation for the upcoming party, I decided to ramp up my workout routine. Instead of my usual two-mile-a-day run, I added an extra mile, plus the stairs at Lantern Bay Park.

I had to get up and out early for my Saturday run. Aidan was coming over. His mid-term final was Monday, and he was feeling a little anxious. I quickly dressed in my work-out clothes, stuck my earbuds in, and blasted my music. Maggie pranced around me while I tied up my laces. Grabbing her leash, I dashed toward the front door and ran right into Aidan, literally.

Maggie's leash dropped from my hand as my head smacked into his firm chest, knocking him against the door. He caught himself before he fell, but held onto me in the process. Aidan steadied himself and continued to hold me in an intimate embrace. He took a deep breath, leaned in, and smelled my hair. Aidan touched my cheek with the tips of his fingers then gently removed an ear bud from one ear.

"Are you okay?"

"I'm fine," I whispered. I was expecting him to let

me go, but he didn't. Just like our night in the harbor, I felt overwhelmed. He held my gaze, but I snapped myself back into reality and shifted away from him, breaking the contact of our bodies. I bent down, picked up Maggie's leash, and stepped outside the door.

"Sorry, Aidan." I laughed it off. "You're early."

"I thought I'd hang with Mason until you were ready."

"Okay, I'll make it quick. I should be back in about forty minutes." I didn't look back, but I could feel his eyes on me as I picked up my pace and jogged away.

****

When I stopped at my usual stretching pole, my heart revved up at the sight of Mr. Dimples loading up his jeep. The back was open, and he was meticulously placing camping gear in the trunk space. California weather was always pretty good, but here it was early December, and he was going tent camping? My mind drifted, and I felt myself smile when I thought about how fun it would be to help him stay warm. A few minutes later I realized I was just standing there, staring like an idiot. I pulled myself together, remembered I had to get back to Aidan, and pushed the mental image of Mr. Hottie out of my head. I gave Maggie a tug, and we were on our way.

****

"You don't think we should get together one more time before mid-terms?" Aidan was nervously tapping his pencil on the desk.

"Nah, you're gonna do great." I handed Aidan his book and swept the eraser shavings on the floor.

Aidan placed the book in his backpack and tossed it next to my bed.

"Are you okay, Aidan? You've seem kinda out of it." I wasn't sure if he was acting strange because of the incident at the front door, or if it was something else. I gingerly took the pencil from his grasp, placed it in my coffee cup pencil holder, and shifted in my seat so I could give him my full attention.

"I'm alright…"

"I can tell something's bugging you. What's wrong?" "Forget it, Liz…"

"No, tell me," I pleaded.

Aidan glanced my way but didn't respond.

"How 'bout if I tell you some deep dark secret of mine and then you tell me why you're so upset?" I bargained.

"It doesn't work like that."

"C'mon, Aidan, please? I'm sure it'll make you feel better."

A pained expression crossed his face, and after a few minutes he murmured, "It's my mom." He ran a hand through his hair and rubbed the back of his neck. "She's back in rehab."

"Rehab… for what?" "Meth."

"Meth? I can't believe you've never said anything."

"It's not something you tell people." His arms were crossed, and he was focused on my bookcase across the room.

"How long has she been…?"

"She started when I was about four." Aidan's eyes shifted from the bookcase to me.

"After my mom had me, she struggled with weight and started using. I was too young to remember any of it… besides… she was good at hiding it. When my dad finally figured things out, he put her in rehab, thinking it would fix everything. It did for a while, I guess, but it didn't last long, and eventually she'd start up again. My dad was gone a lot, so by the time I was seven, I was taking more care of her than she was of me. The sad part is, when I was a kid, I knew she wanted to quit... she was such a good mom when she wasn't using, but she chose the drug over me... and my dad."

"What about your dad? Does he...?" "No, never."

"How long were they married?"

"They got divorced when I was eight. I remember... I must have been about twelve. I was visiting her for the weekend, and she went on and on preaching to me about not doing drugs. Even then, I knew she was high as a kite. Such a hypocrite." He scowled.

"I can't even tell you how many times she's been in and out of rehab. This time I thought she'd do it, but here we are again — I'm so sick of it!" His fist slammed down on my desk, rattling my pencil cup.

"I'm sorry." I reached forward and placed my hand on his knee.

Aidan held my gaze, his pained eyes widened.

"When's the last time you saw your mom?"

"I talk to her more than I see her. The last time we talked, she was doing so well... but now... it's so frustrating. I worry about her all the time. I wish she could just get her life together. Every time things are going well for her, she ends up using again." Aidan placed his head in his hands. "Maybe this time she'll do it... I don't know. I just don't know anymore." His last sentence came out in a whisper.

My heart filled with compassion, watching his emotions unfold before me. His declaration tore me apart, so open and vulnerable.

He placed his hand over mine and held them. When he gazed into my eyes, his expression was broken and sad. After what seemed like minutes, he leaned in close.

My heart raced; the warmth of his breath was inches from my face.

"Aidan… wait…"

"Liz…" His lips hovered over mine.

Common sense deserted me as I focused on the sadness in his eyes and the desperation in his voice.

I felt myself tremble, then I whispered, "I've never been kissed before."

Aidan's eyes softened as he slowly brought his lips to mine. He cradled the back of my neck with his hand and gave me feather- light kisses. I closed my eyes, the warmth of his tongue skimmed across my tense lips, coaxing them to open.

I responded, awkwardly at first, but Aidan didn't seem to care. His lips sealed over mine as my first kiss rolled into the next. I reached up, finally able to touch his hair. It was softer than I had imagined. I ran my hands down the silky strands to his strong shoulders and muscular arms. My grasp tightened, then he pulled me in close.

A soft moan escaped his lips as he kissed me again. His hands traveled to the small of my back, and he tightened his grip. He peppered my neck with kisses, and his warm breath whispered, "You're beautiful."

I felt myself shudder, and he kissed me again. I wasn't sure how much time had passed.

Eventually, Aidan pulled away. "I've wanted to do that for a while."

His honesty surprised me, and I instantly responded. "Me too."

We held each other for a few more minutes, and he stroked my hair.

"So… what's your secret?" he prompted. "I lied to you."

"Lied to me?"

I felt his body tense with my confession. "Yes… I guess you were part of the reason I wanted to lose my weight. I mean… I always wanted to. But, after I watched all those girls swarming around you, I wanted to know what it felt like to be one of them."

Aidan hugged me tighter. "You're so much more than that," he whispered. Aidan kissed my forehead before he shifted and glanced at my alarm clock. "It's almost noon. I gotta be at work by 1:00. I'd better get going."

My heart was still racing as we walked to the front door. Aidan took a step outside the door before he leaned over and sweetly kissed me on the lips. "I'll see ya, Liz."

I closed the door, peered out the front window and watched him leave. Sad as it was to hear Aidan's confession, I knew it was a good thing. *He opened up to me… shared his past… and kissed me.* My thoughts jumped to Melissa. Excitement filled me when I reached for my cell, but then… I placed it back in my pocket. What was I going to say to her? She didn't want me with Aidan. But, how could I keep this from her? I walked in the kitchen and grabbed a diet soda from the fridge. I popped the top and took a long sip, contemplating if I should text her or not. The vibration of my cell phone freed me from my thoughts.

Aidan: *Are you alright?*
Me: *Yes.*

Aidan: *I didn't mean to dump all that crap on you.*
Me: *It's okay.*

Staring at my cell phone, I had hoped he'd text me something more, but that was it. I sipped my soda as I climbed the stairs and had a brief feeling of regret but immediately dismissed it. I placed my drink on my bedside table and lay down. My eyes closed, and a smile crept across my face. It felt good knowing Aidan had confided in me, and I must be special to him... and my first kiss... was better than I had imagined.

****

The week prior to our birthday flew by. Between school, studying for midterms, and practicing for the church's Christmas concert, I hardly had time to think about anything else... except Aidan.

I hadn't seen him since the night we'd kissed. I tried to find him at school, but I never saw him. He didn't park in his usual parking space. He was never in the lunchroom surrounded by his entourage. I even went to the grassy area of the lawn where the popular kids hung out. No luck.

My final attempt to confront him was when I went to his house. His truck was there. I knocked, but he didn't answer the door.

By mid-week, I questioned if that day in my room had even happened at all. I was mad at myself for being taken in by him. Now I knew I was one of many. I wasn't special. My humiliation was complete when I received a text from him thanking me for helping him pass calculus with a B. I felt like a fool. My only consolation was I'd never told Melissa. At least I didn't have to deal with that embarrassment.

The music drifted into my room from the garage below. Today I would finally get some answers. He couldn't avoid me. I knew Aidan wouldn't miss practice, and I was desperate to talk to him. Spurred on by anger, I hurried downstairs. When I opened the garage door, my eyes focused on the old brown couch. The sound of Derek's drums and Mason's voice swirled around me. I plopped down on the worn-out cushions and allowed my gaze to find Aidan.

He didn't show.

Leaving the garage, I went back to my bedroom, kicked off my boots, crawled into bed, and pulled my blanket around me. Staring at the ceiling, the tears began to fall.

I want him to be the sweet guy who opened up to me. Trusted me with his secrets and looked into my eyes like he truly cared. But that isn't him. I'm mad for letting my guard down. Believing he is different and for kissing him. What a fool I am... a stupid, stupid fool.

Chapter Seven

I braced myself against the wall and slipped on my black pumps. The eye shadow and three coats of mascara I'd applied made my light green eyes pop. Taking Melissa's advice, I let my hair dry naturally. The hair product I'd used took away the frizz, leaving behind soft loose curls that fell midway down my back. After I slipped in a pair of silver hoop earrings, I turned to look at my back in the mirror. I loved how this dress fit me and loved the crisscross design. But most of all, I loved that I had lost the weight.

Melissa came over to drive with us to the party. She and Mason were in the family room, standing by the stone fireplace. Mason was wearing dark jeans, an untucked, white-collared shirt, and a charcoal blazer. Melissa wore a strapless teal party dress with a glittery-tulle skirt. Anyone else wearing it would have looked ridiculous, but sassy Melissa could pull it off. She was the perfect combination of cute and sexy.

My parents were seated on the couch as I walked into the room. All eyes focused on me. I would think I'd be fine standing in front of my family, but the attention still made me uncomfortable.

Mason smiled while Melissa scurried toward me. "Liz! I knew that dress was perfect. Spin around so I can see the back."

I obeyed Melissa's command as my parents

approached me together. They both hugged me. My mom stepped back, then my father kissed my forehead.

"You look beautiful." My dad handed me a small box wrapped in pink paper with a white bow.

After I opened it, I locked eyes with my father. "I wanted to be the first man in your life to give you diamonds." They were beautiful, petite, diamond-stud earrings. Classic.

With tears in my eyes, I hugged my father. "Thank you, Daddy." I glanced over at my mom and watched a tear roll down her cheek.

"Happy birthday, sweetie." She walked over and gave me another hug.

Mason lifted his arm and shook his wrist at me. "Look what I got!" He sounded like he was ten. My parents had given him a beautiful set of silver cufflinks.

After I exchanged my hoop earrings with my diamond studs, we headed out the door to the party.

****

The parking on Beach Road was already packed. Space was limited, so most kids had to park far away and hoof it up to Kyle's. After driving up the street twice with no luck, Mason pulled up to the front of the house.

"Okay, girls. Out."

"Oh, Mason, I could walk." I pouted.

"I don't think so, Liz." Mason glanced down at my heels. "I'll be right back. I don't want to spend our eighteenth birthday in the emergency room." Mason drove away, leaving Melissa and I huddled together in the driveway.

Even in my four-inch heels, Melissa towered over me. I was starting to get nervous.

Melissa must have sensed my anxiety. She reached

around and gave me a side hug. "It's gonna be fun. Try not to worry."

"I know. I think I just need to get in there and get this over with."

"Here comes Mason." Melissa smiled. Mason jogged up and kissed her on the lips. Then he reached for my arm and escorted us both into the party.

Entering Kyle's house, we were met with roaring applause, shouts of "Happy Birthday", whistles, and howling. Mason and Melissa walked in with ease and grace. Knowing my face was beet-red, I continued to clutch Mason's arm to keep me from wobbling. Kyle and Derek were the first to greet us.

I released Mason's arm as Kyle gave me a warm hug. "You look beautiful, Liz."

"Thanks, Kyle," I whispered.

The next thing I knew, I was being spun around. Derek's dirty laugh echoed in my ear.

"Lizzie, you're smokin'." He chuckled and slapped me on the butt. I glanced toward Melissa. She giggled and rolled her eyes. Walking through the crowded family room, I saw several familiar faces from school. About sixty people were milling around.

I only knew a few of them. No sign of Aidan.

This wasn't the first time I had been in Kyle's home, but the beauty of it had always taken my breath away. The family room had floor-to-ceiling windows that showcased a panoramic view of the Pacific Ocean. French doors opened up to a spacious wrap-around patio with steps that led to the sand.

I approached the kitchen and was met with the kind, blue eyes of Kyle's mother.

"Mrs. King, Thank you for all of this." I motioned

to everything.

"Nonsense, Lizzie. You know how much we love you and Mason." She hugged me tight. "You look beautiful. You've lost so much weight, and your dress is stunning!"

"Thank you."

"Would you like something to drink?" she asked while leading me into her enormous kitchen.

"Not yet, but thank you."

"Well, help yourself when you're ready." She smiled and left me in her kitchen while several people filled their plates with food.

The aroma of garlic and spices increased as I approached the beautiful silver chafing dishes that covered the marble kitchen island. All my favorite comfort foods. Mini pizzas, pasta, meatballs, and garlic bread. My attention focused across the kitchen to the dessert table. Cake pops, cupcakes, and brownies. On a small round table sat a beautiful sheet cake with red, white, and black icing. The words *Happy 18th, Mason and Elizabeth* were written in beautiful script. I knew I was going off my diet tonight, big time. I made a mental note I would run extra hard tomorrow to make up for the calories I was going to consume.

I walked from the kitchen to the outside patio and was met with a huge black and silver banner that screamed *Happy Birthday, Mason and Elizabeth*. Market lights were strung back and forth, illuminating the spacious deck, and several tiki torches lined the sand. The party was in full swing. Bruno Mars was blasting through the speakers and a couple of guys were starting a bonfire near the ocean. Derek and Kyle were setting up outside to play a few songs. It seemed like more partygoers had arrived because the place was packed.

I sat at a small table near a space heater. Melissa and Mason were mingling, but when Melissa caught my eye, she made a beeline straight toward me.

"Oh no, no, no, Lizzie, you're not sitting at this table all night!" Melissa grabbed my arm and led me to the makeshift dance floor.

She started to shimmy around me "It's time to par-tay!" She squealed.

Of course, I was mortified. What little I knew of dancing I had learned from goofing around with Melissa and practicing in front of my mirror. Embarrassed, I swayed from side to side, praying not to fall. In heels, it was the best I could do.

Mason soon joined us with a couple of his friends. I quickly dispelled my own inadequacy while witnessing the spectacle of the two guys dancing before me. One of them moved in close and shouted over the music.

"We've never met. I'm Mason's friend, Brandon."

I took a small step back, but bumped into someone. "I'm Liz."

"I know who you are. You're the birthday girl. Wanna dance?" He smiled.

"Okay," I shyly replied.

Brandon was a good-looking guy. Tall, muscular with dark hair and dark brown eyes. His cologne was a bit overpowering, but I guessed it was better than the alternative.

The music changed from one song to the next, and I realized I was having fun. My feet were killing me, but I didn't care. I had been keeping track of how many guys I'd danced with. Currently I was at seven. I smiled at Melissa when she and Mason were dancing intimately even though the song was upbeat.

I was laughing, sweating, and dancing my butt off. This was the best time I'd ever had.

Then my heart stopped.

I felt a lump in my throat and a pit in my stomach when I saw him, dressed in black jeans and a black button-down shirt. He was movie-star perfect as he sauntered across the dance floor. When I tore my gaze from him, I noticed the accessory that graced his forearm. A leggy blonde wearing a short red dress. *Figures.*

I was torn between wanting to excuse myself and run or torture myself and stay. Foolishly, I opted for the latter. My heart twisted with jealousy watching Aidan gyrate to the music while his pretty dance partner sexually rubbed up against him. The pain was agonizing. Like a train wreck. I wanted to look away, but I couldn't.

Brandon had cut in when the last song had ended. The music had changed, and a slow song hummed through the speakers. Brandon moved in close. His shirt was damp with the smell of sweat and lingering cologne. He pulled me in close, but I backed away, putting some distance between us. Brandon's size blocked my vision from Aidan, and I was thankful. I decided when the song ended, I was getting off the dance floor. The torture of watching Aidan and Ms. Red Dress had been enough.

I thanked Brandon, but before I could make it back to my small table, a firm hand gripped my elbow and spun me around.

"Dance with me," Aidan said, sounding more like a statement rather than a question.

"What for?" I couldn't hide the disdain in my voice. "One dance, please," he begged.

"Forget it, Aidan. I'm done with you." My voice was glacial.

I snapped my arm from his grasp and walked off the dance floor.

Without glancing back, I heard the whiny voice of the leggy blonde, "Ai-da-a-an, let's dance."

"Bump N' Grind" blasted through the speakers.

Oh, that's just perfect.

The adrenaline was coursing through my veins. I wanted to run from the party, but I knew I couldn't. In an attempt to calm myself down, I kicked off my heels and headed toward the bonfire. The cool sand under my aching feet was soothing. A group of kids were huddled around the pit, and in the distance a couple was making out. I stood before the blazing flames and breathed in the combination of salty sea air mingled with the pungent smell of smoke. The dancing flames of the fire mesmerized me.

Unaware of how long I'd been standing there, I emerged from my trance with the sounds of the crackling fire and the pull of Melissa tugging my arm.

"C'mon, Lizzie, I've been looking all over for you. It's time to blow out the candles!"

We walked back to the house. I could think of only one thing. *When will this party be over?*

Chapter Eight

Tonight was our last performance with Lance. Our congregation would be saying goodbye to the only music director they had ever known. Lance had been serving on staff since the church was planted three years ago. Spencer Hayes had been introduced last week. Apparently, he'd caused quite a stir. Everyone was abuzz with anticipation for him coming on board. Mason met him and liked him instantly. I, however, hadn't been able to meet him. Two days after the disastrous birthday party, I'd come down with strep throat.

I'd spent my first week of winter break laid up in bed, sucking down ice cubes and drinking chicken broth. Aidan had heard from Mason I was sick, and that's when the texting had started. The first few texts from Aidan had been innocent enough.

Hey, Lizzie, I heard you were sick.
How are you? Are you feeling better?

I deleted them unanswered.
By midweek, his texts were groveling.

I'm sorry. Can I see you? Please?
Again, I deleted them.
At the end of the week, I could almost feel his rage.

Why won't you answer me?
Can you at least answer my texts?
Will you let me try and explain?"

Delete.
Delete.
Delete.
Finally, the texting stopped.

****

The church was beautiful. Behind the podium, three decorated Christmas trees lit the stage. Twinkling lights reflected off the slick black surface of the baby grand piano. Fresh evergreen swags were draped throughout the sanctuary. The scent of pine filled the air, and a lone candle illuminated a small nativity.

After the performance, I was finally going to meet Spencer. He was sitting in the audience with his family. Thankfully, I felt good. Surprisingly good, considering how I'd felt just a few days ago. I'd barely said two words last week, hoping not to strain my vocal cords, knowing tonight I was closing out the performance with "Silent Night."

Lance had been a nervous wreck because I had been so ill, but when I nailed the song during rehearsal, he'd been relieved. After our practice ended we'd had a private going away party for Lance. I'd been an emotional mess, and all the guys had broken down. Lance had teared up when we presented him with a heartfelt video montage of our best moments together.

The church lights dimmed as I took center stage. When I glanced over at Lance, his kind brown eyes were filled with emotion. Lance knew I hated the limelight, but he'd used every tactic he had to get me to solo.

Finally, he'd cashed in the guilt card, knowing since this was his last night, I'd never refuse him. My usual custom was to hide behind the safety of my piano, but tonight that wasn't the case. I wiped my palms on my green dress then tried to adjust my mic, but my hands kept fumbling. Mason approached me to help. He lowered the mic then covered it with his hand.

"You okay?" he whispered.

"I'm freakin' out, Mason — I can't do this." I must have looked terrified because the concern in Mason's eyes seemed worried on my behalf. "It's packed out there."

"Liz, stop it. You're good. Just suck it up. Close your eyes during the whole song if you need to. Pretend you're at home. Whatever it takes. But you have to do this." Mason looked at me wide-eyed. "Breathe, Liz."

I took a deep breath and nodded at Mason. "You ready?"

I nodded.

Mason stepped back, picked up his guitar, and began strumming the chords.

My hair was pulled up in a twisted bun, and a few loose curls framed my face. I nervously chewed my thumbnail, and seconds later the spotlight was on me. My hands trembled while I reached for the mic stand and held onto it for support. I gathered all the confidence within me, closed my eyes, and began to sing. I wanted to run from the stage when I heard the quivering in my voice, but thankfully by the second chorus, it subsided. When the song neared the end, my nerves had tapered off as my hands dropped to my side. Lance silenced the instruments, and I finished the song a cappella.

When I finally opened my eyes, they were met with

thunderous applause. Relieved the song was over, I stepped back, hoping to take the attention off me. I motioned for Lance to join me, and within seconds, everyone was on their feet in adoration for this sweet man they loved. I gave him a warm embrace and told him for the last time I would miss him. I stepped back, allowing the church to pay homage to Lance. Overcome with grief, I wiped away my tears and exited the stage. When I turned the corner toward the hallway, I was met with the piercing blue eyes of Aidan Mitchell.

Stunned, I stood with my mouth gaping. Aidan was standing before me looking as gorgeous as ever. I closed my mouth while the last few tears fell from my eyes. An awkward silence filled the space between us. Aidan seemed anxious, but he spoke first.

"You wouldn't text me back, and I had to see you. I didn't know what else to do. I knew you'd be singing tonight. That's why I'm here." Tension swept across his beautiful face while he stared at me. I wiped the last of my tears away and rubbed my temples.

"What do you want from me, Aidan? What could you possibly have to say to me?"

Aidan reached out and tried to stroke my arm, but I backed away. His eyes roamed over my face, and he murmured, "I'm sorry."

"Fine." I brushed past him then headed toward the exit door.

Aidan came after me and placed his hands on the door, closing me in. "Will you just listen to me? Please?" He groaned in frustration. "I just want to talk to you to clear things up." His tone was desperate but guarded.

The pent-up anger from the last week was bubbling up inside me. Even Aidan's sheepish expression didn't faze me as my emotions became freely unleashed. "To clear up what? That you treated me like crap? That you kissed me, and I never heard from you again? That on my birthday you showed up with some whore, who was all over you on the dance floor? Is that what you want to clear up? Well, we're clear. Perfectly clear!"

I pushed him away, leaving Aidan in the wake of my fury then exited the door. The December air chilled me as I walked into the night.

****

After an uncomfortable night of tossing and turning, unable to sleep any longer, I finally got up. A thick veil of fog had rolled in offshore, covering my morning running route with a cloud-like mass. I was at my usual streetlamp, stretching out my legs while Maggie sniffed around. The visibility was so poor if Maggie was more than six feet in front of me, I couldn't see her. She didn't seem to mind, and neither did I.

Maggie and I jogged past my hot neighbor's house. The garage was open and the jeep was there, but the motorcycle was gone. I scanned the streets on my way to the creek bed, hoping to get a glimpse of him, but no luck. Trying to rid my mind from thoughts of Aidan, I put in my ear buds and blasted my music. It didn't help.

I kept replaying what had happened last night in my head. I had never yelled at anyone before, and the guilt was all-consuming. I wouldn't even listen to Aidan, and that wasn't me. I was usually so reasonable and understanding, giving people the benefit of the doubt. In a snap decision, I took my cell phone from my pocket. It was still early, but I didn't care. I tapped out a text to him before I changed my mind.

Me: *I'm ready to listen.*
Aidan: *Now?*

I was surprised Aidan texted me back so quickly, it was only 7:04 a.m.

Me: *Coffee place in the harbor at ten-thirty.*
Aidan: *Great. Thanks, Liz.*

The guilt was gone, and I immediately felt better. With this renewed sense of freedom, I surrendered myself to the run. The fog had lifted, and sweat was beading down my forehead. I was running in sync to the music, like a well-oiled machine, but then, I stopped.

Ahead in the distance, I saw a black and tan mangy dog sniffing around some trashcans. I removed my ear buds and slowly backed away, whispering Maggie's name. I silently prayed the stray dog didn't see us, but my prayer was unanswered. The dog glanced up and was headed our way.

I watched in horror while this raging animal charged with angry eyes fixed on my sweet Maggie. Adrenaline coursed through my veins, and my heart pounded. My eyes darted around, nervously looking for a place to run.

The dog was bearing down fast, but I knew I couldn't outrun it. My trembling hand reached in a frantic attempt for the pepper spray. My efforts were met with no avail as the impact of this unprovoked aggressive dog collided with me. The force of the blow knocked me to ground, causing me to drop the leash. Pain exploded from the back of my head as it slammed against the concrete. I staggered to my feet, clutching my head. I could feel blood trickling between my fingers. Maggie let out a yelp then rolled on her back in submission.

The snarling mongrel lunged forward, latching onto the soft fleshy fur at the base of Maggie's neck. Maggie cried out and rolled to her feet, then I grabbed the leash and yanked her back. Maggie's instincts kicked in, and she savagely attacked the aggressive animal. Tears streamed down my face, and I screamed for somebody to help me. Maggie's yellow coat was covered with splotches of red blood. I was vaguely aware a few cars had pulled to the side of the road.

Someone was yelling to call an ambulance. The sound of stomping feet ran past me toward the vicious dog. I heard the dog yelp as it ran toward the creek bed. Maggie was lying limp a few feet away, whimpering. I tried to reach her, but I stumbled. A strong warm arm caught me before I fell to the ground.

"Be still, darlin', you're hurt." I was wrapped in the arms of a soft leather jacket, looking into the most beautiful eyes I had ever seen.

I choked out the words, "My dog, Maggie," before I slipped into the darkness.

Chapter Nine

My eyelids fluttered open to the tearstained face of my mother.

"How do you feel, Liz? Does your head hurt?"

I lifted my hand to silence her before I turned my head toward the floor and violently threw up. Mom ran out of the room to get the nurse.

My head ached, and my body felt heavy. My left arm was bandaged from forearm to elbow, and my right arm was stuck with an IV. I was wearing an itchy hospital gown, covered with a thin blanket. Surveying the sterile environment, tears rolled down my cheeks. My immediate thought was of Maggie.

Mom hurried back to my bedside, a nurse followed behind her. I wiped my tears away before the nurse reached the bed.

"Hi, Elizabeth, I'm Katelyn." Nurse Katelyn seemed to be in her mid-twenties, with wavy red hair pulled back in a ponytail and kind blue eyes. She checked my vital signs, told us the doctor would be in shortly, and cleaned up the vomit.

"Mom, what happened to... Maggie?" I could barely get the words out. I held my breath and waited for her to respond.

"Melissa and Mason took her to Dr. Wheaton. He's stitching her up now. He said she's going to be fine."

I breathed a sigh of relief followed by tears.

"Oh, Mom, I was so scared. I thought she… was…"

"Sh-h-h, sweetie, she's hurt, but she's gonna be okay." Mom glanced toward the door as my dad anxiously walked into the room.

"How's my girl?" Dad rubbed my blanket-covered leg as his eyes narrowed in concern.

"My head hurts, and I feel dizzy. What's wrong with me?"

As if on cue, the doctor walked through the door. Dr. Lee was a soft-spoken man who explained I had a concussion, stitches from the wound on the back of my head, and several cuts and abrasions. During Dr. Lee's examination of me, I glanced at my parents.

"How did I get here?"

Mom glanced to my dad then back at me. "You don't remember being in the ambulance?"

"No, not at all. I remember screaming and trying to get Maggie away from that dog."

"You were so brave. We're just so thankful you're okay." She turned her attention to the doctor. "She is going to be okay. Right, Doctor?" Mom seemed anxious as she questioned Dr. Lee.

Dr. Lee focused his attention on my parents. "We're going to keep her overnight for observation. I'm sure she is going to be fine. If her night goes well, she'll be discharged in the morning." Dr. Lee scribbled a few notes on a clipboard before he exited the room.

After I relived what I could remember from the dogfight, my parents kept me company for a while. Dad even joked about how I was a little warrior. When I told them I was tired, they each kissed me on my head and said they would be back later that night.

My sleep was interrupted with the gentle probing of

Nurse Katelyn. She checked my vitals and refilled my water jug. I glanced at the clock in the room while she replaced my IV bag.

It was 4:38 p.m. *Aidan!*

"Katelyn, do you know where my stuff is?"

"Yes, all your personal belongings are in this drawer." Nurse Katelyn bent down to the table next to my bed. She pulled out a large plastic bag.

I cringed when I saw my bloodstained workout clothes.

She glanced at the cell phone and told me it was against hospital policy to use it. She put the bag next to me and said with a wink, "Don't get caught."

When she exited the room, I grabbed the phone.

Five missed texts. The first four were from Aidan.

10:28: *I'm here. I'll order you a nonfat latte.*
10:35: *I'm sitting outside.*
10:45: *Your latte is getting cold.*
11:02: *I can't believe you stood me up.*

Melissa's text was last.

4:25: *Mason and I are on our way to pick up Maggie. We'll be at the hospital soon. I love you.*

Several missed calls and messages, but the only one I listened to was Aidan's at 11:28 a.m.

"I can't believe you. You text me and wake me up, tell me you'll meet me, and you don't show up? Is this your way of getting back at me? Thanks... thanks a lot."

I tried to call Aidan, but the cell service was so bad it wouldn't go through. I tapped out a text and hoped it had enough power to reach him.

Me: *I'm at the hospital.*
Aidan: *What happened?*
Me: *My phone's gonna die. I'll tell you later.*
Aidan: *Saddleback or Mission?*
Me: *Mission.*
Aidan: *I'm on my way.*

I put my cell phone back in the drawer then I gingerly got out of bed. Clutching the IV stand for support, I rolled my way into the bathroom. I stood at the sink and gasped in horror at my reflection.

Thin red scrapes covered the left side of my forehead, and I was bruised above my cheekbone. I touched the back of my head and felt a swollen egg-sized lump. My hair was a matted mess. I felt a bandage, and, for a second, I wondered how much hair they'd had to shave off to stitch me up.

Desperate for a toothbrush, I swished some cool water in my mouth and spit. I tried to untangle the matted mess of hair with my fingers but gave up when the standing became too much. I rolled myself back to bed and carefully climbed back in.

About a half an hour later, Aidan walked in the door. As usual, he looked amazing. Thankfully, I wasn't hooked up to a heart monitor, or it would have been beeping out of control. He winced when he saw me.

Aidan's eyes were fixed on mine. His voice was soft and soothing while he stroked the bare skin of my arm, careful to avoid the IV line. "What happened?" he asked.

I proceeded to tell him what I could remember. His expression ranged from pained to relief when I told him I was going to be fine, and Maggie was okay, too.

Aidan moved his chair and leaned in close. He picked up a loose strand of my hair and tucked it behind my ear. He stared at me for a long time as if he were struggling for words.

I whispered, "Talk to me..."

Aidan exhaled before he began. "I was scared, Liz, scared of how I was feeling for you." Shamefaced, Aidan paused for a moment. "You know me, usually if I hang out with a girl, it ends up as a hook-up. I never told anyone about my mom, my life... it scared the crap out of me." He reached for my hand and held it while the pad of his thumb swept back and forth. "I'm sorry for being such a jerk at your party. Dancing with that girl. I know I hurt you. After I kissed you in your room, I knew you'd expect things to be different between us. I wasn't ready for a relationship. Or, I thought I wasn't ready. I was an idiot, and, like a fool, I pushed you away. I didn't realize how much I cared about you until I cut you out of my life. I feel like I lost my best friend." Aidan paused and shifted in his seat, "I know I hurt you, and I hate myself for it. I'm so sorry. I wish I could go back and change every stupid thing I did, but I can't. All I can do is ask you to forgive me and hope you can."

We sat in silence for a few minutes. I tried to absorb his words. His gaze met mine and he let out a deep breath. He seemed so vulnerable and stripped bare.

"I miss you, Liz. I miss everything about you. Do you think we could start over?" The desperation in his voice was undeniable.

Aidan was still holding my hand when Melissa and

Mason walked through the door. I didn't have time to respond. My eyes focused on a wide-eyed Melissa, and when I glanced at Mason, his stunned expression was locked on our clasped hands.

"What's going on? What are you doing here, Aidan?" Mason's troubled tone was starting to sound annoyed.

Aidan's chair screeched as he got up. I felt the warmth of his hand leave mine as he pulled away.

"I heard Liz was hurt, and I needed to talk to her."

Mason ran a hand through his hair as Melissa left his side to stand by me.

"About what?" Mason's unblinking eyes were locked on Aidan.

Aidan approached him. "This doesn't have anything to do with you, Mason."

Melissa and I both watched the tension build between them.

Mason took a step forward.

"Yeah, I think it does. When I walk in here and see you holding hands with my sister? It has a lot to do with me."

"I care about her." Aidan glanced at me then back to Mason.

"Sure ya do." Mason smirked.

"You can be such a jerk sometimes." Aidan bit back.

"Me? I'm not the one who sleeps with anything with a pulse.

And if you think my sister is going to be the next…"

"Stop it!" I cried. All eyes focused on me. "I can't listen to this right now. Please, just stop," I begged.

The room was silent. Melissa had to move out of the way when Aidan walked boldly to my bedside. He leaned down, the warmth of his breath against my ear then whispered, "Just think about what I've said."

The words lingered through my mind as Aidan gently kissed my head. He brushed past my scowling brother and exited the room.

Mason took a few calming breaths before he approached me. "What the… Liz. I don't want you with Aidan… you know how he is. He treats girls like crap."

Melissa stroked his arm and told him to calm down. Mason didn't seem to hear her.

"Tell me what's going on."

My eyes welled with tears. I was in no mood to fight with Mason, especially since I knew he was right.

Melissa grabbed Mason's arm harder. "Mason! Leave her alone. You can talk about this later."

"I need some air."

Melissa and I watched as Mason stalked from the room. She turned back to me and gave my hand a firm squeeze.

"Are you okay?" Melissa asked as she comforted me with a sympathetic smile. "What happened?"

Unsure if she was asking about the dogfight or Aidan, I again retold my experience of earlier that day. An awkward silence was between us, but knowing how inquisitive Melissa was, I started in before she had time to ask me any questions.

"I wanted to tell you about Aidan, but knowing how you felt about him, I just couldn't. I was trying to figure things out on my own. I was doing pretty good with everything, until now." I sighed. "Now I don't know what to do."

Melissa was absorbed in my words. I filled her in on every detail leading up to that day. She leaned back in her chair and exhaled.

"I'm just worried about you, Liz. What if you decide to give Aidan a chance and he hurts you? Do you think he can change?"

"I don't know, Melissa. I still need to talk to him."

My parents walked in the room. Dad was holding a bunch of balloons, and Mom was holding a bag. Melissa got up, but I reached for her arm, and she leaned in close.

"Could you fill Mason in on everything? He might take it better coming from you."

"I'm not so sure about that, but I'll do my best." She said goodbye to my parents and me then left the room.

A few minutes later Mason came back and approached my bed. My dad was tying the balloons to a table and my mom was pulling out clothes and toiletries from the overnight bag.

"I'm sorry I lost my temper. I just want the best for you, and I don't think Aidan is it."

A few tears fell from my eyes when Mason reached down and hugged me. "I'm so glad you're alright," he whispered.

I sobbed while my brother held me.

****

The next morning, Dr. Lee examined me one last time and gave me the green light to go home. A nurse I'd never seen before handed my mom discharge papers, information regarding wound care, along with a prescription for antibiotics. By the time we walked out of the hospital doors, it was almost 3:00 p.m. My body ached, and my head still throbbed, but knowing I would be home soon made me feel better.

Mom helped me walk through our front door. A gimpy Maggie immediately greeted me. Tears fell as I coaxed her back to her bed and inspected her sutures. My face nestled into hers, and I caressed her soft fur and covered her in kisses. She looked horrible, but her injuries didn't seem to affect her mood. She was still as playful as ever. I told her to stay. My mom helped me up the stairs. We headed straight to my bathroom.

"Thank you, Mom... but I'm okay now." "Alright, sweetie, I'll check on you in a bit."

When my mom shut the door, I turned the bathtub on full blast. Before the hot water covered the room with steam, I stared at myself in the mirror above the sink. My bruise looked worse today than yesterday. It was an array of colors ranging from a muted yellow to a garish purple. *Lovely.*

I removed my clothes, thankful my mom had brought me a front-button shirtdress from her closet. I balanced myself against the wall and placed one pointed toe in the hot water. The other foot soon followed, and I eased down into the water. With a towel rolled up behind my neck, I leaned back against the tub and rested my bandaged arm on the ledge. I closed my eyes and let the hot water envelope my aching body while the steam billowed around me. My thoughts were consumed with Aidan.

He wants to start over. He misses me. He's sorry for how he's treated me. He's never shared about his life with anyone, but he did, with me.

A knock at the door freed me from my dilemma. It was my mom asking me if I was okay. I told her I was fine, because I was. Finally, I knew exactly what I was going to do.

Chapter Ten

I'd texted Aidan earlier and told him I had thought about what he'd said and was ready to see him. He wanted to pick me up after he got off work, but since Mason was home, I decided meeting him elsewhere would be better. My mom was happy to bring me to meet him. Aidan had charmed her months ago during our tutoring sessions and band practice. She adored him.

"Ouch! Careful, Mom." I jerked my head away when my mom pulled the brush through my damp hair.

"Oh, Liz, I can't believe you got your hair wet when the doctor told you not to!"

"I couldn't handle how my hair felt. I had to wash it. It was gross. Besides, I was careful."

My mom inspected the back of my head and strategically placed my hair away from the stitches. "Your stitches look good, but still — I wish you hadn't. You have to be careful." Mom scanned the floor and picked up my dirty clothes. "What time do you want me to drop you off at the harbor?"

"How about in an hour?" I handed her my wet towels. "Do you need me to pick you up?"

"No, Aidan can bring me home."

"Okay." My mom took a step toward me. Her anxious eyes roamed over my bruise and the scrapes on my forehead. "Are you sure you feel good enough to go out?"

"I feel fine, Mom."

"Okay," she muttered. Her arms were overloaded with my dirty clothes as she exited my room.

I closed the door behind her, put on a green t-shirt, jeans, boots, and my black pea-coat with a red-and-green tartan scarf. Since Christmas was only a few days away, I thought I'd try and make myself look festive. I glanced at my reflection one last time.

My hair looked pretty good, considering it had been a matted mess just an hour before. I applied some mascara and eyeliner, hoping to distract from the scrapes on my forehead and bruise on my face, but I still looked a fright. Oh, well. This was as good as I was going to get.

****

I was about to go inside the small café when my phone chimed with a text.

Aidan: *You there?*

Me: *Yes, what do you want to drink?*

Aidan: *Nothing. Get us a table and sit. I'll get our drinks.*

Me: *I can get them.*

Aidan: *Sit. I'll be there in five.*

The brisk air of the early evening felt cool against my bruised cheek. I buttoned up my coat and took a seat under one of the green café umbrellas. A gentle breeze carried the aroma of coffee through the air. The railings surrounding the harbor looked beautiful. They were draped with decorated garland and holiday bows. The annual Christmas boat parade had been a few weeks ago, so most of the sailboats were covered in twinkling lights. The harbor was bustling with shoppers, couples walking arm in arm, and plenty of tourists.

In anticipation of Aidan's arrival, I chewed my thumbnail. He'd be here any minute. I was prepared with what I wanted to say to him, but I only hoped my decision was the right one. In the middle of my internal pep talk, I spotted him while he casually maneuvered his way through the crowded walkway. I watched in awe as each female between the ages of fourteen and forty noticed him. Even from a distance, he took my breath away. When he got closer to the café, he scanned the tables, and when his eyes met mine, he flashed me a smile that lit up his face.

Aidan seemed nervous when he approached the table. His hands were stuffed in his front pockets as he rocked on his heels. He hesitated before he leaned over the table and gave me a gentle kiss on the cheek. His blond hair was slicked back, apparently still damp from a recent shower. He smelled clean, and his breath was minty-fresh.

In a whisper he said, "Hi," then stood up and glanced toward the coffee house.

"Non-fat latte, right?" "Yes, please." I smiled.

He fished in his back pocket, grabbed his wallet, and headed into the café. He returned a few minutes later with two steaming paper cups. He placed my latte in front of me and sat down. The sweet aroma drifted between us. Using the steam from the cup, I warmed my hands.

"Are you cold?" "A little bit."

Aidan took my hands in his and rubbed them together. "How are you feeling? You look so much better." His eyes swept over me.

"Thanks, I feel pretty good. I just wish I didn't look

so beat up."

"You're still beautiful, bruises and all."

I took a deep breath and began the dialogue I'd rehearsed in my head all afternoon, except I decided to change my opening statement after his recent compliment.

"Was I not beautiful before?" I took a sip of my latte. It warmed my insides while it slid down my throat. I glanced at Aidan as he moved his chair closer toward mine.

"You were always beautiful. I was just too stupid to see it." Aidan was silent for a few minutes and his eyes shifted from mine to his steaming cup.

I took a deep breath and gazed over the boats docked in the harbor. I gave myself a few more minutes before I finally spoke up. "I thought about everything you said. You said you were scared. I'm scared too." When I twisted my body toward him, his eyes met mine. "Just look at you. Girls are always going to be throwing themselves at you. We've even joked about it."

Aidan held my hand. "Other girls don't matter to me. I want you. Can't you see that?" he countered.

"I came here tonight to tell you to forget about me, about us.

That I didn't trust you, and we'd be better off just friends."

Aidan eyed me cautiously. Several things ran through my mind, but the most unbelievable was he wanted me. I wanted to trust him because he seemed so sincere, but he had already hurt me and I was so worried it would happen again. Part of my subconscious was screaming *Don't be stupid. Don't fall for him,* and the other part was screaming *Don't be stupid. Go for it.*

"I want to believe you, but I'm scared."

Aidan pulled me into his arms and kissed me on my forehead then whispered, "I'm scared too, but let's try."

I felt myself getting caught in his spell. I reached up and pushed him back so I could look him in the eyes.

"Why did you try and kiss Melissa?" I could tell he was shocked I knew about what had almost happened between them.

After a few minutes he answered. "I don't know. I kept watching how she and Mason were together. I wasn't thinking. I guess I wanted, ya know, what they have together, but what they have, I want with you."

He answered me with such sincerity I believed him. Maybe I was being a fool, but I believed him. Aidan pulled me into his arms and rubbed my back.

"Please, Liz, forgive me. Give me a chance."

We sat in silence until I whispered, "Just don't hurt me." I felt his body relax. Then he kissed me softly on the lips.

We sat nestled together, gazing over the festive lights. Our coffee was cold, and the café workers started closing the umbrellas for the night.

"Do you feel up to taking a walk?" Aidan murmured. "Sure."

I picked up our cups and threw them in the trash. Aidan reached for my hand and we strolled through the twinkling lights of the harbor. The soft moonlight was shining against the rippling water. Aidan stopped me in front of a railing near the water's edge. He wrapped his arms around me and hugged me from behind.

"I've never wanted a relationship before. I promise not to hurt you," he whispered.

I leaned back into his firm chest while he gave me

slow soft kisses from my neck to my cheek. I turned to face him, and his kisses moved to my lips. I reached my arms under his hoodie to feel his warm muscular back. Aidan's touch was firm as he gripped my back, aligning my body with his. He kissed me more aggressively and accidentally bumped my bruised cheek. I winced back in pain. He released me and lightly traced the outline of my bruise with the tips of his fingers.

"Sorry." He gazed down at me with a look of concern. "I'd better get you home." He placed his hand on the small of my back and led me toward the parking lot. "Time to face the music," he said with a wry smile.

"What are you talking about?" I cocked my head and tilted it to the side.

"Your brother." He opened the passenger side door of his truck and motioned for me to get inside.

"I'll handle Mason. Don't worry about him."

"I saw how ticked he was. He's not going to take out his anger on you because I've been such an idiot."

His assertive tone was firm, and I chose not to argue. "Okay… but, Mason can be pretty stubborn."

Aidan leaned in and gave me a big smile. "And I can be extremely persuasive."

Then he closed the passenger side door. I watched him as he walked to his side of the truck.

That's what I'm afraid of.

Chapter Eleven

Last night turned into an extremely long night. When Aidan and I walked in the door, Melissa and Mason were cuddling on the couch. We were able to tell them both we were giving our relationship a chance. Easy or not, it was what I wanted.

Everything was out in the open. Aidan and I didn't want to start our relationship with lies, so with my hand in his, Aidan confessed to almost kissing Melissa. I was proud of him for wanting to own up to his mistake. Aidan did his best to try and explain his stupidity, and after a tense twenty minutes, the worst part of the conversation was over. There was nothing more to hide.

Aidan apologized to both Mason and Melissa and even said my brother could throw a punch at him. Mason didn't, of course, but I thought he appreciated the opportunity just the same.

By the end of the evening, everyone had accepted our decision. The last words I heard my brother say were: "If you hurt her, I'll kill you."

Our relationship was just beginning, so Mason and Melissa were going to need some time to trust Aidan and, if I was honest with myself, it was going to take time for me, too. But, I was happy. For the first time in a long, long time, I was happy.

****

Christmas was just a few days away. Aidan and I

hadn't done any shopping yet, so we decided to make our first official date a shopping one. Not the most romantic but strolling the mall hand in hand with Aidan didn't sound so bad either. He was going to pick me up at 1:00 p.m. Random Plan was playing later that night, so we had to be back reasonably early.

Surprisingly, my hair still looked pretty good, so I just pulled the sides back and camouflaged the stitches with a few strands of loose curls. My bruise was still prominent in color but, thankfully, the swelling had gone down. The bandage on my arm was bulky, so I decided to replace the large gauze strip with a latex one. Rifling through my drawers, I pulled out a cream-colored sweater, jeans, and grabbed my grey shoes.

I headed downstairs to check on Maggie and drink a protein shake before Aidan arrived. A beautiful arrangement of sunflowers sat on the kitchen island. Even though my parents had been married for twenty-two years, my dad still brought my mom flowers for no reason at all. So, seeing the beautiful bouquet didn't faze me until my mother said the flowers were for me.

"What?" I gasped.

Mom was emptying the dishwasher. "They were delivered earlier this morning when you were sleeping." My mom stopped what she was doing, gave me a huge grin, and handed me the card. I ripped it open and read the note.

Elizabeth,
I'm looking forward to officially meeting you.
I hope you're feeling better soon.
Spencer Hayes

I stared at my mom in surprise and handed her the card. She read the short message, smiled, and handed it back to me.

"How sweet. Your dad and I can't wait to meet him. Mason says he's great."

I grabbed a protein shake from the fridge and my mom left to go back upstairs. I drank my shake and reread the card again.

I'm looking forward to officially meeting you.

I downed the rest of my shake, picked up my flowers, and carried them upstairs to the bedside table. Maggie barked as the doorbell rang. I walked downstairs, gave Maggie a few gentle rubs, and opened the door. The adorable smile of my boyfriend made my heart beat a little faster.

"Ready?" he said, reaching for my hand.

"Yep." I gave Aidan's hand a squeeze, then he guided me to the truck.

When he opened the passenger door, he held my gaze as I leaned inside. He smiled before he softly brushed his lips to mine. I reached my arms around his neck and closed my eyes, allowing him to deepen the kiss. My insides trembled when Aidan's body was firmly pressed against mine. I felt the seat behind me, and, without breaking our kiss, he effortlessly lifted me so I was now sitting with my legs apart, and he was between them. His hand found its way to the small of my back beneath my sweater. I stilled at the contact, and then he kissed me again.

Aidan backed away then murmured, "We'd better stop, or we'll never get out of here."

I nodded and exhaled a breathy "Okay."

My heart was pounding, watching Aidan get into the truck. He turned his gaze to mine and winked before he put the key in the ignition. No doubt about it... I needed to talk to Aidan. My innocence was already hanging on by a thread, and it was only our first date.

****

"That was insane!" Aidan sounded exhausted. He carried all my packages up the stairs to my room, dropped them on the bed, and eyed the sunflowers on my bedside table.

"From your parents?" he asked while taking a sniff.

"Not exactly." I give him a half-smile.

"Oh?" He sounded surprised. "May I?" He raised an eyebrow and picked up the card.

I shrugged. "Sure."

Aidan studied the card. "Who's Spencer?"

"He's the new guy in charge of the band at church."

"What's he like?" Aidan approached me while I sat on the edge of my bed.

"I haven't met him yet, but Mason likes him a lot."

Aidan moved the bags aside then gently laid me down. "Well, as long as *you* don't like him a lot, we're good."

I giggled when Aidan crawled up beside me and covered my neck in kisses.

****

Aidan leaned against his truck as I drank in the sight of him. "You're sure you don't want to drive together tonight? I can come back and pick you up." He pulled me into his chest and planted a quick soft kiss on my lips.

"I need to go to church and pick up a few packages. I'll just meet you there."

"Okay, gorgeous girl. I'll see you tonight."

I smiled and watched him as he got in his truck and drove away.

****

It felt like I hadn't driven in forever. I cranked up the volume and sang along with the music then headed to church.

Lance had sent me a text earlier in the day. He'd wanted to let me know he had left Mason and me a Christmas gift. With all the chaos of his last night, he'd forgotten to give them to us. His text said to pick them up in the music room.

I pulled into the empty parking lot and entered through the back door. It seemed eerie to walk the halls of the church when no one other than the staff was there. I walked quickly toward the music room.

When I approached the door, the sound of an acoustic guitar and a man's soulful voice overwhelmed me. I reached up to knock but stopped. Not wanting to disturb whoever was behind the door, I took a step back to walk away. But the voice was drawing me in. Curiosity had my hand on the doorknob, and, with a click, it was open. The music became louder when I stepped inside the small room.

His voice was filled with such emotion. The pitch was smooth, yet when he hit the high notes, there was a roughness in his tone, making it sound seductive. His back was toward me, so I continued to watch him unnoticed.

The song was sexy, far too sexy to be played in the music room at church. Listening to his soulful voice and the provocative lyrics made me feel like I was invading his privacy, rather than casually observing. My gaze was still fixed on him while I backed away to walk out of the room. I reached behind me to grab the door handle, but my hand slipped, causing a thud. My head bumped against the door, and I heard myself cry out in pain.

Abruptly, the music stopped. He spun around, and our eyes met. Within seconds, he was up on his feet. The next thing I knew, he was at my side. Gradually, I sunk to the floor.

"Are you okay, Elizabeth?" Anxious grey eyes were locked on mine. I was tongue-tied for a minute, trying to process all the information spinning around in my head.

"I think so." I reached up to touch the back of my head to make sure my stitches weren't bleeding.

"Here, let me."

He kneeled and carefully examined my wound. The proximity of his body next to mine, combined with his warm subtle scent, was making me nervous. From my peripheral vision, I could see his chiseled jaw was covered in light stubble and his full bottom lip was tense with concern. He sighed a breath of relief.

"No blood. I think you're good." A dimpled smile crossed his face, then he sat down next to me. Both of us were leaning against the wall, my knees bent, his legs outstretched.

"Do you feel dizzy?"

I could still hear the concern in his voice. I was lost for a minute in the unusual color of his eyes.

A part of me wanted to laugh. Looking at this Adonis of a man? *I'd say I'm dizzy.* All I could squeak out was "A little bit."

He nodded and scanned my face with those beautiful grey eyes.

"You're Spencer? You're my... neighbor?"

"Yes." He chuckled. "Finally, I get to meet the mysterious Elizabeth Ryan." Usually I preferred the name, Liz, but the way his sultry voice caressed my full name, I didn't mind.

"What? Mysterious?" I answered.

"Do you have any idea how many times I've tried to meet you?"

"Well, no, not exactly," I shyly responded.

He twisted his body to look at me. "You were sick the first week I got here. After the Christmas concert, I came backstage to meet you. One minute you were singing on stage, and the next you were gone. And then, the dog attack."

"Wait. You were there?"

"I was there." He nodded. "I just wish I'd been able to get to you sooner. If I had, maybe all this," he motioned to my injuries with his hand, "wouldn't have happened. I had to kick the mutt to get him away from your dog."

I glanced down at Spencer's feet. He was wearing heavy, black motorcycle boots. I shuddered at the thought of being kicked with them.

"Anyway, after the Christmas concert, I knew who you were, so when the ambulance came, I told them your name. I felt terrible I couldn't stay to make sure you were okay, but I had to leave town. I got back yesterday, sent you the flowers I'm assuming you got today, and well, here we are."

"I'm sorry. I didn't mean to barge in on you while you were singing." I cocked my head to look at him. "By the way, what was the song you were singing?"

"Oh that." Now he was embarrassed. "It's a song called 'Unbroken Promises.' Like it?"

His dimpled smile made me blush. "Yes. Not sure the song is right for church." I raised an eyebrow at him.

"Well, I thought I was alone." He smiled while he held out his hand to help me up.

I glanced at his muscular arms, knowing his tattoos were hidden under the long-sleeved thermal he was wearing.

The wrapped Christmas presents were on the table. "This is actually what I came here for." I checked the tags, picked up the packages, and gave him a small smile. Spencer grabbed a well- worn, brown leather jacket from the back of a chair, put it on, and reached out to take the packages from me.

"Let me hold those for ya, darlin'."

Clearly he wasn't Southern, and hearing the term of endearment coming out of this tatted-up guy made it sound all the sweeter. Spencer juggled the gifts in one arm so he could open the door for me. We walked down the hallway toward the parking lot together. He was Aidan's height, and their body types were almost identical, but that's where the similarities ended. Aidan was a blond, pretty boy with delicate features. Spencer, with his dark brown hair and strong facial features, was more masculine. Although, when he flashed his dimples, there was a boyish quality about him. They were both ridiculously attractive… *seriously*.

Spencer walked me to my car and put the packages in the back seat. He took a step toward me and gave me the once-over.

"Are you sure you aren't dizzy anymore? You'll be okay to drive?"

"I'm fine and thank you for the beautiful flowers." I smiled. "Beautiful flowers for a beautiful girl," he said, and I felt myself blush. Then he took a step toward me as he whispered, "Merry Christmas."

I inhaled his delicious scent one more time and murmured, "Merry Christmas, Spencer."

I sat in my car for a minute and watched him until he fired up his bike and rode away.

****

The restaurant was packed. Since winter break was still in full force, most of the kids from school were there. I noticed the cute brunette Aidan had flirted with a few weeks ago. She'd become quite a fixture. I tried to push the image from my mind while Melissa and I scanned the crowded venue, looking for a place to sit.

From the back of the stage, Mason's head popped up. He pointed to a small table he'd saved for us. The regulars, primarily college-age girls, were coming up to greet the guys. Mason never seemed to let the attention go to his head, while Derek ate it up, and Kyle seemed uncomfortable.

The minute Kyle saw Melissa and me, he stepped off the stage and maneuvered his way to our table. Kyle was more like me. He enjoyed being in the band, but the attention overwhelmed him. I guess that's part of the reason he'd always been a favorite of mine.

Kyle asked me about the dogfight and how I was feeling. I went into autopilot, retelling my story, breaking eye contact now and then to glance over the room. Aidan was here. I had seen his truck in the parking lot. But with each passing minute, I became uneasy, my imagination was getting the best of me. The onslaught of mental images of Aidan consumed my brain: behind the building, in his truck, the bathroom, anywhere, with some girl. Suddenly, from behind me, warm hands clasped my shoulders and startled me. Smooth, clean-shaven skin was against my cheek.

"How's my girl?" His voice was a whisper.

My fears diminished as Aidan nuzzled my ear, sending chills down my spine.

"What's going on?" Kyle gasped. His eyes darted from me to Aidan. Out of the corner of my eye, I could see Melissa smirking in that you-made-your-bed-now-lie-in-it kind of way.

"Well…" I stammered out, but Mason cut in and interrupted me.

"C'mon, guys, it's time for the set to start."

Aidan gave me a quick kiss on the cheek, and they headed toward the stage.

For the first time since I'd made the decision to become Aidan's girlfriend, I was embarrassed. The look in Kyle's eyes made me feel like a fool. I knew what he was thinking. It's what everyone was thinking. I had just been thinking the same thing a few minutes ago.

Aidan picked up his bass, and I watched as the adoring fans drooled over my boyfriend. Then reality hit me. If Aidan and I were going to have a chance at our relationship working, I was going to have to put his past behind us and, as hard as it was going to be… trust him. If I didn't, being a couple would never work. When the thought crossed my mind, our eyes met, and a slow sexy smile spread across his face. It made my heart melt.

The guys were singing the usual fan favorites and throwing in a few holiday songs here and there. Earsplitting cries came from a few of the college girls while Mason sang a romantic ballad.

"How do you handle that, Melissa?" I motioned to the girls panting over my brother.

Melissa shrugged. "I trust him." She smiled and continued to watch Mason finish the song.

Trust… such a small word but it meant everything in a relationship.

I mulled over what Melissa had said, Mason finished his song, and Aidan approached him. Aidan covered the mic with his hand, and they talked for a minute. Mason said something to Derek and Kyle, then he stepped away from the mic, smiled at Aidan, and left him front and center. The college girls who were squealing for Mason now focused their attention on Aidan with just as much enthusiasm. Aidan cleared his throat and adjusted the mic.

"This song is called 'If the Moon Fell Down Tonight.' I'd like to dedicate it to my girlfriend, Liz."

A few of the girls from school gasped. There was a murmuring of disbelief echoing through the bar. I was acutely aware all eyes were on me. The cute brunette was wide-eyed and fuming. Melissa was in shock, but I think in a good way.

When Aidan began to sing, I was overcome with emotion. I blocked out everyone around me and focused on nothing but his beautiful blue eyes. His gaze never left mine as he sang this sweet love song to me. My eyes welled up, and a few tears rolled down my cheeks.

When the song ended, Aidan stepped off the stage. The silence in the bar was deafening. Aidan shuffled through the crowd and headed my way. When he reached me, he leaned down and kissed me on the lips. He pulled back so we were nose to nose and whispered, "Merry Christmas, Liz."

The last thing I remembered hearing was Derek yelling out, "Oh yeah!" A few people laughed as the restaurant erupted with cheers.

Chapter Twelve

"Perhaps you'd like to join us, Miss Ryan? I believe winter break is over."

I was jolted from my thoughts to the stern brown eyes and disparaging tone of my AP Government teacher, Mr. Reyes. He was a good teacher, from what I'd heard, but he intimidated even the most arrogant students. My fear was I had just slipped into the I've-got-my-eye-on-you category.

"Yes, sir," I replied with a soft voice and quickly sat up straight. Melissa caught my eye from across the room. She raised an eyebrow and gave me a smirk. I could tell she was enjoying my embarrassment — she always referred to me as such a nerd. Mr. Reyes didn't miss a beat and continued to drone on about what was expected of us this semester.

I slipped back into my thoughts but kept my eyes focused on the stoic disciplinarian. A slight smile crossed my face while I twiddled with the beautiful tanzanite necklace Aidan had given me for Christmas. At first, I'd hesitated to accept the generous gift, but he'd said it was to make up for not getting me a birthday present. Arguably, as a combination gift, I had to accept it. I had told him singing to me at the restaurant had been gift enough. He'd ignored my argument as he'd slipped the necklace on while he'd distracted me with gentle kisses in the process.

New Year's Eve had been a bust because Aidan had had to work at the hotel. So I'd been pleasantly surprised when I awoke a little after 2:00 a.m. to the warm arms and whisper of "Happy New Year" from my attentive boyfriend.

My eyes had widened as I'd whispered, "How did you get in here?"

Aidan had chuckled. "The key under the rock. Mason and I had to use it once." He'd shrugged.

"I thought you'd either think I was incredibly sweet or super creepy. Well?"

The soft moonlight through my window had made his blue eyes glisten.

"Sweet and a little creepy." I'd giggled.

"I'll accept that, but I'd better go. I'll see you tomorrow." He'd smiled and given me a quick kiss on the lips before he'd said goodnight and closed my door...

The bell rang, bringing me out of my thoughts, and Melissa was at my seat in a heartbeat.

"Lizzie got in trouble, Lizzie got in trouble," she taunted in her most sing-songy way.

I just rolled my eyes.

"Whatcha thinkin' about, Liz?" She still had the sing-songy tone to her voice.

"What do you think?" I fluttered my eyelashes at her.

"I'd say you've got it bad for the boy." We each giggled, exiting the classroom.

"Yeah, I guess I do." I smiled.

"Well, he sure has blown me away. The change in him is crazy! Do you know how many hearts are breaking all over this campus because you have tamed the untamable Aidan Mitchell?"

"I just hate the way everyone is talking about me. I went from being Mason's twin to Aidan's girlfriend. No one knows who I am." A twinge of discontentment ran through me.

"Oh, Liz, you're the girl with the hot boyfriend and even hotter brother!" She laughed then nudged my arm with hers. "C'mon, let's get moving. My next class is in the D Building."

Melissa and I picked up the pace as we headed toward the quad.

****

"Hurry up, Liz! Or, I'm leaving without you." Mason banged on the bathroom door again.

"I'll be done in a minute!" I hollered back. I ran down the hallway in my robe, yelling at Mason I'd be ready in ten minutes.

Spencer was having the band meet at church tonight for the first time since Lance left.

The image of him singing in the music room flashed before my eyes while I was getting dressed.

What a voice… face… eyes.

I shook my head for a second to dislodge the memory. It didn't quite work, but Mason's banging on my door did.

"I'm leaving, Liz, you can drive yourself!" yelled Mason. "Noooo, five minutes!" I pleaded.

"Hurry up!"

Fearing Mason's wrath, I hustled, scrambling into my clothes. I bent over and blow-dried my hair, trying to get most of the dampness out before Mason started banging on my door again. With a flip of my head, I stood up, smoothed my hair down, and applied mascara, blush and red lipstick. In stride, I grabbed my black pea-coat and ran out my door as Mason was headed my way, shaking his keys.

"Okay, I'm ready," I squealed, brushing past him toward the front door.

****

When Mason and I entered the music room, Spencer was already going over a few things with Jake and Matt. Mason shot me a dirty look. I mouthed "*Sorry.*" Spencer glanced up at us.

"Hey, guys, come on over." He grabbed a couple of folding chairs, and Mason and I took a seat while he went over his plans for the year. Spencer was wearing a striped, button-down dress shirt, dark jeans, and black deck shoes. His jaw was covered in a day's worth of stubble, and his dark brown hair was a shaggy mess, but it looked good. Too good.

The guys seemed to like him immediately. The conversation flowed, the guys approved of the song choices, and by the end of the evening, they were all joking around together like they had been friends for years. Afterwards, Spencer was folding up the chairs and motioned me over.

"Can you stay a little longer, Elizabeth? I want to practice a few songs with you."

"Mason and I drove together…"

"No problem, I can give you a ride home."

The thought of my arms wrapped around Spencer, speeding through the night, was temping.

"On the motorcycle?" I sounded so hopeful. *Idiot.*

"No." He chuckled. "I drove the jeep."

Spencer and I said goodbye to the guys. They walked out the back door, and we headed to the stage. He took a seat at the piano and rolled up his sleeves a bit.

I was able to get a glimpse of the script writing on his forearm, but I still couldn't make out the words. I thought it said *fight,* or something like that. For the first time, I saw that he had a small tattoo wrapped around the ring finger of his left hand. Maybe it was a word written in script, but I couldn't tell.

Spencer caught my eye. I was so curious, but he didn't comment, so I looked away. Feeling unsure if I should join him on the bench or stand next to the piano, I decided to stay standing, waiting for his instruction. Spencer smiled and motioned for me to sit next to him.

"C'mere, Elizabeth, have a seat."

Sliding in next to him, the scent of his cologne surrounded me, making it difficult for me to focus.

"I was thinking we could work on a duet. I'm not sure which song yet, but I wanted us to practice so we could get comfortable singing together." He cupped his chin and tapped his long index finger over his lips. "Hmm... what should we sing?" Spencer's eyes widened as he focused on me. "Do you know the song 'Hazy'?"

I swallowed hard. I knew exactly the song he was talking about.

What's with him and these intimate love songs?

I felt myself cringe with embarrassment. "Yeah, I know it."

My face must have looked priceless.

With a glint in his eye, Spencer started tapping out the song and gave me a nod to begin. His gaze didn't leave mine. Usually, I would crumble under such scrutiny, but his eyes were encouraging, and I found myself wanting to please him. I continued to sing this intimate love song. My part of the duet faded out, and Spencer's began. The warmth of his soulful voice mesmerized me. He stopped playing and laughed.

"What?" I blurted out.

"You're supposed to come in on that part." I giggled. "Oops."

Spencer gave me a confident smile. "See, that's why we need to practice. I almost lost it with your singing too. Let's start again."

I started the song one more time but stopped. "Now what?" He chuckled.

Not until we'd run through the song a second time did my brain register the words I was singing.

"Elizabeth, what's wrong?"

With downcast eyes I whispered, "The song. The words. I fell and hurt myself. Everything was hazy." Although it was a love song, the words brought me back to the dog attack. Acknowledgement registered across Spencer's face.

"I wasn't thinking. I'm sorry."

After a few moments, my eyes focused on his. "I never thanked you, Spencer. I don't even remember you being there. But… thank you. If you hadn't come…"

"You're welcome, darlin'."

Spencer's words cut into mine. I could tell he was uncomfortable with the gratitude I had bestowed upon him.

A shy smile crossed his face, then he sat up straight and began to play again. "How about a few more songs and we'll call it a night?"

"Sure."

When Spencer and I finished, it was almost eleven o'clock. He led me to his red jeep and opened the passenger-side door for me.

"Sorry, Elizabeth, I didn't mean to keep you so

long." "That's okay. It was fun."

He leaned in before closing the door. I was hit with the scent of his cologne and his dimpled smile. "It was, wasn't it?"

Spencer sang along with the song on the radio, and I couldn't help but think he sounded better than the actual artist singing. When we entered our neighborhood, I pointed to my house. He pulled to the curb and shifted his body to face mine.

"We need to work out a time to practice. I was thinkin' Wednesday nights. Would that work for you?"

I thought about it for a moment. Aidan worked Wednesdays, so that wouldn't interfere with him. "Yeah, that's great."

"Do you mind if we practice at my house? It'd be easier, but if you're uncomfortable…"

"No, that's fine."

"Perfect. I'll see ya Wednesday. Eight?"

I opened the door and slid off the seat. "Okay." "Night, darlin'."

"Night." I closed the door and walked up the driveway.

Spencer didn't pull away from the curb until my foot was inside the door.

****

Maggie happily greeted me, but my parents were already in bed. I went in the kitchen to get a glass of water. I took a drink then headed up the stairs. Mason's light was on and his door was open, but he wasn't home. I shut his light off, walked into my room, and placed my water glass on my bedside table. I pulled my phone from my coat pocket. When my cell powered up, it vibrated. Four missed texts and two missed calls, all from Aidan.

I didn't have time to read them before my phone vibrated again.

"Hello."

"Are you home?" Aidan's tone was chipped. "Yes-s-s." I dragged out the word as I answered him.

"Meet me outside." I didn't have time to respond. He had already hung up.

Maggie was at my heels as I ran downstairs. When I opened the door, I was met with his icy gaze. Stepping outside, I closed the door while he walked toward me.

"Why haven't you texted me?"

"Umm… I didn't know you texted me. My phone's been off. I was practicing at church. I just got home." I knew I was babbling, but I felt under attack and had no idea why.

Aidan's blue eyes were shrewd, assessing. After what seemed like minutes, his gaze softened and he reached out and held me.

"I was worried about you. I hadn't heard from you since earlier today. I texted Mason and Melissa, but they never texted me back. Then I thought I'd come over to find out where you were."

I pulled myself back so I could look him in the eyes. "Are you mad at me?"

Aidan kissed my forehead and exhaled a sign of relief. "No, I was just worried. When I didn't hear from you, it made me crazy." He ran a hand through his hair. "Oh man, I sound like such a stalker."

Aidan cupped my face with his hands and brushed his lips against mine. He backed me up against the door and deepened the kiss. Our bodies were pressed up against each other as he continued to give me an onslaught of vigorous kisses.

I gasped. "Aidan. Stop. Stop."

"I'm sorry." He held me for a long time. I could feel his beating heart while my head rested on his chest. Finally he whispered, "I'm glad you're home safe... I'd better go."

He kissed me one last time before he turned and walked toward his truck. I went back in the house. My troubled thoughts confused me as I climbed the stairs.

Chapter Thirteen

Maggie was so jumpy, but I didn't blame her. She had been cooped up in the house since the attack. I'd been back in my routine the day Dr. Lee had removed my stitches and given me the go ahead. It had been a few weeks for me, but since this was Maggie's first day out, I'd decided to take it slow. When we approached the house where the dogfight had been, I stopped. Usually, I would cross the street and run by it without giving it a second look. Today, I decided to exorcise the demons that haunted me. Maggie sniffed the grass, and I wondered if she could remember any of it. Did animals remember trauma? It didn't seem to affect her. At first, I hadn't thought it had affected me either. But it had.

I used to run with both ear buds stuck in my ears and my music blasting. Now I only ran with one, leaving the other ear bud dangling behind me. My pepper spray was now in my pocket instead of clipped to Maggie's leash, and when I ran, I scanned the area like I was the Terminator.

I wrapped my arms around myself when I approached the area where Maggie once lay bleeding. I crouched down and let my hand skim across the damp blades of grass. Maggie sat next to me and put her sweet face next to mine. Overcome with emotion, I fell to my knees and cried. Not just a few tears. I sobbed. I was aware time was passing, and this was going to be the extent of our walk today, but I didn't care. Wiping the last of my tears away, I was startled by the touch of a warm hand on my shoulder.

"Are you alright, darlin'?" The gentle voice of concern and the feel of his touch sent me over the edge. I was thrown back into uncontrollable weeping. When I stood, Spencer held me in his strong arms. Overcome with emotions, my head rested on his shoulder while I continued to sob.

"Shhh, you're safe. You're safe." He repeated those words over and over while he stroked my hair.

The scent of his soft leather jacket mingled with freshly showered skin was comforting to me. When I shed my last tear, I looked up into his smoky, grey eyes.

"I feel like an idiot." I stepped back, breaking the connection of our bodies as I wiped my nose with the back of my sleeve.

"Don't, Elizabeth. When you've gone through anything tragic, you never know when it's going to hit you. Trust me, I know."

I thought about his words for a minute and then glanced at his tear-stained jacket.

"I'm sorry about all that." I motioned to his sleeve.

He glanced down at his left arm and shrugged. "That's okay. It just gives it more character."

Spencer and I walked toward his motorcycle with Maggie following behind. In my emotional fit, I hadn't even heard him pull up. He zipped up his jacket and grabbed his helmet.

"So, tonight? Eight o'clock?"

I took a step back. Spencer put on his helmet and straddled the bike.

"Yeah, I'll see you tonight."

Spencer gave me a dimpled smile, started up the bike, and rode away.

****

Memories of Mrs. Chapman flooded my mind. The front door still had the pewter knocker I had tapped to let her know I was there. I couldn't bring myself to use it. I swallowed the lump in my throat before I rang the bell.

After my crying jag from the morning, I felt a little awkward when Spencer opened the door. My embarrassment soon faded when my eyes locked with his, and he welcomed me inside. The inside of the home was so different than I had remembered. The first thing that caught my attention was the baby grand piano I had coveted on move-in day. A peaceful feeling flowed through me as Spencer walked me past his living area. It was so comfortable and inviting. A deep green sofa and love seat surrounded an oversized dark leather ottoman. Hanging above the couch was an assortment of black-and-white photographs, mostly pictures of waterfalls and a beautiful mountain landscape.

I glanced around the house, hoping to see his little brothers, but they were nowhere in sight. Spencer led me into the kitchen.

"Something to drink?" he asked. "Sure."

Spencer opened the fridge and grabbed a bottle of orange juice and held it up. I nodded and sat on a barstool next to the kitchen island. He filled our glasses with ice, while I continued to observe my surroundings. The tan color in the living area flowed through the kitchen as well. Stainless steel appliances took the once-dated house and gave it a modern feel. The change in the home was shocking. The hardwood floors were the only reminder Mrs. Chapman had ever lived there.

"Where are your brothers?" I asked. Spencer stood on the opposite side of the island, and he handed me my glass.

"My brothers live with my mom."

I was taken aback by his answer. "Oh, I just assumed you lived with your family."

Spencer shook his head. "Nope, just me." He leaned against the island and sipped his orange juice.

"This place is yours?" I couldn't hide the curiosity in my voice.

There was an awkward silence between us, and I felt horrible for being so nosey. All I could think of was how did a twenty-one-year-old college student afford all this?

"I didn't mean to pry. I was just surprised. It's just a lot for someone so young." Spencer's relaxed stance became tense.

"Let's get started." His usual gentle tone became curt. "I'm sorry, Spencer, that was rude of me."

He gave me a nod, and I followed him as he walked into the living room.

Spencer slid across the piano bench and motioned for me to sit by his side. He was wearing a long-sleeved, white-and-grey- striped cotton shirt. No chance of checking out his tattoos. I couldn't even figure out the script on his ring finger, but after the comment about his finances, there was no way I was asking about it.

We spent the next hour rehearsing for Sunday's service. The earlier awkwardness was gone, and I felt the kindhearted Spencer coming back to me. He brought out sheet music for the song "Lead Me To The Cross" and handed me the lyrics.

"I want you to sing this. Not at your usual hiding place behind the piano either. Front and center, like you did at the Christmas concert. I'll accompany you with my guitar." His tone was authoritative.

My heart was racing. The thought of having to sing again was terrifying.

Spencer slid off the piano bench and padded down the hallway. Seconds later, he returned with his acoustic guitar. He sat on the edge of the piano bench and began to play.

"It's not something I'm comfortable with," I mumbled and began nibbling my thumbnail.

Spencer stopped playing. "I know all about that, Elizabeth. Lance filled me in. We're going to get you comfortable. You have a beautiful voice. It's time you quit hiding it. Now stand up. Eyes on me."

I took a deep breath, tense green eyes focused on encouraging grey, and with a nod from Spencer, I began. I didn't know if it was the beautiful song or the confidence that he was willing me, but when I finished, Spencer was beaming with such enthusiasm I felt myself grinning like a little kid.

"Well, what do you know? Elizabeth Ryan is finding her voice." He smiled before he said, "Let's do it again."

We ran through the song a few more times until Spencer leaned over to check the clock. It was 10:16 p.m.

"I guess we'd better call it a night." He leaned his guitar against the wall as I walked toward the front door and reached for the doorknob.

"I'll see you Sunday, Spencer." I smiled back at him and stepped outside.

"Hold up, darlin'." He quickly made his way toward me.

"I wouldn't be a gentleman if I let you walk home alone. Let's go." Spencer placed his hand on the small of my back and guided me toward the sidewalk then walked me safely home.

****

Aidan was so busy with work all week so, other than school, we hadn't been able to spend any time together. I could tell he was frustrated, so we planned an all-day date for Saturday. He was coming over at 11:00 a.m. so we could go to brunch.

I missed Aidan and wanted to look my best for him, so I took extra time getting ready. I knew he liked me in dresses, and since the weather was beginning to change from winter to spring, I was happy to wear one for him. I put on a sassy little blue sleeveless dress made from a stretchy fabric that hugged me in all the right places. Looking at my reflection in the mirror, I knew he'd love it.

I'd never been big on makeup, and since Aidan had said I didn't need it, I just applied some mascara and a pale shade of red lipstick. I slipped on a pair of nude, strappy sandals and gave my head a shake. My loose curls fell around my shoulders, cascading down to the middle of my back. I headed downstairs just as I heard the doorbell ring and Maggie bark.

When I opened the door, Aidan's mouth dropped. Just the reaction I had hoped for. I fluttered my eyelashes and gave him my best sexy smile. He clutched his heart like he was having a heart attack and pulled me into his arms.

"You're stunning." He leaned in and kissed me with so much passion I knew my lipstick was gone.

"Let me look at you." I breathed.

Aidan stepped back and spun around so I could admire him. He was wearing a white-collared shirt and

117

black jeans. His hair was slicked back and had that just-showered scent I loved so much.

"You'll do," I teased.

Aidan swatted my butt as I walked past him toward the truck.

****

After a filling brunch, we walked around the harbor talking, kissing, and making up for lost time. I suggested a run at the park to relieve the guilt I felt for eating far too much. Aidan hated that I was going to change out of my tight-fitting dress, but I pacified him with the promise to wear it Sunday night when the guys played. We went to my house so I could change into my usual workout gear and then headed to his house.

As we entered, Aidan and I passed by his father, who was lounging on the couch watching CNN.

"Hi, Mr. Mitchell," I said en route to Aidan's bedroom. How ya doin', Lizzie?" he smiled.

"I'm good, sir, thank you."

No wonder Aidan was so attractive. His father had sandy- blond hair, expressive blue eyes like his son, and was extremely handsome. Aidan's new stepmom, Natalie, was beautiful too. Aidan had told me she was thirty-five, but she could pass for someone in their late twenties. She had shoulder-length dark hair cut in flirty layers that framed her big brown eyes. Every time I'd seen her, she'd looked perfect. She was what my mom called a trophy wife.

When we entered his room, Aidan unbuttoned his shirt and tossed it on the floor. He grabbed a t-shirt from an open drawer and a pair of running shorts. He began to unbutton his jeans. My eyes focused from the top button of his jeans, past his defined abs, and finally settled on his darkening blue eyes.

"I don't think so…" My cheeks felt flushed. Aidan lunged toward me and we fell on his bed. "What's a matter, Liz. Am I too much for you?"

I squirmed beneath him. "Somethin' like that." I giggled.

Aidan's lips were soon on mine. My hands roamed across his shirtless body as he parted my legs with his jean-covered knee and held his body over mine. One of his hands found its way under my t-shirt while he continued to distract me with his heated kisses. The next thing I knew, we were rolling around on his bed. I could feel my pulse quickening but knew we needed to stop. I was barely able to break my mouth free as I gasped.

"Aidan… wait."

Aidan groaned then rolled his body from mine. "You're killin' me, Liz. You're killin' me."

I reached for him and placed my head on his bare chest. "I'm sorry," I whispered.

Aidan caressed my hair as his breathing returned to normal. "You're so beautiful, Liz. I can't help but want you."

I was at a loss for words. All I could think to do was bury my face in the crook of his neck. I looked up into his eyes. "I know what you want… but… I'm not ready."

I hugged him but felt him tense up. He exhaled and pulled away from me. He moved to the edge of the bed, sat with his feet on the floor, and his back toward me.

I crawled across the bed and rested my head on his muscular back. My hair curled down his right arm. I whispered, "I care about you so much. I just feel like this is all moving so fast." I kissed his shoulder and moved so we were sitting side by side. "Please let's take things slow, Aidan. Please."

"Okay," he answered. There was a reluctant tone in his voice, then he grabbed his clothes and went into the bathroom to change.

****

The tension between Aidan and me seemed to be gone when we made our second loop up the stairs at the park. Aidan took my hand and pulled me over to a stone bench overlooking the Pacific. I sat while he stretched out and placed his head on my lap. I bent down and kissed him on the lips.

"You make me happy," he said with a smile.

I leaned in close for another kiss and a ringlet of my hair tickled his face. "You make me happy too."

He placed the dangling hair behind my ear. "Do I?"

"Of course you do." I gazed out over the ocean watching the sailboats catch the wind while I ran my fingers through his soft hair. "I'm just worried. I know what you want... what you're used to... but..."

"But?"

It took me a minute to finish what I needed to say. "I know this sounds crazy, but... I grew up in a home where doing... that... is what you do when you're married."

I breathed a sigh of relief. I'd wanted to say that to him for weeks. My innocence had been taken down a notch, but I wasn't ready for going-all-the-way. I exhaled and asked him the question that had haunted me since he'd first asked me to be his girlfriend. "Do you think you can be with me and not do... that?" I couldn't say the word... how was I supposed to do the word?

Aidan moved his head from my lap and sat up. He was quiet for a long time.

"I don't think I can." His answer floored me.

"I didn't finish, Liz. I don't think I can... but... I'll try."

We stayed on the bench until sunset. As we watched the sun slip into the ocean, I could feel Aidan Mitchell slipping deeper into my heart.

Chapter Fourteen

My anxiety increased listening to Pastor Dan finish up the sermon. It had taken everything in me to sing the solo performance at the Christmas concert, and here I was again. Spencer approached the piano bench and slid in next to me as I wiped my trembling hands back and forth on my black skirt. He placed his hand over mine.

"You're going to do fine," he whispered. "If you get nervous, pretend it's just us, like we've practiced."

I nodded while fiddling with my necklace from Aidan.

Spencer's hand left mine and gestured it was time to begin.

Mason moved the podium to the side and whispered, "You've got this, Liz."

Jake adjusted the mic in front of me, and I took a deep breath. Spencer grabbed a stool and placed it far enough in front of me so eye contact wouldn't be a problem. I stood in front of the mic and cleared my throat, mentally trying to prepare myself. The stage light focused on me as Spencer began to play. I hesitated and bypassed the lead-in of the song.

My wide green eyes met calming grey. Spencer gave me an encouraging smile and began again. This time my gaze never left his. I could almost feel the confidence he was willing me through the depths of his eyes. When he strummed the last chorus, his mouth curved into a smile, then the song was over. Spencer was beaming with pride. I bit the edge of my bottom lip and gave him a shy smile. The lights rose, and my focus turned from Spencer to the enthusiastic audience. Stepping back from the mic, I looked over the congregation. My focal point went from a sea of faceless faces to one. I felt my heart quicken when I gazed into the blue eyes I had come to adore. My thoughts were racing from *He's gorgeous to what's he doing here?*

Spencer approached me with a quick hug and a whispered, "You did great, darlin'." His warm eyes looked deep into mine. "It's just the beginning, Elizabeth." Spencer laughed as he watched my smile fade into fear. He just shook his head then picked up the mic and walked off the stage.

My eyes found Aidan, but his breathtaking smile had been replaced with a compressed thin line. I raised one finger to signal I'd be with him in a minute.

I rushed into the music room to get my purse and almost ran into Spencer in the process. "Sorry, Spencer."

All the guys applauded and told me I did a great job. I thanked them and grabbed my bag. Spencer caught my eye as I headed toward the door.

"What's the hurry?" Spencer said with a smile. He was in the process of untangling an electrical cord.

I felt uncomfortable. I wasn't hiding the fact I had a boyfriend. The subject just never came up.

I barely made eye contact before I murmured, "My boyfriend's waiting for me."

Spencer gasped but tried to cover it up with a cough.

I glanced at him before I walked out the door and our eyes met. He seemed so caught off-guard it made my heart ache. His expression went from shock to confusion.

I walked down the hallway, lost in my thoughts. The look on Spencer's face haunted me.

****

Aidan was still standing where I'd last seen him, only now his arms were folded.

"Are you okay?" I reached out for him, but he backed up a step.

"Who's the guy that was hugging you?"

"Oh, that's just Spencer." I tried to sound as indifferent as I could.

"The guy that gave you the flowers?" His voice dripped with animosity.

"Aidan, it's no big deal. He's the music director." The instant the words left my mouth I felt disloyal to Spencer. He was so much more than that. I turned my back on Aidan in an attempt to head toward the exit door, but he hurried to my side and hissed in my ear.

"No big deal? You're clueless, Liz. That guy's into you."

The sounds of Aidan's footsteps followed me as I pushed through the exit door and headed toward my car. "I'm not doing this, Aidan. It was nothing."

He was right on my heels. I stormed through the parking lot, and when we passed his truck, he grabbed my arm and told me to get inside.

"Why? So you can yell at me? No thanks." I took a few steps. "Liz, stop! I didn't come here to fight with you."

Church had let out, and the parking lot was becoming crowded. I didn't want to cause a scene, so I stopped.

"Well, then quit it. I didn't do anything. Why are you so mad at me anyway?"

"Let's talk in the truck." Aidan took my hand, walked me toward his truck, and held the passenger door open for me. I hopped inside as he climbed in the driver's seat.

"I haven't had the best morning, and I wanted to see you. But when I saw the way you and that guy were looking at each other, it ticked me off."

"Aidan, I'm supposed to look at him. He leads us. We all look to him, for direction. That's all it is." The image of Spencer's pained expression flashed through my mind.

"How old is that guy?"

"Twenty-one." My eyes drifted over the parking lot, watching the cars pull away. I turned back to Aidan. "There's nothing to worry about, so please don't." I reached across the seat and placed my hand on his knee. "Don't be upset."

Aidan fiddled with his hands and sighed. His shoulders slumped as he looked up at me. "I'm sorry… I'm just in a bad mood. Let's get outta here, do something fun," he said with less tension in his voice. "Do you want to go to the beach?"

"Sure. How about if you pick me up in twenty minutes?" Aidan's demeanor quickly changed, and I was thankful.

"Perfect!"

He gave me a quick kiss on the lips and walked me back to my car. "I'll go home, grab my stuff, and come back to get you."

"Alright, I'll see you in a bit."

As I pulled out of the parking lot, Spencer was walking toward his motorcycle. Seeing him caused a sadness that shook me to the core.

125

****

Aidan laid a couple of striped beach towels on the sand while I pulled my hair back in a ponytail. He looked amazing, wearing a white t-shirt and turquoise swim trunks. I was wearing a pink bikini, jean shorts, and my grey zip-up hoodie. It was warm enough to get some sun but too cold to go in the ocean. He bent forward, removed his t-shirt, and tossed it on the sand. I drank in the sight of his broad shoulders and sculpted six-pack. He grabbed my hand as he lay down on the towel, pulling me with him.

He hovered over me on one elbow as he kissed a path from my neck, traveling to my cheek and finally to my lips. His tongue gently glided over mine while our bare legs were entwined. Aidan pulled away, giving me a gentle kiss then leaned back on his elbow.

He seemed distant, and I wondered if he was still upset about this morning.

"Are you okay?"

After several quiet minutes, he answered me. "I heard from my mom today."

"Oh? How's she doing?"

I know he heard my question, but emotionally he seemed miles away. I ran my hand through his hair and was quiet until he was ready to speak.

"She seems up... happy... ready to take on the world." "That's good. Isn't it?"

"I've heard it before... it's hard to believe... that's all." "Maybe this time she'll stick with it." His raised eyebrow and skeptical expression made me feel bad he had lost all hope in his mother.

"How were things with your first stepmom?"

"That would be, Jennifer. She had twin girls, Erin

and Erica. Whiny little brats, completely spoiled. Their marriage only lasted a couple of years. I couldn't stand living with them. My dad was gone a lot on business, so Jennifer let me do whatever I wanted. I think my dad married her just so he didn't have to worry about me so much."

"Did you ever live with your real mom?"

"Only when she wasn't using, so not very often. Weekends mostly, I hope she stays clean this time, but…"

I reached up and pulled him close. His head lazily fell to my shoulder, and his breathing slowed while I ran my fingers though his hair. I wanted to comfort him, tell him everything was going to be okay, but I had no idea what the future would be like for his mom and didn't know what to say to him. So I just held him, hoping it would be enough.

The sun warmed us as Aidan brought his lips to mine. He began giving me soft, slow kisses that heated my already-warm body. I shifted beneath him while my hands ran down the length of his arms, and I pulled him in close. I wanted him to forget about this morning, his conversation with his mom, and focus on nothing but us. Feeling far too warm, I unzipped my hoodie. Aidan's gaze went from my green eyes to my flimsy pink bikini top. He rolled from his elbow to his back and threw one arm over his eyes.

"Crap, Liz, what are you doin' to me?"

The agony in his tone made me giggle. I lifted his arm to peek at him. One dilated blue eye fixed on mine, and I gave him a flirtatious smile.

"Too much?" I couldn't hide the humor in my voice. "That's it!"

The next thing I knew, Aidan was after me at full speed as I ran down the beach laughing.

The hours passed while we sat on the sand watching the tide come in. I found myself lost in his eyes when he leaned in and sealed his lips over mine.

"Thanks for listening… ya know… about my mom." Aidan held my hand and brought it to his lips with a soft kiss.

"Sure."

"I loved hearing you sing today. I've always wanted you to sing with the band. You know that, right?"

"I know you do. It's just hard for me." With my free hand I began picking up handfuls of sand and letting it sift through my fingers.

"Do you even know how good you are?"

"Oh, Aidan." I sighed. I released my hand from his and brushed the sand away before I kissed him on the lips.

Aidan deepened the kiss, and after a few minutes, he gave me a sweet smile. "This turned out to be a great day." He hopped up and grabbed my hand. "Time to get ready for the show."

We picked up our towels and headed back to his truck.

The last thing Aidan said to me when he dropped me off was "Don't forget. You promised to wear the blue dress." His smile was wicked.

****

The venue was packed, but Melissa and I got there early to claim our usual table. There she was, the cute brunette who'd hungrily gawked at my off-limits' boyfriend. Derek was surrounded by a bunch of college girls and loving it. Kyle and Mason were talking off to the side of the stage, and when my eyes saw Aidan, his lips curved into a seductive smile. Gracefully, he weaved through the crowd, not taking his eyes from mine.

"You're beautiful," he whispered. With the tip of his index finger, Aidan traced the sunburned skin on my shoulder. "Does this hurt?" He kissed the area where his finger had just been.

"A lil' bit." I smiled.

"How about here?" He moved his lips to the opposite red shoulder and gently kissed it.

I answered, "A lil' bit."

Aidan gave me a sly smile then cupped my face with his hands. He brushed the pads of his thumbs across my rosy cheeks. Leaning forward, he kissed the side of my face.

"How about here?" He stopped briefly to kiss the tip of my nose before kissing the opposite cheek. "Or here?"

Smiling, my final response repeated, "A lil' bit."

"Shoot. I missed my opportunity to cover this body in sunscreen."

A loud cough came from behind us. Aidan and I both glanced down at Melissa, sitting at the table.

"Ya know, I'm sitting right here." She rolled her eyes. "Just makin' sure my girl is okay."

Aidan gave me one last kiss before he made his way back on the stage. The guys began their set as I took a seat.

"You both are so cute it kinda makes me a little sick." Melissa took a sip of her soda.

"Well, now you know what it feels like to hang out with you and Mason."

"Are we that sickening?" "Pretty much."

Melissa raised her glass to mine and clinked it.

"Here's to being sickeningly happy." We both giggled then continued to watch the guys play.

The crowd began moving about, and a couple of college guys were sitting at the bar, drinking and flirting with a few girls. My eyes met the gaze of one of them. He was handsome with dark hair and brown eyes surrounded by thick black eyelashes. He smiled at me. My eyes went to Aidan's, but thankfully he didn't see anything.

As the set continued, the handsome stranger kept looking my way. Feeling uncomfortable, I shifted my chair to avoid any further eye contact. Melissa and I were having a good time singing along and cheering for the guys until the unoccupied chair next to me moved. A voice I didn't recognize asked me my name as he sat down in the empty chair.

"Elizabeth," I responded while glancing up into his intense dark eyes. Instinctively, I knew his eyes weren't the only ones focused on me. When I glanced at the stage, a shudder ran through me. The eyes that had showed such care and concern not more than twenty minutes ago were now a fiery blue.

"Hello, Elizabeth." He glanced at Melissa. "And you are?" "Melissa."

"Nice to meet you. I'm Dominic." He shifted his chair so he was facing me.

Fending off the advances of the opposite sex was something I knew nothing about. Having no idea how to handle this situation, I anxiously glanced at Melissa for some help. Sensing my anxiety, she tapped Dominic on the shoulder.

"Dominic?"

He looked over his shoulder at Melissa. "We're not

interested."

"Are you two together?" he asked with a smirk.

Melissa raised an eyebrow at him. "You wish. Listen, our boyfriends are up there." She nodded toward the stage. "So I suggest you move along."

Dominic looked me over before he got up from the chair. "Well, that's too bad. Ladies..." While Dominic made his way back to the bar, I breathed a sigh of relief, reached over, and thanked Melissa.

The minute the song was over, my adrenalin spiked when I watched Aidan rush to the bar to confront the handsome stranger.

"Crap!" In desperation I jumped up and waved my hand at Mason, motioning toward Aidan.

Mason spoke into the mic, telling the crowd the band was going to take a ten-minute break. He then maneuvered his way toward the bar. I shoved my way toward Aidan with Melissa muttering behind me. Aidan's voice was beginning to escalate as we all approached him at the same time. Mason grabbed Aidan by the arm and pushed him through the venue toward the exit door. Melissa and I followed.

"What's your problem, Aidan? Do you want us to lose this gig?" Mason was trying to rein in his temper, but I knew he was fuming.

"What am I supposed to do? Just sit back and let some player come on to my girl?" Aidan was furious.

Flustered, Mason rubbed his hand through his hair.

"Hey, Aidan, nothing happened. You have got to get it together and calm down." Mason gave him a few minutes to let the words sink in.

I approached Aidan and hugged him. After a moment, his body went from rigid and tense to somewhat relaxed.

Mason slapped him on the shoulder. "You okay now, buddy?"

Aidan gave him a head nod and an apology.

"I'll deal with the guy at the bar. You've got about five minutes."

Mason and Melissa went back inside, but not before Melissa made eye contact with me. By the look on her face, I knew a conversation with her was in the near future.

Aidan held me tight but didn't say anything.

After a few minutes, I spoke. "Aidan, you have to stop being so jealous. Please don't be this way."

"I know, Liz. I guess it just got to me. First it was Spencer and now this guy. I've never felt this way before. I hate the thought of someone taking you away from me."

I stood on my tiptoes and kissed his lips. "Aidan, I'm not going anywhere."

He smiled at me, his eyes finally softening. He brought his lips to mine and kissed me as though I was the air he breathed. He wrapped his arm around my waist and we walked back inside the club together. I forcibly dragged my thoughts from what could have happened. I squeezed him a little tighter, hoping the worst was over, and we could move on from here.

****

Melissa's text came in just as I was crawling into bed. Four words.

We need to talk.

Her message caused a heavy breath to leave my

lungs. Melissa's many attempts to corner me hadn't worked. Aidan had never left my side, causing Melissa's no-nonsense approach to have to be put on hold. I was thankful... I hated confrontation and certainly hadn't wanted to hash it out in the restaurant. Her constant glances had me on edge but having had Aidan within earshot had assured me that *the conversation* wouldn't happen tonight.

My fingers hovered over my cell before I tapped out my reply.

Saturday, Lantern Bay, 11:30 a.m.

The thought of having Melissa browbeat me with questions seemed more tolerable in the open air and serene setting of my favorite park.

Can't wait.

I considered answering her but just placed my cell on my bedside table and drifted off into a troubled sleep.

****

I stood on the sidewalk outside Spencer's house and inhaled a few deep breaths, desperately trying to will the anxiety to leave my body. But nothing seemed to work. I hated that I'd caused that look in his eyes. I knew I hadn't done anything wrong, but I was so riddled with guilt. I hated myself for not mentioning Aidan to him sooner.

When I moved closer to the door, I heard him playing his guitar and singing the song "What I Know," one of my favorites. Without warning, my eyes pooled with tears while I listened to him sing.

There was no denying Spencer and I had a special bond, but that was all it was. I had never led him on or flirted with him. So why did I feel so awful? I leaned against the door and closed my eyes. Spencer was singing with such passion I couldn't bring myself to knock until he was finished. It took me a minute to blink back the tears and compose myself. I turned around and rang the bell. I swallowed hard as the door opened. Our eyes met and held for a moment before Spencer spoke.

"C'mon in, darl… Elizabeth." His smile dimmed.

My heart sank when I realized the sweet endearment that used to roll off his tongue was gone. Being the perfect gentleman, Spencer offered me something to drink and motioned me to the kitchen. I sat on the barstool and asked for some ice water. My mind was racing trying to decide if I should bring up the elephant in the room. I didn't have to drag out the inevitable because Spencer did it for me.

"How long have you and your boyfriend been together?" His frankness surprised me.

"About three months." Spencer handed me my water, and I took a small sip. He ran his hand across the stubble of his jaw and then rubbed the back of his neck.

"The fun stage." Spencer's expression was unreadable as he picked up his glass and filled it with ice.

Feeling uncomfortable, and to take the focus off me, I took another sip of my water and asked, "Do you have a girlfriend?"

Spencer filled his glass with some orange juice, took a sip, and placed his glass on the kitchen island.

"Nope."

He didn't elaborate on the fact, which left me even more curious.

Spencer leaned back against the counter, eyeing me. He pushed up his long sleeves before he crossed his arms over his firm chest. His gaze made me feel stripped bare of any conscious thought.

"We haven't talked about Sunday. How did you feel during your solo?"

"Didn't like it," I responded. Spencer gave me a knowing smile.

"Yes, I understand. But like I've already told you, we're going to get you comfortable. Lance didn't push you. I want to help you with your confidence." Spencer's stance changed, and his eyes softened. "You trust me, don't you?"

There was a softness in his tone that I was thankful to hear. "Yes, I trust you."

"Good. Let's practice next week's solo." He gave me a dimpled grin and walked into the living room.

I followed behind. Spencer picked up his guitar and began to play. My eyes focused on what little I could see of his tattoo, a lighthouse.

Spencer and I ran through my solo several times, and when he was satisfied, we moved to the piano and practiced a duet together. I was feeling more confident and excited to sing with him. With his good looks and soulful voice, he should just scrap college and go for rock star. I smiled at the thought as Spencer glanced my way.

"What's the smile for?"

"Oh nothing. Can I ask you something?" I got up and stretched then plopped myself down on his comfortable couch.

"Sure." Spencer slid his long legs over the piano bench so we were facing each other.

"What made you decide to choose the tattoos you have?"

His expression changed as his grey eyes turned from mine to the floor. He exhaled and glanced at the clock.

"It's getting late, Elizabeth, how about if I tell you about that another time?"

Sensing his apprehension, I stood. He got up and opened the front door.

"Okay."

I walked through the door with Spencer behind me. Our walk to my house was quiet. When we arrived, our eyes met.

"Thank you for walking me home."

Spencer seemed distant, lost in his thoughts. "Sure," he answered. He waited on the sidewalk until I was inside. I peeked out the front window and watched him stuff his hands in his front pockets, turn, and walk away. My last thought was of Spencer walking into an empty house. The sadness consumed me.

Chapter Fifteen

It was a beautiful day. The temperature was in the mid- seventies, and the park was bustling with activity: Mommy and Me class, kids playing soccer, and several people running the stairs. Having left early to get in a quick run had proved to be a good idea. I was already feeling less anxious for my talk with Melissa. My cell phone vibrated as I jogged up the last few steps of the stairs.

Melissa: *Running late. I'll be there in about 30 minutes.*
Me: *No problem.*
Melissa: *I'll text you when I'm leaving.*
Me: *Okay.*

One more lap around the park, and maybe she'd be here. I stuffed my cell in my pocket and took off. I slowed, making my way around the bend, then stopped dead in my tracks. In the distance was Spencer. He was laughing and playing football with his little brothers. Spencer always seemed so reserved, seeing him enjoying himself, playful and carefree made my heart swell. His hair was tied back, showing off his handsome face. I'd never seen him in shorts, and I felt my face flush as I gawked at his long, toned legs. Watching him interact with his brothers intrigued me. I took a few steps closer.

I had to see more.

The younger boy finished a granola bar and tossed the wrapper toward a trashcan but missed. He turned and walked away, leaving the discarded paper on the grass. Spencer crouched down to his level and said something to him. The boy seemed upset he had disappointed his older brother. Spencer had him pick up the trash then ruffled the boy's hair and handed him a football. The way he handled his little brother was heartwarming. I found myself wanting to know more about him. Before I knew it, I was headed his way.

Our eyes met, and a slow reserved smile spread across his face. Spencer said something to the older boy and then jogged over to greet me.

"Hey, Elizabeth." I could tell he was surprised to see me. "What are you doing here?" He ran a hand through his hair and adjusted the hairband.

"I like to run here and jog the stairs." I still felt funny telling people I run, but telling Spencer, well, was... nice.

His eyes widened. "Jog the stairs? That's brutal."

"It can be." I took a deep breath. Seizing the opportunity for more information and to take the focus off me, I glanced over at the boys. "I take it those are your brothers?"

His gaze lingered on me for a moment with a funny smile on his face before he glanced over his shoulder. The boys were side by side, about twenty feet away, staring at us. Spencer's social graces kicked in, guiding me to meet his brothers.

Standing in front of them, I was stunned at the family resemblance. The older one reminded me of a mini-Spencer. He had the same grey eyes, but whereas

Spencer had dark brown hair, this boy's hair color was jet black. Spencer introduced me to him first.

"This is Shawn." The boy was a few inches taller than I. He smiled, revealing one prominent dimple on his left cheek. He would have the girls eating out of his hands, if he hadn't already.

"Hi." He put out his hand for me to shake it.

"Hi. How old are you, Shawn?" I let go of his hand. "Fourteen." He smiled.

"Eighth grade?"

"Yep." He fiddled with the football. I could tell Shawn didn't want to make conversation, so I glanced over to the younger boy.

"And this one is Simon," Spencer said, gesturing to his youngest brother.

Simon smiled, and his beautiful blue eyes lit up his face. His hair was a lighter shade of brown, and he had two dimples, just like Spencer. Another lady-killer in the making.

"I'm eleven and in sixth grade."

Spencer gave him a look, and Simon reached out to shake my hand.

"Nice to meet you, Simon." I smiled at his adorable face, and he smiled in return.

"Do you like football? You can play with us if you want to."

Simon was so animated it made me giggle. I was surprised when Shawn chimed in.

"Yeah, we could use a fourth. It could be me and you against the old guy and the kid." Shawn laughed then tossed me the ball.

I glanced at Spencer. He was smiling that sexy smile that made my heart skip a beat.

"Well, I guess I can play for a bit. I'm meeting someone here."

"Boyfriend?" Spencer asked, and his smile disappeared. "Ahh… no, my best friend, Melissa."

Spencer nodded in response as if he was remembering something. "Oh, Mason's girlfriend."

"I'm not sure when she'll be here, but I can play until then." I tossed the ball to Spencer, and after we decided on the boundaries of each end zone, Shawn and I planned our strategy.

Spencer and Simon were about forty feet away from us. Spencer threw the ball, and Shawn ran to receive it. We both took off toward our end zone. I was in front of Shawn, blocking him from Spencer, but Simon ran around me, and with a two-handed touch on Shawn, we were at our first down. My hike to Shawn was a little high, but he was able to grab it. As planned, I ran off to the side of him, then he lobbed it back to me. I saw an opening between Spencer and Simon and made my move. Shawn was cheering in the distance. I picked up speed as I got closer to our end zone. The poundings of Spencer's feet were gaining on me. To lose him, I zigzagged and made a beeline toward our goal.

Shawn was running and shouting "Go, go, go!" A few seconds later he yelled out an enthusiastic "Touchdown!"

I held the ball above my head and gave Shawn a victory high-five. Simon was jumping around laughing, and Spencer's mouth was gaping in disbelief.

Arching an eyebrow with a threatening smile, he leaned in close. "Impressive, Elizabeth, but now it's our turn." He smirked. "C'mon, Simon, it's time for retaliation."

We took our positions at the opposite ends of the field, and Shawn chucked the ball. Spencer caught it with ease and tossed it to Simon. Simon ran with all his might, his protective big brother paving the way. I was able to get one hand on Simon, but he quickly moved to the side and got away. Shawn gained speed and tagged his little brother out as my cell phone vibrated. The Hayes brothers all stopped to catch their breath. All eyes were on me. I glanced down to see it was Aidan, so I stepped away to answer it.

"Hey, baby, were you running?" I answered with a breathy, "Yes."

"Sounds sexy." Aidan laughed. "I'm off work now. Can I come and see you?"

I hesitated for a few seconds and then responded. "Well, Melissa is meeting me at the park. How about later?"

"Okay, we're still on for dinner tonight?"

Spencer's happy demeanor had vanished, and he was closing himself off.

Simon let out a loud whiny "C'mon, Elizabeth," and Spencer shushed him.

"Yes, I'll call you when I get home." "Okay, sounds good. Bye, Liz"

"Bye." I breathed a sigh of relief; thankful Aidan hadn't heard young Simon.

I tried to make light of the interruption and smiled. "Sorry." I couldn't help but notice the look in Spencer's cold, grey eyes.

Simon grabbed the ball from Shawn and got into the hike position. I crouched down in a block stance with Shawn next to me. Simon counted to three and hiked the ball to Spencer. This time Spencer tucked the football under his arm and made his way toward their end zone. Shawn and I both ran after him while he sprinted toward the goal line. Shawn took no prisoners as he grabbed his older brother, causing Spencer to stumble.

In my attempt to catch Spencer, I had gained too much momentum. The next thing I knew, we were in a dog pile with Spencer at the bottom. Everyone was laughing. I was pretty sure Simon jumped on top of me just to get in on the fun. Shawn made his move and grabbed the ball that had tumbled from Spencer's grasp. He took it and ran toward our end zone, laughing.

Simon hopped off me and ran after his older brother yelling "Not fair! Not fair!"

I was still giggling until I felt the contact of Spencer's heated body under mine. The lightheartedness that had been there just seconds ago had changed. My heart rate thudded as our eyes held. His eyes seemed lighter in the sunlight, and I found myself getting lost in them. Time was passing, I expected Spencer to shift his body from mine… but he didn't.

His eyes roamed the contours of my face, while my eyes stayed focused on his. I inhaled sharply when his tongue slowly emerged and moistened his lower lip. Deep within me, I felt an underlying intimacy between us.

Then my cell phone vibrated.

Spencer eyed me cautiously as I rolled off him, breaking our connection, physically and emotionally.

I sat up and read the text.

"That was Melissa, she's on her way." My voice broke, making me look away. I tapped out a text to her to meet me at the stone bench and rose to my feet.

Spencer got up, but kept his eyes on me as the boys

approached us. They were both out of breath and sweaty.

Simon piped up, annoyed. "That was a do-over, Spencer. We weren't playing tackle. Shawn cheated."

"We're done now, buddy. Elizabeth has to go." Spencer broke eye contact with me to look at a sullen looking Simon.

"Aww, can we play next week?"

But before I could answer, Spencer spoke for me. "I don't think so, Simon, and don't pout," he warned him. "Now thank Elizabeth, and I'll take you guys to get something to eat."

Simon was trying hard not to sulk. He gave me a sweet smile and thanked me for playing before he took a few steps back.

Shawn got close to me and smiled. "We totally would have won."

"Totally." I answered back.

He and Simon headed toward the jeep, leaving Spencer and me alone.

Spencer leaned in close. "I think Shawn may have a little crush on you."

I smiled. "They're sweet boys. Thank you for introducing me to them."

Spencer glanced back at his two brothers. "Yep, they're good kids." He paused for a minute.

I thought he might say something else, but he just looked at me for a moment then murmured, "I'll see ya Wednesday, Elizabeth."

"Bye, Spencer."

And with that, he walked across the grass and hopped in his red jeep.

My mind flashed back to the moment we'd shared. *Is it just me? Or did he feel it too?* I need to shake off whatever this is. I jogged to the stone bench.

I hadn't sat here since Aidan and I'd had our awkward, I'm- not-having-sex-with-you conversation. It was hard to believe that he was sticking to his word. We'd had some trying moments, but the change in Aidan was shocking. He had been respectful and always willing to stop before things got out of control.

Who would have thought?

I chewed off my remaining thumbnail while waiting for Melissa's arrival. She was going to want answers regarding Aidan's jealous behavior, and honestly, I wasn't even sure what to say to her. She and Mason had it so easy. With Aidan, things were just... *difficult*. In search of Melissa I spotted her instantly. Although she was hard to miss — she was wearing a pair of short, denim shorts, making her already long legs seem longer. I smiled, watching her make her way to the concrete bench.

"Hey, Liz, sorry you had to wait." Melissa sat, her assessing blue eyes bore into mine.

"That's okay." I was already feeling intimidated under her intense gaze.

True to form, she started in. "So, what's with Aidan?" "What do you mean?"

"What do I mean? Aidan was ready to rip that poor guy's head off Sunday night. When I told the guy you weren't interested, he was respectful and left you alone. Aidan had no reason to go over and harass him. It had already been handled. If Mason hadn't stepped in, things could have been bad and you know it!" Melissa was struggling to contain her anger.

"Aidan can be a little possessive of me, that's all." I shrugged.

"Liz! Are you kidding me? Listen to yourself!"

"I know what you're trying to say, Melissa, and I get it, but Aidan just cares about me. It's just sometimes he gets a little overprotective."

Melissa's expression was approaching *DEFCON 1*. I reached out and placed my hand on her arm.

"I know you're worried about me, but please don't. He's good to me, Melissa. I'm happy."

Melissa's eyes began to soften, a little. "I just don't want you to be with some guy with an out-of-control temper. This is your first boyfriend. Don't get caught up in it. You're smarter than that, Liz."

"I know, Melissa, but things between us are good," I insisted.

Melissa exhaled and I thought I'd pacified her for the time being. "You'll tell me if things get weird between you two, right?"

"Of course."

She leaned toward me and we hugged. "'Cuz ya know I'll beat the crap outta him."

"I know. C'mon, let's run the stairs." I got up and grabbed her arm.

"Ugh."

Reluctantly, Melissa got up and we ran the stairs, leaving the burden that was between us behind.

****

The thought of my date with Aidan excited me. He'd told me to dress nice because he was surprising me and taking me someplace special for our four-month anniversary. I showered, shaved my legs and, for old times' sake, flat-ironed my hair. I had forgotten what a long process it was, but seeing my reflection made me smile.

On my way into the closet, my shoulder bumped my bookcase, causing a framed picture of Mason and me to fall to the floor. It was a picture of us standing in front of the piano. I was fat. My hand slid over the photograph. I was smiling in the picture, but even now looking at it, I remembered I wasn't happy. I placed the picture back on the shelf and tried to shake off the sadness I felt for the fat girl still inside me. As I let my hand glide across the clothes that lined my closet, I began to feel better… until I pulled out my black birthday dress.

Looking it over, I contemplated if I should wear it or not. This dress had such a bad memory attached to it. After a few minutes, I made the decision to wear the dress. That awful memory had to be replaced with a good one. I pulled the dress over my head and shimmied it down my body. Next, I picked up the necklace from Aidan and clasped it around my neck. Since I'd spent most of the afternoon in the park, there was no need for blush. My sun-kissed cheeks against my pale skin were rosy enough. While applying my mascara, an image of Spencer flashed through my mind. I dismissed it.

It was nothing.

I ran down the hallway to my mom's room and gave myself a squirt of her expensive perfume. I needed to hurry: Aidan would be here soon. I dashed back into my bedroom and searched in my closet for my black heels, slipped them on, and exited the closet. My breath caught when I saw Aidan leaning against the doorjamb of my bedroom door. He looked amazing dressed in black dress slacks, a black blazer, and a white dress shirt with a black skinny tie. He was clean-shaven with his hair slicked back. When he saw me, his eyes lit up, and he let out a sexy whistle.

"You look beautiful and smell delicious, good enough to eat."

"You look good too." I nuzzled into the crook of his neck, breathing in the scent of his freshly showered skin. He kissed the top of my head and gazed down at me.

"Are you ready to go?"

"I'm ready. Are you going to tell me where we are going yet?"

He shook his head and held my hand. "You'll know soon enough. Let's go."

While driving to the undisclosed destination, I riddled Aidan with questions. "Is it far?"

"Nope."

"Have you been there before?" He laughed. "Yes."

My eyes narrowed, not sure if I wanted to know the answer to my next question, but I asked it anyway. "Have you taken any other girls there?"

He took his eyes off the road to look at me. "Never." His tone was definitive. I breathed a sigh of relief.

Traveling up Pacific Coast Highway, I giggled. "Are we almost there?"

He reached over and rubbed my leg. "Almost." And with that, Aidan gave me a wink as we rounded the corner onto Carlton Drive.

"Aidan! Are you kidding me? You're taking me to your work?"

We pulled into the long driveway. His smile was infectious as he pulled up to the valet. Immediately, I was greeted by one of Aidan's co-workers, who offered his hand to guide me from the truck. He checked me out and gave Aidan an approving nod. Aidan introduced me to his attractive friend, Tony, and tossed him the keys.

Aidan interlaced his fingers with mine then held my

hand and walked me through the impressive lobby. Two female staff members gave me the once-over from behind the marble reservation desk.

Aidan said, "Hello," and casually walked by them. I was awestruck by the modern decor and lavish beauty of such a stunning hotel.

"Aidan, this is beautiful."

He leaned over and kissed my forehead. "C'mon, we have reservations." He smiled then whisked me through the stunning hotel.

****

The dining room was small, the ambiance romantic. Dark wood surrounded an open wine cellar with circular tables and intimate booths. Classical music hummed through the speakers. The restaurant was full of couples, chatting and enjoying their meal. The hostess sat us at a private booth.

Aidan held my hand while we decided what to order. I leaned in close and whispered to him.

"It's so expensive. Do you want to split something?"

He shook his head. "Don't worry. Get whatever you like." He lifted my hand to his lips and kissed it.

I decided on the grilled sea scallops with wild rice, and Aidan chose a rib-eye steak and a baked potato. The female server brought me some sparkling water and Aidan a soda, along with some crusty bread. I leaned back in the booth, observing the romantic surroundings. I smiled as he swept his thumb back and forth over my hand.

"I wanted to take you someplace special. Happy anniversary. You're so beautiful, Liz." Aidan's eyes shifted to the table and then back to me. "When I saw you at your birthday party wearing that dress, you took my breath away." Aidan squeezed my hand tight. "I'm sorry I was such a jerk that night."

"It's okay, Aidan, everything worked out."

My afternoon with Spencer crept into my thoughts and I hated myself for it. I got up from my side of the booth and slid in next to Aidan. I embraced him, willing the image of Spencer from my mind.

"Hey, are you okay?"

"Yes, I'm fine." I leaned up to kiss him, then our server arrived. She placed our beautifully plated meal in front of us as I got up and went back to my side of the table. I unrolled my silverware from the crisp linen napkin and placed it across my lap. Aidan cut into his steak and placed a small portion on my plate. I returned the gesture with one of my scallops. Aidan wrinkled his nose at me.

"I'm not much of a fish eater." He pouted. "Oh, don't be a baby."

Aidan stabbed the scallop with his fork and placed it in his mouth. I watched his wary expression transform into joy.

"See? Good, huh?" "So good." He smiled.

When I took a bite of my scallop, my mouth watered from the buttery richness that invaded my taste buds. "Mmm… delicious," I murmured.

"Mine too," Aidan agreed then cut into another piece of his steak.

Throughout our meal, the server came back on several occasions to replenish our breadbasket and refill our drinks. When I couldn't eat another bite, I pushed my plate in front of me.

"Would you like dessert?" Aidan asked. "I'm stuffed."

"Me too. How about if we walk around for a bit?"

"I'd like that."

Aidan made eye contact with our server. "May we have the check please?"

"My pleasure," she replied.

****

Aidan took my hand and guided me through the resort. Eventually, we ended up at an outside balcony overlooking the beautiful Pacific. The moon shimmered over endless miles of ocean. Aidan hugged me from behind and wrapped me in his arms. He peppered my neck with kisses, and when his lips reached my earlobe, I was rewarded with a gentle nibble that sent chills down my spine. He shifted me around and grasped the back of my neck and pressed his lips against mine. His eyes burned with a dozen different emotions until his softened gaze settled on my face. He stroked my cheek with the tips of his fingers then brushed the pad of his thumb across my bottom lip before he kissed me again.

Aidan leaned in, the look in his eyes pure. When he whispered, "I love you," I knew he meant it, which made my heart ache even more. I didn't say anything in return.

My rollercoaster of emotions was getting to me. I wasn't sure if what I felt for Aidan was love. I couldn't bring myself to say anything, so after another passion-filled kiss, like a coward, I turned away. He hugged me, and I buried my face in the warmth of his chest. We spent the next hour wrapped in each other's arms as the moonlit sky surrounded us.

Chapter Sixteen

The doorbell rang. Maggie barked, and seconds later Melissa hollered from the steps below.

"Liz, are you up there?"

"Ya, I'll be right down," I yelled from the upstairs landing.

Melissa was scrounging around in the cupboards when I walked into the kitchen. She pulled out a box of crackers but put it back. "I'm starving. Let's go get something to eat. You can tell me about last night in the car."

****

Melissa sucked down her chocolate shake while we waited at the drive-thru for the rest of our food.

"So, he told you he loved you, and you didn't say anything?"

"No… I hugged him. That was it."

Melissa cocked her head to the side, as if she was trying to figure me out. "Liz, you're probably freaked out because of the other night. I'm glad you're not saying, 'I love you' just because he did."

"He's not your favorite. I know that… but I care about him."

Melissa grabbed the bag from the takeout window, handed it to me and pulled away. I opened the bag and grabbed a couple of fries.

"I remember when you told me how it was for you

and Mason. You both couldn't wait to tell each other. I...
I just thought it would be the same for me."

Melissa stuffed her hand deep in the bag and
grabbed a fried zucchini. "How did he seem after? Was
it awkward?"

"No. It was a good night. I just always thought if he
told me, I'd say it back. No hesitation... ya know?"

My mind settled on thoughts of Spencer. I
considered telling Melissa about him but, knowing how
she felt about Aidan, I wasn't going there with her.

"I can't believe he didn't freak out. Maybe there's
hope for him yet." She smirked then took a bite from the
zucchini strip.

Melissa pulled into the driveway. The open garage
door and the guys playing surprised me. I glanced over
at her before she put the car in park.

"Did you know they were practicing today?" "No
idea."

"I feel bad we didn't get them anything."

Melissa held up the bag. "Do you think that'll stop
'em?"

We exited the car and sat on the garage couch. The
minute Melissa opened the bag, Mason and Derek were
hovering over her with outstretched hands. I grabbed a
handful of fries and was able to get two zucchini strips.
Kyle walked from his keyboard toward us. I held up a
zucchini.

"Hey, Kyle, ya want it?"

"No, that's okay." He sat on the arm of the couch.
Melissa was next to me with Mason on her other side.
After Derek tipped the bag in his mouth and ate the
remaining fries, he squished in between Melissa and me.

"Where's Aidan?" I asked.

"On his way," Mason answered.

"What are you guys doing? You never practice on Tuesdays."

"Derek can't make it Sunday."

Derek piped up from his side of the couch. "I gotta hot date."

"But you'll be back before we go on?" Mason eyed Derek. "Yes. I'll be back... daddy."

"Hey, I wouldn't have to be your daddy if you'd show up on time."

Mason got up from the couch and kissed Melissa on the lips before he walked over to the makeshift stage and picked up his guitar. Derek stretched out across the couch and put his head on my lap and his butt on Melissa.

"Cut it out, Derek." I pushed his head off me, but he just put it back. Melissa shoved him, causing him to fall to the floor. Kyle was still next to me with his arm draped across the back of the couch. With the laughter and commotion of Derek's less-than-graceful fall, I never heard Aidan's arrival. A loud cough alerted me to his presence.

He was standing off to the side, half in the garage, half out. I wasn't sure how long he'd been standing there, but by the look on his face, I was sure he had seen Derek's head on my lap. I watched his eyes shift from me to Kyle's arm. His expression was unreadable, but I would have bet money that he wasn't happy. He let out a deep breath as he approached me. Kyle got up and headed over to the keyboard.

"Hi." I saw the disapproval in his eyes. Aidan leaned down and gave me a quick kiss on the lips before he acknowledged the guys and Melissa. He sat next to me and placed his arm around my shoulder while he

153

whispered in my ear.

"I hope I didn't interrupt. Things seemed a little cozy from what I saw."

"Are you serious? Derek?"

Aidan pulled me in close and whispered in my ear. "I'm not talking about Derek."

"What are you talking about?" I tried to keep my voice low. Melissa had gotten up and was chatting with Mason near the keyboard but I didn't want her to question me on this ridiculous conversation we were having.

"I'm talking about Kyle." I glanced at Kyle, who was eyeing us.

"We're friends, Aidan, you know that."

"Oh, I think he'd like to be more than friends." "I thought you were working on this."

"Hey, I'm just telling you the truth. You have no idea, Liz." "Oh, Aidan, let it go." I sighed. Derek hopped behind his drums and started pounding.

"That's my cue." Aidan got up, but not before he glanced at Kyle and branded me with a kiss.

I had to remind myself Aidan was a work in progress. Determined not to let his irrational behavior get to me, I went inside while the guys practiced in the garage.

****

I was singing and practicing at the piano when the grasp of warm hands made my shoulders tense. I continued to play as Aidan slid in next to me. When I finished the song, he leaned in and gave me a kiss.

"That's the first time you didn't stop singing." He smiled. "It's getting easier." I couldn't help but think of Spencer, knowing he was the reason behind my confidence.

"Just wanted to say goodbye before I left for work." Aidan got up and held out his hand. "Walk me to my truck?" he asked.

"Sure."

I got up and followed Aidan out. He leaned against his truck and pulled me in close. His lips enveloped mine, owning me. When I opened my eyes, Kyle was chatting with Mason in the garage. Kyle's eyes met mine again. My eyes widened at Aidan.

"Did you do that on purpose?"

"Do what? I'm just kissing my girl." His mock innocence was insulting.

"I know what you're doing, Aidan. You'd better knock it off."

"I don't know what you're talking about," he protested. Aidan smiled and hopped in the driver's seat of his truck, but before he closed the door, he leaned over and yelled goodbye to Kyle and Mason, making sure he got one more quick kiss in before Kyle looked away. He shut his door while I stood next to the curb with my arms folded in front of me. Aidan flashed me a patronizing grin and blew me a kiss through the window before he drove away.

After he left, I just wanted to clear my head. The best way for me to do that was running. It was still hard for me to believe that I enjoyed running. Feeling the need to pump some positive endorphins through my veins, I put on my usual attire and ran out the door. No Maggie today, just me. When I was overweight, I had heard of *runner's high* and thought it wasn't real. But, here I was, experiencing it and loving it.

The sweat rolled down my face, and my back was

wet with perspiration. I had run hard today. My mind seemed to be clearer, until I made my way up the street toward home.

Spencer's garage door was open, and he was piddling around inside. The thought ran through my mind to ignore him, but when he glanced my way, we made eye contact. He motioned for me to come over. Like a moth to a flame, I couldn't resist. I adjusted my ponytail and wiped the sweat from my forehead with my arm.

"Let me get you a towel. How 'bout some water?"

"That'd be great. Thanks," I breathlessly answered.

Spencer went in the house while I stood in the garage. All his camping gear was out. He was back within a few minutes. He handed me a small hand towel and a bottle of water.

"Thanks." I wiped my forehead and the back of my neck then guzzled the water until it was halfway empty. Spencer grabbed a couple of camping chairs and opened them up. He sat down and patted the chair next to him.

"Take a seat." He smiled. A smooth voice was crooning in the background.

"I like this song," I smiled.

"Me too. I find his music soothing."

After I finished the rest of my water, Spencer motioned for me to hand him the empty bottle.

"More?" he asked.

I shook my head no. He tossed the empty bottle in a nearby recycling bin.

"Have you always been a runner?" His question made me laugh. "What's so funny?"

"I started running about eight months ago."

"The way you run, I would have guessed you've

been doing it for years. What got you interested?"

I wasn't sure I wanted to tell Spencer about my past, so I hesitated for a minute. Then I blurted it out. "I was sick of being fat." I shrugged.

"What?"

"Yep. Lost a little over forty pounds last year." "I don't believe it."

"Trust me. I have plenty of pictures to prove it."

"I would have never thought that. I look at you and always think you're a health nut."

That made me laugh.

"Far from it. I love to eat. That's the problem." "Well, that's good. I hate when girls don't eat."

"Yes, but would you ever date a fat girl?" I lifted an arched eyebrow at him.

"Actually, I have dated a bigger girl."

"I find that hard to believe. What happened to her?"

"It just didn't work out." He shrugged. "Hmm… okay." I scanned his face. "What? Do you want proof?"

He started to rise from the chair, but I grabbed his arm.

"No, no that's okay. That's nice to hear. Most guys aren't like that. Seems they'd rather date someone with beauty on the outside rather than the inside."

"You're lucky then. You've got both." He smiled.

My cheeks felt flushed, and I knew I was red. I wanted to get off the subject, so I glanced around the garage. "Are you going camping?"

"Yeah, I'm taking Shawn and Simon Friday. We're going to San Clemente for a night."

"It's so close. Seems funny you'd go there."

"I know. It's only because school is such a grind, and I can't get away. The boys don't care. They're just happy to sleep in a tent and eat s'mores." He laughed.

"My favorite."

"You should come by, and we'll make you some. In fact, I'll bring my guitar, and we can practice a bit. Ya know, sing songs around the campfire. The boys would love it. You impressed them with your mad football skills. Especially Simon."

"Um... I'll think about it." I began to chew on my thumbnail. "Oh, that's right. Boyfriend."

"Probably not a good idea." That was a no brainer. Aidan would freak for sure. Sensing the shift in Spencer's demeanor I decided to change the subject. "I never told you this, but I was close friends with the woman that used to live here."

"You were?"

"She was good to me, kind and so full of life."
"What happened to her?"

"She passed away... cancer." "I'm sorry," he whispered.

"She always used to tell me that my life was before me... a blank canvas. *'Paint it every color, Lizzie, and have no regrets.'* I loved her so."

"Wise words," he said. I nodded.

"Is it hard for you to be here... in my house?" Spencer's eyes softened with concern.

"No. I love coming here, it feels like... home." My eyes lingered on his.

Spencer squeezed my knee and smiled then leaned his body toward mine. His eyes slid to my lips then back to my gaze, causing me to sheepishly look away.

"I should probably get home." I stood up. "Thanks for the water," I nervously muttered. "I'll see ya tomorrow."

Spencer rose from his chair, and I handed him back the towel.

"See ya," he answered.

I jogged down the driveway. I didn't want to look, but I couldn't help myself. I glanced back over my shoulder. He was standing in the same spot watching me as I jogged away.

Chapter Seventeen

Walking up the street to Spencer's house, I realized I was beginning to look forward to our practice times together. I found myself thinking about him more than I should and longing for him when we were apart. I forcibly pushed the thoughts out of my head, dismissing them as a stupid infatuation.

Spencer was in his driveway washing his jeep when I walked up to his house. When he saw me, he glanced up in surprise.

"Crap! I lost track of time."

"Don't worry about it. Do you want some help?" I picked up a sponge from a bucket full of soapy water and started washing down the jeep before he could answer me.

"Thanks." He smiled.

We made quick work of scrubbing the jeep and hosing it off. Within twenty minutes, we were drying it with some old towels. Spencer's stomach growled.

"Did you hear that?" He laughed. "How could I not?"

"You want to grab some dinner?" Spencer picked up the towels, walked into the garage, and tossed them next to the washing machine. I followed him with the empty bucket and placed it on the floor.

"Okay."

While walking toward the jeep, I let my hand glide

across the seat of the motorcycle. Spencer stopped in front of the sleek, black-and-chrome machine.

"Do you want to take the bike?" he asked.

My eyes grew wide, and a smile spread across my face. Spencer laughed. "I'll take that as a yes."

I was relieved I didn't have to answer. At that moment, all the saliva had left my mouth.

He glanced at what I was wearing. "You'll need a jacket."

"I could run home." Adrenaline was pumping through my veins as I started down the driveway.

"No, no, come back. There's a jacket in the house you can wear, but I need to change."

I followed Spencer in the house, sat on his couch, and waited. A few minutes later he emerged from the hallway with his leather jacket draped over his arm.

"Thanks." I adjusted my ponytail as we made our way back to the garage.

Spencer held out his jacket, and I slipped my arms inside. I was immediately hit with the scent that was uniquely his. The sleeves hung past my hands, and I felt tiny, surrounded by his much-too-large jacket. Spencer smiled and he zipped it up while I wrestled with the sleeves.

He pushed the bike onto the driveway and jogged back inside and grabbed two helmets before he closed the door. He handed me one, and I slipped it over my head.

"Ladies first."

He held the handlebars steady as I hiked my leg up and over. He put his helmet on and straddled the seat. He shifted the bike up straight before snapping the kickstand back with his heavy boot and started it up. The growl of the engine startled me. He glanced back. "You okay?"

"It just scared me, but I'm fine." I spoke above the roar of the engine, so he could hear me.

The thought of the bike speeding down the street made my heartbeat faster.

"You're gonna have to hold onto me."

He reached back and grabbed one of my arms and placed it around his mid-section. My other arm followed suit.

"And if you get scared, just yell in my ear, and I'll stop." "Okay," I yelled over his shoulder while I tightened my hold around his waist.

"Pizza?"

"Sure."

Spencer slowly rode out of our neighborhood and headed toward Pacific Coast Highway. When we'd made it to the coast, he gunned it. I held on tight and tucked myself behind his shoulder. The scent that clung to his leather jacket consumed me.

Speeding down the highway should have been scary, but I found it exhilarating. The wind was whipping past us so fast I imagined the feeling was that of straddling a rocket. The sun was setting over the ocean as we rode through Dana Point and passed Capistrano Beach. We weaved our way through the streets of San Clemente and ended up at Donny's Pizza.

Spencer parked the bike and leaned it to the side then forced the kickstand into place. He dismounted first, removed his helmet, and held out a hand to help me off. I couldn't help but notice his hair still looked good.

"So, what'd you think?"

Before answering, I took off the helmet and handed it to Spencer. Hoping my hair had fared as well as his, I removed the hair band and gave my head a shake, while he anxiously watched. "It was amazing!"

The hesitation on Spencer's face morphed into a dimpled smile. "Awesome! I was a little worried... you were holding me pretty tight." He clipped both helmets on the bike and guided me toward the restaurant.

"Sorry about that, it's just... we were going so fast." I unzipped his leather jacket but kept it on.

"Actually, we never went above the speed limit. It just feels faster." When we entered the doors, Spencer leaned in close to my ear. "I would never put you in danger, Elizabeth." His breathy words sent a chill down my spine.

When the hostess got a look at Spencer, she quickly approached us and smiled at him. She batted her eyelashes and asked if we preferred to sit inside or out.

Spencer looked at me and I shrugged my shoulders. "Out," he answered.

She led us to an outside patio with dark wood beams, surrounded by white twinkle lights. I had eaten here with my family several times. Donny's was a favorite with the locals, and I was happy he had chosen it. The hostess sat us at a small table for two. Spencer pulled out my chair, and I took a seat. He sat across from me. The hostess handed us our menus and asked if we wanted a drink, all the while keeping her eyes focused on Spencer.

"I'll have a root beer please." Finally, she noticed me.

"That sounds good. I'll have the same."

Spencer smiled up at the hostess, and I could have sworn I heard her gasp. We read over our menus for a minute before I looked back at him.

"What would you like?" he asked.

"Do you want to split a pizza and maybe get some pasta?" The garlicky aromas from the kitchen made me realize how hungry I was.

"Perfect. How about a cheese pizza and spaghetti?"

"That sounds good. Do you mind if we get angel hair? It's my favorite."

"Angel hair for an angel." He sat back in his chair and smiled.

His comment embarrassed me. He chuckled at my reaction and stroked the stubble of his chin with one hand.

"It's hard for you to take a compliment, isn't it?"

I shielded my face with the curtain of my hair, looking everywhere but at him. "I guess I'm just not used to it." My face still felt warm.

"I didn't mean to embarrass you. It's just…"

I was thankful when the waitress interrupted our conversation and arrived with our drinks. She introduced herself as Jessie and gave Spencer the once-over while he rattled off our order. I sipped my soda and watched as she shamelessly flirted with him.

He kept his attention focused on me and ignored her. He picked up his root beer, and my eyes glanced over at the script written on his ring finger.

It was so tempting to ask him about the delicate tattoo, but I decided against it. We were having such a good time. I remembered how he'd closed himself off the last time I'd asked, so I thought I'd keep my mouth shut. The food arrived. Spencer divvied up our pizza, while I dished out the pasta.

"I love their pizza." I smiled and took a big bite. Spencer folded his slice in half and took a bite.

"Do you always eat your pizza like that?" He

glanced at his slice and then back to me.

"Lance taught me to eat it this way. He called it the fold-hold, less mess." He shrugged and took another bite.

"I wonder how Lance is doing? I sure miss him."

"I'm sure he's doin' great." He took another bite.

The waitress came back and refilled our sodas while I twirled the pasta around my fork. Spencer finished his pizza and grabbed another slice. My cell phone chimed from my pocket. I hesitated, not wanting to be rude.

"You can get that, if you need too."

I reached in my pocket and pulled out my cell. It was a text from Melissa.

"Boyfriend?" he asked.

"No. Friend." I shut off my ringer and stuffed the phone back in my pocket. There was an awkwardness that surrounded our table after that. Spencer finished up his pasta and the last of the pizza as I placed my fork across my empty plate. I was thankful when the waitress came back and asked if we would like anything else.

"Would you like dessert?" Spencer asked.

"We could split something." That answer seemed to lighten the mood.

"I like your style." He smiled.

"See. Told you. I like to eat. I'll have to pay for it tomorrow, but it's worth it... How 'bout the tiramisu?"

"A girl after my own heart." Spencer glanced up at the waitress and said, "One tiramisu, two forks."

A few minutes later, the waitress returned and placed the dessert between us. We both dug in at the same time. My eyes grew wide while watching Spencer wrap his mouth around the moist cake. The way his tongue slid across his lips and the throaty groan that escaped him made me inhale sharply. My fork hung midair. I was so caught up in watching him I hadn't even taken a bite.

"Mmm... That's good." He suggestively licked his fork.

I had to shake my head to free myself from my wayward thoughts. Finally, I took a bite. Delicious. I savored the taste as I chewed the creamy cake.

Spencer's eyes were transfixed on my lips. When my tongue darted out to retrieve a crumb, he took a deep breath and swallowed. The atmosphere surrounding our innocent dinner was becoming something more. I could almost feel the surge of electricity between us.

To break the spell closing in around us, I put my fork down and grabbed my drink, avoiding the scrutiny of his gaze. Spencer sighed before he looked away.

While sipping my soda, a boisterous laugh caught my attention. It sounded familiar. The laughter turned into a voice I knew all too well. I glanced behind me. My heart began to pound as I shifted in my chair, placing my drink on the table.

Derek.

"Are you alright? You look pale." Spencer picked up on my anxiety. He reached for my hand.

"I'm fine." I withdrew my hand and stood up. "We should go." Adrenaline pulsed through me, and my eyes darted around the patio. The side exit to the parking lot was blocked with patrons. The only way out was the front door.

"I'll meet you at the bike." The distress in my tone made my words sound curt. But at that moment, I didn't care how I sounded. Getting out of the restaurant was my only concern.

The hostess came through with a party of four. I took

advantage of the opportunity, concealed myself behind the group, and walked swiftly past them. My breath escaped me, and I sighed with relief. Within seconds, I was out of the restaurant.

Thankfully, Derek hadn't seen me. If he had, he would have let me know it. What was I thinking? Going out with Spencer? That was the problem. I wasn't thinking. I'd been so caught up in the moment I hadn't even thought of the consequences if Aidan found out. The thought made me shudder.

A few minutes later, Spencer walked past me as he exited the front door.

"Spencer," I called out. The confusion was still apparent on his face. He took a few steps toward me.

"Why'd you run out?" His voice was full of concern. I hesitated before I answered.

"I saw someone. Someone, I didn't want to run into." "Who?" he asked.

My eyes shifted to a group of people exiting the restaurant. I started walking toward the bike with Spencer at my side.

"A guy that's in Mason's band."

Spencer peered straight ahead. He seemed tense around the eyes.

"With your boyfriend?"

"Yes," I whispered.

"I see." Spencer was quiet until we reached the bike. His sudden mood change made me feel like I should apologize. He grabbed the helmets.

"I'm sorry for running out," I said. "It was stupid, but I didn't know what else to do."

He nodded, but his vague expression made me feel uncomfortable. I pulled the hair band out from my pocket and twisted my hair back.

I pulled the helmet over my head. Spencer put on his and straddled the bike then leaned forward, allowing me to get on. The engine growled to life, and I latched my arms around his firm middle. It upset me when his body tensed from my touch. He slowly rode out of the parking lot onto the street.

To shield myself from the wind, I tucked my head behind him. The hum of the engine and the coolness of the night helped distract my jumbled thoughts.

I was thankful when we pulled into our neighborhood and the bike slowed. I wanted us to get back to our normal routine. When we approached the driveway, Spencer opened the garage door. The second he shut the engine, I slipped my leg off and stumbled to the ground. Spencer forced the bike on its kickstand and hopped off to help me.

"You alright?" He pulled my arm and helped me to my feet. "I'm fine."

Embarrassed, I dusted off my behind before I removed my helmet and handed it to him. He removed his and placed them on the seat of the bike. We were both quiet as we walked into the house. I excused myself and made my way down the hallway to his guest bathroom.

After removing the hair band, I separated a few of the tangled strands with my fingers. My cheeks were flushed from the ride, but my hair looked decent. I removed his jacket, smelled it one last time, and exited the bathroom with it draped over my arm.

Spencer was staring out the front window when I returned. He turned to face me when my steps from the carpeted hallway hit the wood floor.

"Ready to start?" he asked, while walking toward

the piano. I nodded, and Spencer slid across the bench.

I placed his jacket over the loveseat and joined him. His mood was hard for me to judge now. It was almost like he was upset but trying not to be. He began tapping out a song that was familiar. He started to sing and nodded when I should start.

When we sang through the song for the third time, I felt a surge of relief. Spencer seemed to be in better spirits, and I was happy he'd chosen a song I already knew. When he seemed satisfied with our performance, he stopped playing and shifted his body to look at me. I could tell he wanted to say something, but he didn't. He exhaled and patted my thigh twice.

"Solo time. You know the song "All I Need Is You," right?" "Yes."

Once again I was relieved I already knew the song. I moved from the piano bench and stood in my usual spot. Spencer picked up his guitar that was leaning against the wall and began to play. We ran through the song twice.

"I think that's enough for today," he said. "Oh, okay."

I walked toward the front door. Spencer reached for the doorknob and opened it for me.

Our walk to my house was quieter than usual. We both seemed to be lost in our thoughts. When we arrived at my driveway, I glanced at Spencer.

"Wait here a sec. I'll be right back." "Okay." He answered.

I quickly walked into my house. When I got inside, I ran up the stairs to my room, grabbed my wallet from my purse, and pulled out a ten-dollar bill. I hurried back downstairs and out the door. When I reached Spencer, I held out the money.

"Here," I said, clutching the folded bill in my hand. Spencer shook his head back and forth.

"Did you think I'd take your money?"

He started backing up, but I followed. I was able to grab his front pocket and stuff the money in it before he could get away. With a smirk and a few steps toward me, Spencer was at my side. He wrapped his arms around me, stuffing the money in my back pocket. We were both laughing, caught up in the moment. I tried to squirm out of his grasp but realized a part of me didn't want to. We both stopped laughing as our friendly struggle turned into something more.

His eyes were locked on mine. I knew I should back away from him, but I couldn't.

He closed his eyes, exhaled, and took a step back, breaking our connection. His voice trailed off as he said, "It was my treat. Goodnight, Elizabeth."

Spencer turned around and walked away, leaving me with my scattered thoughts and ten dollars in my pocket.

Chapter Eighteen

Mason held the back door for me as we entered the church together.

"Thanks, Mason."

We walked down the long hallway toward the music room. I opened the door and stopped so suddenly Mason bumped into me, causing me to stumble to the ground.

"Hey, klutz… what'd ya stop for?" Mason chuckled and helped me up.

Unable to answer, I rose to my feet. My eyes were fixed on what I saw before me.

Spencer was leaning against the table, chatting with an attractive blonde. My gawky entrance caught the attention of them both.

"You alright, Elizabeth?" Spencer asked.

All I could do was nod. When I realized my mouth was hanging open, I immediately closed it. My eyes shifted from Spencer to his friend and then back to Spencer.

"We'll do a quick run-through before the service starts. Just give me a minute." Spencer smiled back at the pretty girl, emphasizing his prominent dimples, and glanced toward us. "Mason, can you and Elizabeth take this stuff to the stage?" He motioned to the mic stand and a few electrical cords. "I'll be right out."

"Sure, Spence." Mason answered him, but I was at a loss for words.

They didn't even notice me when I placed my purse down on the small wooden table. I didn't want to stare, but I couldn't drag my eyes away from them.

"Liz!" Mason's tone made me jump.

"What?" I snapped, as I tore my eyes away from the attractive couple.

"Didn't you hear me? I called your name twice already." Mason handed me the mic stand. "Take this to the stage."

I picked up the mic and walked out of the room, glancing back one more time. In a daze I made my way to the stage and put the mic down. I vaguely remember Jake and Matt saying hi to me while I slid in behind the piano. My mind was so absorbed in what I'd just seen I wasn't sure if I'd even answered them. Mindlessly I tapped on the piano keys, joining them in their practicing.

Why does it matter to me if Spencer is talking to a pretty girl? I should be happy for him. He deserves to be happy.

About the time I was coming to terms with my internal struggle, Spencer and his blond friend came into the church.

"Hey guys, this is a friend of mine, Kara."

Kara smiled a perfect smile and tossed her head to one side, her long blond hair fell midway down her back. She followed Spencer up the steps and reached out and shook hands with Matt and Jake. When Kara turned her back, Matt raised an eyebrow to Jake and smiled. Mason made his way across the stage to greet her. Mason smiled, said hello and introduced himself.

When she approached me, I rose to meet her. I had to tilt my head up to meet her gaze. She was attractive with her tanned skin and deep brown eyes.

"Hi," I said.

"Hi, nice to meet you." She smiled.

"You too," I answered, hoping my reply sounded genuine.

I watched Spencer guide her to a seat, front and center, then I slid back into place behind my piano. When she stood next to him, they looked striking together. He whispered something in her ear, and she giggled. I hadn't noticed what Spencer was wearing until now. He usually dressed casually, but today he was dressed up. I felt a slight tinge of pain and wondered what his plans were after church.

Spencer made his way back to the stage and led us through our first three songs. Each time I looked at Kara, her eyes were always on Spencer.

"Elizabeth, it's solo time." Spencer gave me an encouraging smile and motioned to the mic.

My eyes met his. I glanced at Kara and realized I couldn't do this today. Everyone was looking at me. My gaze went to the exit sign, and I seriously considered sprinting toward the door.

Spencer's soft, grey eyes met mine and saved me from the embarrassment of what could have been. He reached his hand to mine, but I pulled it away. His fleeting expression went from concern to pain in an instant.

I took a few deep breaths and walked to the mic.

I can do this. I can do this. I can do this.

My emotions were all over the place. I needed to focus and get through this. The music began. I reached down from the depths of my soul and put every bit of what I was feeling into each note. I had never sung like this before. Something changed within me as I belted out the song.

When I finished, I opened my eyes to Kara fervently applauding, and I could see the look of awe in the faces of Jake and Matt. Spencer caught my eye, then I whispered into the mic.

"I'll be right back."

Feeling overwhelmed with the need to escape, I made my way to the bathroom. I splashed some cool water on my face and heard a gentle tapping on the door. Gathering all the strength within me I answered, "I'll be right out."

I patted my face dry and opened the door. To my disappointment, it was Mason.

"Hey, are you okay? Spencer asked me to check on you." "I'm fine."

"Liz, that was amazing."

Mason was proud of me, and in the haze of my mixed-up emotions, it felt good. I plastered on a fake smile as we walked back to the stage together.

"You've got some awesome pipes." Mason nudged me, shoulder to shoulder.

"Thanks." I smiled, but this time the smile was real.

****

I had no idea how I made it through the church service. Everything was a blur until I realized it was over. During the whole performance, I hadn't once looked at Spencer. He directed me, and I would obediently comply, but I never made eye contact.

When I exited the stage, my only thought was I wanted out as soon as possible. I dashed to the music room and grabbed my purse, pulled the keys from my bag, and quickly made my way down the long hallway.

My beating heart and the jingling of my keys was all I could hear as my steps quickened. My eyes focused on the exit sign, knowing freedom was steps away. I was just about to push through the door when I heard Spencer call my name. Pretending not to hear him, I pushed myself through the door.

The second my feet hit the pavement, I ran to my car. My trembling hand shoved the key in the ignition, and I made my way out of the parking lot toward the street. When I glanced in my rearview mirror, the last thing I saw was Spencer's confused face darting around the parking lot. I breathed a sigh of relief watching his image slip farther and farther away.

****

As soon as I walked in the door, I texted Aidan. I needed to see him, to reassure myself of the feelings I had for him. This infatuation for Spencer was foolish. I wanted to put it in a box, bury it, and not let it seep out.

Me: *What time are you off today?*
Aidan: *1*
Me: *Feel like going on a run? We can have lunch after?*
Aidan: *Okay. Be there soon.*

****

It was warm outside, so I decided to wear black yoga shorts and a white tank top. I tied up my laces as Maggie entered my room. She sniffed my shoes and started jumping around.

"Not today, girl."

I gave her a few kisses and coaxed her to come up on my bed. She curled up next to me, and I cuddled in her soft fur as I thought about the last twenty-four hours.

Spencer... Kara... Aidan...

My eyes closed, and I felt myself drift off. It seemed like only a few minutes had passed when I was jolted awake by the feel of a warm chest and strong arms spooning around me. Maggie jumped off the bed and Aidan snuggled in close.

"This is my favorite place to be." His sultry words whispered in my ear while he nuzzled my neck.

I stuffed down the visual of Spencer and Kara still lingering in my brain. "Hi," I sleepily whispered.

"Are you sure you want to go for a run? We could just stay here all day." Aidan grinned.

"I'm not sure my parents would approve." "Your mom loves me."

"True, but I don't think my dad would like it. C'mon let's get moving."

I gave him a quick kiss and sat up on the bed. Aidan sat up as Mason entered my room.

"Hey, Aidan."

"Hi, Mason," Aidan answered.

"Why'd you bolt out of church, Liz? Spencer wanted to talk to you."

"About what?"

"He didn't say. He mentioned you sounded amazing. And Kara, she kept going on and on about how good you were."

I glanced over to Aidan, and he had a quizzical look on his face. "Liz, did you solo again?"

"Spencer's making me." "Making you?"

"I hate it, Aidan. I only do it because I have too."

"Oh, he did mention Wednesday. He wanted to make sure you'd be there." Mason said, exiting my room.

"Yeah, I'll be there."

"What's Wednesday?" Aidan questioned.

"Oh, that's just the night we practice." I shrugged it off, hoping he thought *we* meant everyone. I got up and changed the subject.

"We'd better get going. I forgot you guys were playing tonight."

Aidan stood and glanced at my outfit. "Those are pretty short."

I tried to make light of his comment. "Well, enjoy the view because you'll be looking at it the whole time."

"Oh?" He lifted an eyebrow.

I gave him a smile before I took off running down the stairs with Aidan trailing behind me.

****

When we jogged past Spencer's house, I wondered what he and Kara were doing, but dismissed the thought as quickly as it entered my mind.

Running alongside the creek bed, Aidan and I were laughing and having a great time.

A couple of guys I recognized from jogging the trail made eye contact with me and said, "Hi."

I smiled and returned the greeting, not thinking it was a big deal. A few minutes later, a lone jogger ran past, checking me out. I glanced at Aidan. He was quiet, impassive as we continued on our way. We kept running at an even pace until he had to stop and tie his shoe. Taking advantage of the opportunity, I kept running. A couple of guys on bikes whistled at me. I felt my nerves get the best of me when one of them pulled off to the side to chat.

"How's it going?" he asked.

"Goo-ood." My answer came out long and slow. I glanced back at Aidan, who was now rising to his feet.

"Umm, I have a boyfriend. He's back there." I pointed toward Aidan, who was starting to jog toward us.

"Well, that's too bad." He smiled and rode away. Aidan scowled at him when he peddled past. Knowing this exchange could trigger Aidan's temper, I waited until he caught up.

"What'd the guy want?" "Nothing."

"Answer me," he said tightly.

"He just wanted to talk, that's all." I started to jog, hoping we could get past this without a fight.

"Does that happen a lot?" Aidan and I were jogging in sync. "No."

"I find that hard to believe. Every guy that has run past us has checked out your butt. I don't want you jogging here anymore." He snapped.

"What?" I stopped, stunned. "You don't want me jogging here anymore?"

"No, not if you're going to be hit on by every guy that passes you." Aidan's lips were pressed in a thin angry line.

"You've got to be kidding me."

"Am I? Or do you like the attention?"

"You're acting crazy." Unwilling to listen to his nonsense, I started to jog away.

"I'm not done talkin' to you."

My leisurely jog transitioned into a race to get away from him. With each hurried step, I focused on the glimmering Pacific in the distance. The pounding of Aidan's feet was catching up to me, so I ran faster. The sand was in sight, but before I could make it there, his arm reached out and grabbed me. He squeezed my arm tight and swung me around, but I broke free. My feet hit the sand, and I ran a few more feet before he caught me again and crushed his body into mine. I struggled to break free, but he was too strong.

"Aidan, stop it! You're scaring me!" I screamed.

He instantly let me go. I stepped away from him and hunched over, trying to catch my breath. My knees sunk into the sand. Fear replaced anger and brought tears to my eyes. Aidan was at my side in seconds, rocking me back and forth whispering he was sorry. I pushed him back, but he was determined to hold me. I didn't have the strength to move, so I gave up and continued to sob into his damp t-shirt. He covered my face with kisses and whispered repeatedly how sorry he was. Eventually my tears subsided, and my breathing calmed. Aidan cradled my face with his hands and searched my despondent eyes.

"I'm so sorry. I didn't mean to scare you. I was being an idiot. I'm sorry. I'm so sorry," he mumbled. After several silent minutes, Aidan whispered, "Say something."

Still trying to absorb everything, I sat up and noticed the apprehension that covered his face. I thought back on all the conversations we'd had about his mother and how he'd grown up, bouncing from home to home, stepmom to stepmom. He'd always had his father, but what little I knew of Aidan's dad was that of a selfish man.

In the moments that passed, I realized the self-assured Aidan Mitchell was wrapped up in an emotional blanket of anger and pain. I felt myself on the precipice. Do I walk away or try to make us work? There was good in him. I knew there was. Aidan's guarded expression was apologetic and full of regret. He continued to scrutinize my face. Finally, I took a deep breath and whispered, "It's okay."

Aidan breathed a sigh of relief and held me close to his chest, "I'm trying... you know that right?"

When I glanced up and looked into his eyes, they seemed genuine and sincere. I nodded in response to his question, then he bent down and kissed my lips.

He wanted to change... I knew he did. Aidan was trying... it was just going to take time. As I continued to search his face, I realized I was willing to give him that... and truly, what more could I ask of him?

****

Melissa and I sat at our usual table while the guys brought in their gear and set up. The regulars were milling around and, of course, the cute brunette... she seemed to have a usual table too.

Aidan had been more attentive than necessary, and it hadn't gone unnoticed by the inquisitive Melissa. "What's with the pretty boy?"

"He's just being more amazing than usual."

"Cut the crap. He seems all nervous and awkward around you. Did something happen?"

I felt vulnerable, and the truth was I wanted to talk to her about what had happened. I glanced up to the stage to see where Aidan was and leaned in closer to Melissa. "Today, while we were jogging, some guy came on to me, and Aidan freaked out."

"What do you mean by freaked out?" She eyed me with caution. "Did he fight the guy... or... hurt you?"

"No... no." My mind flashed to Aidan's firm grip on my arm, but I dismissed it. "He was just jealous, like that night in the bar."

I could see anger beginning to surface in her eyes. "And...?" "I think he still feels bad. That's why he's acting the way he is."

Melissa leaned back in her chair, her eyes still on mine. "I'm glad he feels bad, but he's still doing it. You said you wouldn't put up with it… and here you are."

I could hear the skepticism in her tone.

"How many chances are you going to give him?" "I don't know."

"What if he loses it again?" Melissa glanced at Aidan and back to me.

I was silent while I contemplated her question. Over the past few hours, I had asked myself the same thing at least twenty times. I was willing to give Aidan time to change, but if he freaked out like that again, I just didn't know. Hearing Melissa ask me brought the definitive answer I had been searching for. With certainty I knew.

"I would break up with him." I stared into Melissa's eyes with such assurance that her body relaxed as she breathed a sigh of relief.

Chapter Nineteen

"Holy crap! Ninety-five bucks a piece?" Aidan glanced at the poster and shook his head.

"I can pay for my ticket, Aidan."

"No, no. Of course I'm paying for you. It's just crazy how pricy it is." Aidan kissed the top of my head as we walked down the locker-covered hallway.

"Well, it *is* prom. It's always a rip-off," I shrugged.

"True. At least I get to see you dressed up. It'll be worth it." Aidan smiled and held my hand while we walked to the office to buy our tickets. He stuffed the tickets in his wallet and walked me through the school to the parking lot. I unlocked my car door, got inside, and started it up.

"So, I'll see you later? Movie night at my house?" Aidan bent down so we were eye to eye through my open window.

"Yep, I'll be over in a few hours." I leaned my head out and kissed him goodbye.

****

On my way to Aidan's, I couldn't help but look at Spencer's house. I pulled off next to the curb and parked my car.

Is he lounging on the couch? Is he singing at the piano or playing the guitar?

Now it seemed my imagination was getting the best of me. Each time I thought of Spencer, I thought of Kara.

I imagined him telling her everything, singing to her, laughing with her, and kissing her. I was surprised at how much my thoughts pained me. Deep down I knew he was entitled to be happy and have someone. I just hated how much it bothered me.

****

"What's wrong, Liz? You've been out of it since the movie started." Aidan pulled me in close as the credits started to roll. He grabbed the remote and clicked off the TV.

"I'm just tired." I snuggled in next to him and breathed in his fresh scent.

"Come here," Aidan said while he lay back on the couch and pulled me onto his chest.

Spencer kept creeping in and I hated myself for it. To distract the direction of my thoughts, I crawled up Aidan's body and kissed him teasingly, allowing my tongue to taste his as our kiss deepened into more. Hopeful to lose myself in him, I ran my hands under his t-shirt and pressed my body firmly against his. His hands cupped my backside while he peppered my neck with nips and kisses. I felt a few of his fingers lightly trail under the waistband of my underwear as he brought his lips back to mine. Aidan pulled back. His heated gaze roamed my face. He looked at me with such passion I knew my eyes mirrored the same. "My dad and Natalie are still up. Do you want to go in my room?" His words came out slow and seductive.

Everything within my body screamed to keep going, but my head said *Stop!* I knew if I didn't get up and go home, we'd end up doing something I would regret. I took a deep breath and sat back up.

"No, Aidan, we shouldn't," I breathlessly

whispered.

"I love you, Liz," Aidan said, and he kissed me again. I peered up at him through my long dark lashes. He pulled back. His eyes narrowed while he studied my face. "That's the second time I've told you that, and you haven't said anything."

"I…" But before I could respond, a burst of light from the kitchen distracted me. It was Natalie, and she glanced into the family room.

"Don't mind me. I just need a glass of water." Aidan rolled his eyes and got up, extending a hand to help me. Together we silently walked outside. Aidan leaned against my car and pulled me toward him.

"Well?" His gaze met mine. "I care about you."

"Care about me? What does that even mean? I love you and you care about me? Oh, that's just perfect!" He huffed.

"Aidan, I…"

"I haven't looked at another girl since we've been together.

His anger rose as he interrupted me.

I stepped back.

He began pacing back and forth.

"You've asked me to work on my jealousy. I'm working on my jealousy. You wanted to take it slow, and we're taking it slow. Ten minutes ago, you were all over me. Then you tell me we should stop, so we stopped. I'm trying here, Liz! I just don't know what you want from me." Aidan stopped in front of me with his arms folded. The frustration on his face was evident.

I rubbed his arm to apologize. "Aidan, I… I love you're doing all this for me." His arms were tense but I continued to rub my hand back and forth. "I just… I don't know. We've only been together a few months. I just can't say it. Not yet." I pulled his arms down and moved in close wrapping my arms around him. "You're special to me. So special." I squeezed him tight. "I'm just not ready to say that, but you mean so much to me... you do."

After a few minutes, his rigid body became slack, and he hugged me back.

"I'm sorry I haven't said it yet. Please don't be mad at me." I stood on my tiptoes so I could kiss his cheek. "Are we okay?"

Aidan breathed out and said, "Yes," then kissed the top of my head. He stepped back so he could look me in the eye. "Ya know what's so ironic? Girls have tossed those words around to me, and I thought nothing of it, and the only girl I want to hear it from won't say it."

"No, it just means when I do say those words, I'll mean it from the depths of my soul."

Aidan leaned his forehead against mine. "I guess that'll be worth the wait then." He smiled and grabbed my car door and opened it. "So, will I see you tomorrow?"

"Remember, I'm prom-dress shopping with Melissa?"

"Oh, yeah. Alright then, I'll see you at the club." Aidan kissed my lips before I got in my car. "Pick out something sexy." He winked.

"I'll think about it." I smirked. "I'll see you tomorrow night.

Bye, Aidan."

"Night, Liz."

****

Melissa pulled my arm as she weaved our way

through the crowded mall.

"C'mon, just one more store." She gasped.

She was so wound up. Each store was crammed full of prom dresses. To Melissa it must have felt like the mother ship had landed. I had already found a dress I liked, but Melissa said I couldn't make an accurate decision until I had seen everything. I stopped counting after store number seven.

"I love that one! That's perfect for you!" Melissa squealed.

A strapless maroon gown that gathered on one side — it was elegant and had just a bit of shimmer. I had to admit, I loved it too.

"C'mon, let's go back to the store with the blue, glittery dress. I think that's the one I want." Melissa grabbed my arm once again, and we were headed back to store number three or maybe it was four.

The idea that I was going to prom was still hard for me to believe. I never thought it would happen, and here I was, walking out of the mall with a beautiful dress draped over my arm.

****

Derek tucked himself behind his drums and began tapping out their first song. The guys followed suit as Mason took the stage. A few of the regulars moved in close, and little Miss Brunette was front and center. Mason was crooning one of Melissa's favorites. I smiled when she sang along. Aidan caught my eye but still seemed pained from the other night. I gave him an encouraging smile, and it seemed to help lighten his mood. The music slowed and, as Mason finished the song, I watched all the females within ten feet of my brother swoon. Melissa and I made eye contact and laughed.

Glancing over the crowded venue, I couldn't help but feel a sense of pride that Random Plan had such a loyal following. I began to hum along with the next song as I watched the crowd join in. My humming immediately stopped when my focal point zeroed in on a familiar tatted arm casually draped around the back of a wooden chair. My heartbeat stopped. Wisps of perfect blond hair were delicately cascading over that arm.

I tried to focus on the crowd, the music, Aidan — anything to keep my mind occupied and my gaze from the intimate table for two. My mind was racing, overcome with curiosity. A shiver ran though me, I crouched down in my chair and turned my gaze to the small round table. Mesmerized, I couldn't look away.

Kara was invading Spencer's personal space, leaning in, batting her eyelashes, and smiling her perfect smile. Yes, she seemed interested, but was he?

"Liz, what are you looking at?" Melissa broke my spellbound trance.

"Um… oh, our bandleader is here." I tried to sound casual then gestured over to the table in the back of the room.

"Whoa! I've got to get to church more." Melissa laughed. "Yes, you do." I gave her a patronizing smirk.

"That's the guy you practice with on Wednesday nights?

You never told me he was such a hottie. Is that his girlfriend?" "I'm not sure." I glanced back at them.

Melissa continued to stare, "Well, if she isn't, I can tell she wants to be." Melissa rolled her eyes and motioned for me to glance back at the table.

Kara had completely shifted her body toward

Spencer and was twirling her hair around one slender finger. About the same time I was trying to determine if Spencer was interested in her or not, he shifted his chair. From across the room, our eyes met. Spencer held my gaze. I matched his long, fixed stare as unemotionally as possible until the roar of the crowd broke in, causing me to turn away. I focused my attention on Aidan until Mason finished the song and spoke into the mic.

"We've got a special friend here tonight. Let's see if we can get him up for a song." The crowd glanced around and continued to eagerly applaud.

"C'mon up, Spencer." Mason smiled across the room.

I glanced back to their table. Kara was beaming as Spencer confidently took the stage. A few of the college girls howled and whistled. Mason handed Spencer his guitar then pulled up a stool. He caught my eye while he adjusted the mic.

"I've got one condition. I'd like to make this a duet."

My heart started to pound when I realized what was about to happen.

"Elizabeth Ryan, will you please join me?" The crowd cheered, Melissa gasped, and Aidan's expression was of stunned irritation.

I must have had an out of body experience because the next thing I knew I was sitting on a stool with Spencer whispering in my ear. I wasn't sure if I shuddered from the feel of his warm breath against my skin or the fear bubbling up inside me. I exhaled a deep breath, hoping to calm my nerves.

"I hear you sing this song to yourself all the time. You can do this." Spencer took a step back and began to strum the intro to the song, "Need You Now."

My voice came out in a whisper and was shaky from nerves. At that moment… I hated him. I closed my eyes, shutting everyone out, and continued to sing. I was able to calm down my breathing as Spencer sang. When it was my turn to sing again, I was relieved. I felt the trembling in my voice taper off. The song seemed to go on forever, but I just kept singing.

When I finally opened my eyes, Spencer gave me a nod and a proud smile. As we finished the song, we were met with an outpouring of applause, and everyone stood in admiration. Spencer joined my side and leaned in close.

"You did it, Elizabeth." He smiled.

I couldn't help but smile too. My emotions were of relief and gratification. But my smile soon faded. I glanced around the stage, looking for Aidan, and he was gone.

Chapter Twenty

My eyes darted around the bar. The applause continued, and the regulars started chanting for another song. Spencer smiled and covered the mic with one hand.

"They love you, Elizabeth." He was beaming with pride.

I was torn between staying or going to look for Aidan. I smiled at Spencer and whispered, "I have to go," and walked off the stage.

Melissa grabbed my arm as I reached for my purse. "Where are you going?"

"I need to find Aidan."

Melissa blocked my way. "Didn't you say you'd leave him if he kept up with this jealousy crap?"

"I just need to see him, Melissa. That had to be hard for him.

I want to make sure he's okay."

Melissa disapprovingly shook her head and reluctantly let me pass.

****

I rushed out to the parking lot. Relief washed over me when I saw Aidan's truck still there. The windows were shut, so I stood on my tiptoes and peeked inside. I couldn't see anything and reached for the door. It was locked. My eyes scanned the parking lot. Finally, my eyes found his. He maneuvered his way through the cars. He was coming toward me with such a vengeance I wasn't sure what was going to happen. Within seconds I was trapped between Aidan and his truck.

Aidan narrowed his eyes at me and yelled, "What was that, Liz? I've been begging you... begging you to sing with me, and you sing with him? I am so mad at you!" He cursed under his breath, and, with a clenched fist, slammed his hand against his truck. I tried to step to the side, fearing for my safety, but with each step I took, Aidan closed the distance between us.

I stared into his furious eyes and finally was able to speak. "I had no idea that was going to happen. What else was I supposed to do?"

I glanced down at his tendons bulging on his forearms. He bent down and brought his face to mine.

"Is there something going on with you two?" His penetrating eyes were fixed on mine. "Answer me." His tone was ominous as he placed his hands on my arms and began to squeeze.

Before I could answer, Mason was jogging toward us. "Aidan, get back in there. We have to finish our set." Mason's gaze went from me to Aidan. His stance went from casual to stern. "What's going on?" he questioned.

Aidan released me and backed away then unlocked the door of his truck. "Nothing's going on. I'm out!"

He climbed in, glanced at me, and angrily tossed a cellophane-wrapped rose out his door. I watched as a card slowly drifted to the pavement below. He slammed his door, started up the truck, and revved the engine. Both Mason and I jumped back when his truck peeled out of the parking spot. His wheels screeched, racing out of the driveway onto Pacific Coast Highway.

Mason stared at me in confusion. "What happened?"

"He's mad. Mad I sang with Spencer." I leaned

down and picked up the rose and the card. "I don't blame him. He's wanted me to sing with you guys forever. I feel awful."

Mason wrapped his arm around me.

"We've all wanted you to sing with us. You finally did it.

What's the big deal?"

"Think about it, Mason. I was up there singing a romantic duet with another guy. I shouldn't have done it." My eyes met Mason's and he shook his head.

"Don't feel like that. He should be proud of you." In the distance, we heard Melissa yelling Mason's name from across the parking lot. Mason waved, and Melissa headed our way.

"I gotta get back in there. For what it's worth, you sounded awesome." Mason jogged back to Melissa, they talked for a few minutes, and then she walked toward me.

"He's gone?"

There was such surprise in her tone I just looked at her and shrugged. Melissa glanced at the rose I had cradled in my arms.

"What's with the rose?"

I just shook my head at Melissa's confused expression.

"He basically threw it at me before he left." I started walking toward my car with Melissa next to me. I unlocked the doors, and we both got inside.

Melissa gave me her *what now* look. "He'll be okay. Just give him time." Melissa looked at me and shook her head.

I thought about her comment in the club just moments before. I knew what she was thinking. I still held the card in my hand.

"Are you gonna open it?" she asked.

Without answering her, I took a deep breath and ripped open the envelope. I studied the card face. It was a picture of a black grand piano with a red rose sitting atop it. It was so me. I loved it. When I saw his handwriting, I started to cry.

Dear Liz,
These last few months have been the best in my life.
Even though you're not ready to say the words, it doesn't mean I can't.
I love you,
Aidan

I reread the card a few times while tears rolled down my cheeks. I handed it to Melissa. After a few minutes she spoke.

"What are you gonna do, Liz?"

"Go find him. Apologize. Hope he forgives me." I wiped my tears away with my sleeve.

Melissa sighed and started to speak then took a deep breath.

A moment passed.

"Do you want me to go with you?" Her tone didn't reflect the kindness of her words.

"No, I'll be alright." I reached out and hugged her. She opened the door, got out, and leaned back in.

"Call me if you need me. Let me know what happens." I nodded, and she closed the door.

Before I drove out of the parking lot, I texted Aidan. No response. I tried to call. He didn't answer. I went to his house. No truck. His favorite beaches were farther down PCH, and I drove by each one. I never found him.

After that, I even went to Lantern Bay Park. He wasn't there.

My cell phone vibrated with several text messages. They were from Melissa and Mason. I texted them both and added an extra text to Mason, asking him to cover for me. It was after midnight, and I knew my parents would wonder where I was.

Just before I made it home, I decided to turn around and check Aidan's house one more time. When my headlights reflected off his truck, I was relieved. I parked behind him and pulled out my cell phone. When I walked to his front door, I texted him.

Me: *I'm here. Please let me in.*

I waited… and waited.
No reply.
I tried to call. He wouldn't answer.

When I realized I wouldn't be hearing from Aidan tonight, I stuffed my cell in my front pocket and grabbed my keys. Movement from a car parked across the street caught my attention. The soft glow from an overhead streetlamp surrounded a white sedan. Suspicion focused my eyes on the car as I slowly walked across the street. I took a step forward and peered through the dirty car window.

Lost in a sea of desire, the two lovers were unaware of my presence. My heart pounded while I witnessed the betrayal before me. The adrenaline pumped so quickly through my veins I felt dizzy from the sudden rush. Fearing I might pass out, I reached out and put my hand against the car to steady myself. The unexpected jolt caused the two to look my way. I took a step back, but not before the lustful brown eyes of the brunette met mine. A slight smile crept across her face that made me feel like I might be sick.

My instincts told me to run, but my feet wouldn't move. I was vaguely aware the car door was opening and Aidan was coming my way. I staggered across the street, praying I wouldn't fall. Aidan called my name. Stunned, I stared at him while he zipped up his pants, and I took off running. Tears were streaming down my face as I reached for the handle of my car. Aidan grabbed me before I could get inside. He spun me around, and I snapped away from his grasp. We stood in silence as his eyes met mine. The top button of his pants was undone and his tan shirt hung open. In the distance, I heard the steps of heels clicking our way.

"I guess I'm gonna take off, Aidan. Unless you'll be finished here soon." The brunette chuckled.

"Give it a rest, Nina." Aidan's jaw tensed. His gaze never left mine.

I stood, shell-shocked.

The white sedan drove away, leaving us alone with nothing but anger and pain between us. My eyes filled with tears. I lowered my head and began to sob. Aidan reached out and grabbed me. I pushed back and stared into his eyes.

"I trusted you! I trusted you!" I cried out while I gasped between sobs. "And you humiliated me." He smelled of cheap perfume, and it sickened me. The feel of his touch made my skin crawl. I pushed him with all my strength and seethed. "Don't touch me!"

He dropped his arms and let me go.

I wrapped my arms around myself in an attempt to calm down. When my sobbing stopped, I finally questioned him.

"Why?" I wiped my tearstained face with the back of my hand.

"I don't know, Liz. I was so mad when I left the club, and Nina followed me."

He choked out his flimsy excuse like that was supposed to make it better. My eyes roamed over his bare chest while his shirt blew in the breeze. He disgusted me.

"Have you been seeing her the whole time?"

"Would you believe me if I told you this was the first time?" Aidan buttoned a few buttons of his shirt and stuffed his hands in his front pockets.

"Probably not," I confessed. "Well, it was."

"Is that supposed to make it better?" I snapped.

"I don't know. I messed up." Aidan pulled his hands from his pockets and rubbed his face then took a step toward me.

"I'm so sorry. I love…" But before Aidan could finish, I silenced him with my lifted hand.

"Don't. Don't say that to me."

"Liz. Please." Aidan's voice cracked. Tears were falling down his cheeks. "Please, forgive me… please."

Aidan's remorseful demeanor didn't affect me. I couldn't bear to look at him anymore. I closed my eyes and inhaled the balmy night air. The uncertainty of what was to come was swirling between us. I knew it was up to me. I knew what I had to do. I took a step toward Aidan, swallowed hard, and with certainty I spoke. "It's over." I unclasped my necklace and held it in front of him.

He slowly opened his hand. I dropped it in his palm, turned around, and got in my car. The last thing I remember seeing was Aidan's slumped silhouette reflected in my rearview mirror.

Chapter Twenty-One

Mason nudged me. "Liz, are you going to school?" My eyes didn't want to open. I tried and was able to squint up at him. His face showed concern. "What happened last night? Are you okay?" My bed dipped down with the weight of Mason next to me. I wasn't ready to talk to him about what had happened. I wiped the sleep from my eyes and blinked up at him.

"I'm alright." *A lie*. "I'll tell you everything later. Will you tell Mom I'm sick?" The palms of my hands continued to rub my eyes. My bed shifted again when Mason got up.

"Yeah, I'll tell her. Maggie wants in. Do you want her?" I glanced toward the door.

"Sure. C'mon girl." Maggie jumped up on the bed.

My door closed just as the tears began to fall. I wiped them away, knowing my mom would be in my room any minute. While petting Maggie, my hand skimmed across the area where she had been attacked. I sat up and inspected the scar.

My mom peeked in my room as I was kissing Maggie's snout.

"What's wrong, sweetie?"

"I'm just not feeling well." I didn't make eye contact. One look at me and my mom would know I had been crying. I curled my body around Maggie.

"Stomach? Head? What?" Mom asked from the

doorway. "Cramps."

"Oh, alright. I'll get the heating pad."

"No, Mom, if I need it, I'll get it. I just want to go back to sleep."

"Alright, Liz. I'll see you when I get home from work." "Bye, Mom." I pushed Maggie off the bed.

"Bye, sweetie." Maggie followed my mom and she closed my door.

When I knew the house was empty, I finally got up. My pounding head was in desperate need of some aspirin. I padded down the hallway to the bathroom and opened the medicine cabinet. Slurping the water from the faucet, I downed two tablets. My puffy eyes and splotchy red face assured me I'd made the right decision to skip school today. I turned on the shower and stepped inside. The hot water washed away my tears while I sobbed.

What will I to say to everyone? That they were right? That Aidan is a cheater? Am I any better? I hadn't acted on my feelings, but I still felt them. No — I refuse to believe that. I didn't cheat, he did! Images of Nina wrapped in Aidan's arms made me sick. *I hate him for betraying me. I hate that I trusted him, and I hate that I cared.*

The sudden rush of icy water chilled my anger. I wrapped myself in my purple bathrobe and climbed back in my bed. Scrolling through my cell, there were several texts from Melissa and two from Mason. Aidan had texted me six times. His all said the same thing.

Please forgive me.

****

"Liz, what are you doing?" my mom asked. I didn't even hear her open the front door. I glanced down at the open carton of chocolate ice cream and dropped the spoon.

"I... guess I was hungry." I glanced down at the open carton and wondered how much ice cream I had consumed.

"I came home for lunch and wanted to check on you. At least get a bowl." Mom opened the cupboard.

"No, no, Mom. I'm good. I'm done." I got up from the table, put the lid back on the ice cream, and shoved it back in the freezer.

"Are you feeling any better?" Mom grabbed a piece of cold chicken from the fridge and began constructing a sandwich.

"Yeah, but I think I'll go lie back down." "Okay, honey."

The second I climbed back into my bed, I burst into tears. Not again. Not because of what happened with Aidan. I wasn't going to let myself go down that road like before. No matter how I felt, I wasn't going to eat my feelings. I was going to feel them. I allowed myself to cry until I heard my mom yell from the stairs below she was leaving. I yelled back. "Bye, Mom." I wiped my tears away and got out of bed.

The wilted rose on my desk looked as sad as I felt. I decided to put it out of its misery and throw it away. With the rose in hand, I went downstairs and out the back door. Before I tossed it to its death, I gave it one last sniff and watched it fall atop grass clippings in the green-waste trashcan.

It was a warm day, so I decided to get out of the house. Back upstairs, I went to my room and put on a white sundress. I thought it might make me feel better if I at least dressed cute. My flip-flops looked comfortable, so I slipped them on and headed out the door toward my car. I threw my purse in the passenger seat and started up my car. It didn't matter where I was going. I just wanted to go.

Mindlessly, I drove past the park, the harbor, and then down the coast. I ended up at Hole in the Fence Beach. Since I had no idea where I was headed, I didn't have a towel. I took off my flip-flops and let my toes sink into the sand. My eyes caught the attention of a couple walking hand-in-hand up the beach. Before I realized it, tears were threatening to fall.

A text from Melissa pulled me from my grief. She told me she would be stopping by after school.

What am I going to tell her? What am I going to tell Mason?

I didn't want to tell them about Nina. Mason would kill Aidan. I decided I would just say I couldn't handle how jealous he was. That was believable. Because it was true.

Reluctantly, I texted Aidan. I didn't want him spilling the beans to Mason to clear his conscience.

Me: telling Mason and Melissa we broke up because of your jealousy. I'm leaving your whore of a girlfriend out of it.

I knew he'd get mad when he read it, but I didn't care. A text from Aidan came through seconds later.

Aidan: *Can I see you? Please?*

I never answered him.

****

When I walked in the house, Mason and Melissa were sitting on the couch waiting for me. I hated I couldn't tell them the truth, but I knew my brother. He had let it slide when Aidan had confessed about trying to kiss Melissa. I knew it was because we were together then. Now Aidan wouldn't be so lucky.

Melissa got up from the couch and hugged me. "Are you okay?" she whispered.

I shook my head, yes, even though it wasn't true. "What happened last night?"

I sat down and leaned my head back against the couch.

"I found him at his house. We argued, and I told him I couldn't handle how jealous he was. I had given him enough chances, and I was sick of it."

I glanced at Melissa and Mason, hoping they would take what I'd said and not question me too much. It seemed to work.

They both began talking over each other about the incident in the bar and how Aidan was always possessively watching me.

Melissa ended the Aidan-bashing with her last statement. "That's just not healthy."

I looked at Mason and asked, "Did you see him today?" Mason shook his head no.

Mason glanced at Melissa and asked, "How about you?"

"I saw him from a distance. He was walking toward the parking lot. I think he left after second period." Melissa shifted toward me. "Have you heard from him?"

"He texted me. He wants me to forgive him." I shrugged.

Maggie came over and laid her face on my lap. I

rubbed the top of her head. Mason sat up and took a deep breath.

"I hate to bring this up, but I need to talk to Aidan. I know he said he was out of the band, but I still want him in. Are you okay with that? Or should we find someone else? It's your call, Liz."

I looked at Mason for a few minutes before I answered. "It's fine. It'll be hard... but, it's fine." I turned my gaze to Maggie as she went and curled up on her bed in the corner.

"Alright," Mason answered.

Maggie popped her head up seconds before the doorbell rang. Mason and Melissa both stared at me. Mason got up.

"I'll get it."

I didn't have to open the door to know Aidan was the one behind it.

Melissa was wide-eyed, and I nervously chewed my bottom lip. We could hear soft murmuring coming from the front room. Melissa was the first to get up and hurry toward the door. I followed.

"She doesn't want to see you."

Melissa stood next to my brother, blocking my view.

"Five minutes, that's all I want." Aidan sounded desperate.

I maneuvered myself in front of Melissa and reached for Mason's arm. His solid muscles were tense.

"I'll talk to him," I whispered.

Mason let out a breath and backed away. Melissa glanced at me before she slipped her arm around Mason's waist and walked back into the family room.

I stepped outside and closed the door behind me. Other than Aidan's bloodshot eyes, he looked perfect. He was wearing the blue, button-down shirt I'd bought him for Christmas. *My favorite.* I stared into his red-rimmed eyes and found his expression so pained it was hard to look at him.

"You asked for five minutes," I said icily.

Aidan took a few steps away from the door and motioned to the driveway.

"Can we go for a walk?"

I wrapped my arms around myself and didn't move from the front door.

"Please," he begged.

The look on his face was pleading. I took a step forward, and Aidan sighed in relief. When we exited the driveway, I made sure to walk in the opposite direction of Spencer's house. I knew running into him wouldn't be good.

Aidan tried to hold my hand. I jerked my head to look at him. His eyes softened as he whispered, "Habit."

The silence between us became more uncomfortable with each step. Five minutes was up ten minutes ago. We were nearing a small park in the neighborhood. It was empty.

Aidan glanced at me. "How about if we sit over there?"

He motioned to a slatted-wood bench. We walked over, and I sat down close to the end. Aidan sat. He had more room on his side than I did. He bent forward, head down, elbows on his knees. After several minutes he spoke.

"Why can't you forgive me?"

His good looks and tormented expression were beginning to cloud my judgment. The unwanted pull of compassion was softening my heart.

"Aidan, you cheated on me. I can't trust you anymore."

Aidan tried to interrupt me, but I just continued. "I can't trust you."

Again, he tried to say something. My tone became more amplified as I slowly spoke. "I. Can't. Trust. You."

"You're my best friend. You're everything to me."

Even though I was angry his words were killing me. Before I could think straight, he reached out and hugged me. I felt his body go limp while he sobbed in my arms.

"What do I do, Liz? I love you... I love you." He whimpered. My shoulder was wet with his tears. He was so broken I felt myself weakening. To protect myself, I allowed the walls to go up, which was easy to do with the images of Nina seared in my brain.

My body stiffened as I pushed myself away from him.

"You should have thought of that before you had sex with Nina in her car."

He reached for me and tried to hold me again. I moved from his grasp and stood up.

"I've gotta go. Your five minutes are up." I walked away just before the tears started to fall.

Chapter Twenty-Two

School was the most difficult for me. Melissa and Mason tried to make it better. They made sure one of them was always with me: when I walked to class, walked to the parking lot, walked to brunch. Like I couldn't function without them. Near the end of day two of their constant shadowing, I couldn't take it anymore. I took the opportunity to confront them when they were both escorting me to my economics class.

"Look, you guys, I know you're trying to be nice, but your constant hovering is starting to get to me."

They both appeared wounded with my honesty. It almost made me laugh. Almost.

"It is?" Melissa asked.

"Ya, kinda." I smiled. "I'm doing okay. It's hard, but I'm not falling apart, so please, ease up." I glanced at Mason and hesitated before I asked, "Do you know how Aidan's doing?"

"I've been checking on him. I just didn't want to tell you about it. It felt... I don't know... disloyal." I reached out and rubbed his arm.

"No, Mason, I would never think that." "Are you sure you want to hear this?"

I wasn't sure, but I shook my head yes anyway.

"Not good." The bell rang for class. "He's a mess. I didn't realize how much he loved you."

"Mason, stop. I can't hear any more." Compassion

started to overwhelm me as I backed away from them both. "We should get to class. I'll see you guys later."

****

The last few days had been heart-wrenching. I was thankful it was practice night. I was looking forward to getting my mind off Aidan. When I approached Spencer's house, there was an unfamiliar car in the driveway. My curiosity was soon put to rest when the blond beauty, Kara, opened the door.

"Hi, Elizabeth, it's nice to see you again. You and Spencer were fantastic the other night." Kara smiled a perfect smile and invited me in. So graceful and poised. I felt gawky in her presence.

"Thank you." I glanced around, looking for Spencer, but I didn't see him.

"Why don't you have a seat?" Kara motioned to the couch. "Spencer will be right out. Can I get you something to drink?"

I watched her, so at ease and comfortable in Spencer's home, but I was still confused.

Who is she to him?

"No, thank you, I'm fine." With as much grace as I could muster, I walked to the couch, but since my eyes were still focused on Kara, I stumbled and slammed my knee into the coffee table. *Klutz.*

"Are you alright?" Kara came to my side and put her hand on my shoulder.

"I'm just clumsy." I tried to laugh it off while I rubbed my jean-covered leg. The coffee table was pushed over a bit, so I moved it back to its previous position and sat down on the couch.

Kara was prattling on, filling the void of Spencer's absence. I nodded, smiled, and rubbed my knee as she continued to gush about mine and Spencer's duet at the club. When she spoke about our performance, I had to shake off my thoughts of Aidan. It pained me to think of him.

I was thankful when Spencer emerged from the back room. His hair was damp, he was wearing faded ripped jeans and a tight green t-shirt. His colorful tatted arms were fully exposed.

"Sorry about the wait, Elizabeth. We'll start in a minute." Spencer's gaze met mine and then focused back on Kara. "I'll walk you out, Kara."

Kara turned, smiled, and told me goodbye before Spencer closed the door behind them and walked her out the door.

Still stumped and curious, I was up from the couch and at the front door in seconds. One eye peered through the peephole. My eye focused through the small opening, and my heart sank, my question answered.

A few feet from the front door Spencer was locked in an embrace with Kara. I stepped back quickly, ran back to the couch, and tried to calm myself down before he returned. My heart was beating out of control, and my stomach was in knots. Feeling panicked, I got up and escaped to the bathroom. I had to get out of his living room before I lost it. I closed the toilet seat lid, sat down, and put my head between my legs to calm myself down.

Maybe I should tell Spencer to forget it and get out of here. "Elizabeth?" Spencer called my name, but, still feeling out of sorts, I didn't answer. "Elizabeth?" he called again.

I heard his footsteps approach the bathroom door but, thankfully, he walked away. I gave myself another minute before I opened the door and headed down the hallway. Spencer was strumming his guitar.

"Sorry, I had to use the bathroom," I quietly murmured.

"No problem." He stopped playing and put his guitar down. "Elizabeth?" Spencer got up and stood in front of me. He placed both hands on my shoulders and stared deep into my eyes. "I'm sorry."

"For what?" I stepped back, but he closed the distance between us.

"For making you sing the other night. I shouldn't have put you on the spot." Spencer was inches from my face, his eyes focused on mine.

"It's fine." My voice came out in a whisper as I backed away from him. I wasn't about to tell him Aidan and I had broken up after that.

"Are you sure you're, okay?"

"I'm good, Spencer. We're fine. I was nervous, scared, but you know how I am."

Spencer reached out and softly trailed his knuckles down my cheek. "Yes, I do know how you are."

"Should we start?" I asked while I backed away. Spencer nodded and picked up his guitar.

We eased back into our practice time, and when he was satisfied with our performance, we moved to the couch. It felt good to talk and laugh with him. I hadn't laughed in days. Spencer even did an impression of how I looked Sunday night before I approached the stage. Tears were rolling down my cheeks from the laughter. I was certain his impression of me was spot on. Spencer plopped down on the couch and rejoined me.

"I have to admit…" He laughed. "At one point, I thought you were going to kill me." He smiled his boyish smile with dimples in full view.

"Trust me, I wanted to."

Spencer placed a hand on my thigh and rubbed my leg, grazing my knee. I winced back in pain.

"Are you okay?" He quickly removed his hand.

"I hit my leg on the coffee table earlier. It must be bruised." I rolled up my pant leg to exam it. A small cut was dotted with dried blood, but with the recent friction of pulling up my pant leg, it began to bleed again.

Spencer stood up and held out his hand to help me up. "Come with me," he commanded.

We walked into the bathroom I'd been in earlier. I sat down on the closed toilet seat while Spencer rifled through the medicine cabinet. He placed a bandage, a few cotton balls, and some antiseptic cream on the small counter.

"Spencer, I'm fine. I bump into things all the time." "Apparently you do." He smiled.

Spencer doused the cotton ball with hot water, applied a small amount of soap to it, and bent to his knees. He gently brushed the cotton back and forth, cleaning off the small abrasion, and leaned down to blow his warm breath across the scrape. A shiver ran through me as Spencer's grey eyes shot up to mine and held my gaze. After what seemed like minutes, he averted his eyes and continued to focus on the task at hand. He applied the antiseptic cream and placed the bandage over it.

"All better," he said.

A wisp of dark hair fell in front of his eyes. Without thinking I brushed it back with the tips of my fingers. Spencer's eyes met mine again, this time with an intensity that left me feeling helpless. The confines of the small bathroom were getting to me. As much as it pained me, I tore my gaze from his and stood up. Spencer stumbled and fell on his backside.

"Oops, I'm sorry." I reached out a hand. Spencer lightly chuckled.

Thankful for the diversion, I helped Spencer to his feet and exited the bathroom.

"It's still pretty early. Can I get you something to drink?" He gestured to the kitchen, and I took a seat on a stool.

Spencer opened the fridge and held up a carton of orange juice and a bottled water. I opted for the water, and he poured it into a glass over ice. Spencer pulled up a stool and placed his orange juice on the island. My eyes followed him, and I focused on his colorful, tatted arms.

I don't know what possessed me, but I slid off the barstool and, without my gaze leaving his, I approached him. I placed my hand on his arm and pushed up the left sleeve of his green t-shirt, revealing his muscular, tatted bicep. His eyes were on mine as he slowly outstretched his sculpted arm, giving me the opportunity to continue my inspection.

Spencer's approval had me eager with enthusiasm. I traced the outline of the lighthouse with the tip of my index finger, and goose bumps rose on his flesh. I turned his arm and admired the detailed script and beautiful foliage. Again, I traced the outline, but this time my attention was on the elegant wording. *Fight, Faith, Finish.* I felt like I should stop, but I couldn't. Seizing my moment, I picked up his hand, finally able to study the script encircling his ring finger. *Amato.* I mouthed the word and looked into his heated gaze. Realization crept in, and I immediately backed away, ashamed.

"I'm so sorry. I don't know what I was doing. I

wasn't thinking." I dashed toward the front door muttering. "I'm so sorry. I should go." In my haste, I bumped into a small table. A potted plant fell to the hardwood floor and shattered, scattering ceramic pieces and dirt everywhere. I fell to my knees and began picking up the destroyed planter. I could feel the tears starting to come while embarrassment and shame washed over me. The familiar touch of Spencer's warm hand was on my shoulder.

"Hey, it's okay," he whispered. Spencer's compassionate eyes focused on mine as he brought me back up to my feet.

"It's not a big deal, Elizabeth. It's just a plant." Spencer brushed a tear from my face. I couldn't look at him. His handsome face and tender heart overwhelmed me.

"I'm so sick of you seeing me cry." I wiped the rest of my tears and backed away from him.

"There is nothing wrong with tears, Elizabeth. Tears cleanse the soul." His words were like a blanket that warmed me.

"Thank you, Spencer." I smiled when he walked past me to get a broom. After we cleaned up the mess, we sat back down at the kitchen island.

"Will you tell me about your tattoos?"

Spencer glanced down at his arm, picked up his glass, and tilted his head. "Follow me."

Intrigued, I grabbed my water and followed him down the hallway to his bedroom. Spencer motioned to the bed. "Sit."

I did as I was told and sat on the edge of his bed. Spencer took my water and placed it on the bedside table, next to his orange juice. He entered his closet, and I heard him moving things around. I took the opportunity to inspect the surroundings of his bedroom. The floor-to-ceiling bookcase was packed with an impressive collection of authors. Some were familiar to me. Some weren't. I loved that he was a reader because I was one too.

Throughout the bookcase were several groupings of framed pictures.

Spencer's furniture was a dark wood, and the walls were painted a light shade of tan. It seemed to flow with the rest of the house. His bedspread was tan and black striped flannel. His desk area was stacked with papers, open college books, a small desk lamp, and a computer. To the side of the desk was his electric guitar.

Spencer emerged from the closet with a photo album in hand, and he placed it on the bed. He walked over to the photographs on the bookcase and grabbed one. He took a sip of his orange juice, inhaled a deep breath, and sat next to me. He handed me the framed picture, allowing me to study the image. It was a lighthouse, the same one Spencer had inked on his arm. The artist had done an amazing job, because the likeness was identical. Standing in the foreground was a family. Spencer cleared his throat before he pointed to each person in the picture.

"This is my mom, Sharon, my father, Matthew, my sister, Sierra. You know these two, Shawn and Simon. This is me." Spencer's expression was that of pride and despair.

"What a beautiful family," I whispered. Spencer's father had the same facial features, same prominent dimples, and the same grey eyes.

"How old are you here?"

Spencer hesitated before he answered. "It was about

a year before my father died, so I was eleven." He was quiet for a few minutes, looking at the picture.

"I'm so sorry, Spencer." I placed my hand on his tatted arm. "You don't have to tell me anymore."

"No, Elizabeth, I want you to know. The first time you asked me I wasn't ready, but I am now." Spencer cleared his throat again before he began to tell me about his pained past.

"My father was on his way home from picking up Sierra from dance class." Spencer softly laughed at the memory. "Sierra loved to dance. She was always spinning around. It used to drive me nuts." He shook his head and rolled his eyes at the memory. "Anyway, they were driving down the street, and a car on the opposite side was waiting to turn left. An SUV tried to go around the car, but it was going too fast. It swerved, hit the curb, skidded across the street and slammed into my dad's car head on. My dad died instantly." Spencer's voice was just above a whisper. "Sierra hung on for two days before she passed away." After a few silent minutes, he exhaled and began again. "The guy that killed them had been drinking. He was just under the legal limit. He had a good lawyer, ended up pleading *No Contest*, was sentenced to eleven years for vehicular manslaughter, and was out on good behavior in seven." Spencer shook his head back and forth.

I picked up the frame and glanced over the picture again. "How old was Sierra?"

"Sierra was eight, Shawn was four, and Simon was just a baby."

It all started to make sense to me. Spencer's protective nature. The way he took care of his brothers.

"So you helped raise your brothers?"

"Not at first. I was pretty messed up after Dad and Sierra died. We all were."

Spencer got up from the bed and placed the photograph back on the bookshelf. He grabbed the photo album and sat back on the bed, leaning against the headboard. He motioned for me to join him. I crawled up along his side, and he placed the album between us. He began to show me more pictures of the lighthouse. He pointed to a picture of his parents standing in front of it. They were young, and it was just the two of them.

"My dad had a thing for lighthouses. He and my mom met here." Spencer turned the album so I was able to look over all the pictures. "This is Pigeon Point Lighthouse in Northern California. They both were staying at the youth hostel there." Spencer showed me several pictures of the housing, more of the lighthouse, and several group shots. I gasped when I recognized a young, familiar face."

"Is this Lance?"

"Yes, they were best friends."

"Lance never mentioned he knew you."

"I asked him not to. I wanted to interview with the church on my own. I didn't want Lance to influence them." Spencer shrugged.

I brought the album closer so I could get a better look. "Look how thin Lance is." I smiled.

"I know, right?" Spencer laughed. "He's a good old guy." "Did Lance help your mom when you were growing up?" I closed the album and gave Spencer my full attention.

"More than you know." Spencer leaned his head back against the headboard.

"What do you mean?"

"After Dad and Sierra passed, I was in shock. Not wanting to believe it. I wouldn't talk about it, wouldn't acknowledge it. Lance was always there to check in on me, on all of us." Spencer shook his head in disbelief. "Lance gave me my first guitar and taught me to play. I was such a jerk to him, but he never gave up on me."

Spencer turned his gaze toward me, and those same stray hairs fell against his forehead. I resisted the urge to move them while he continued on with his story.

"My mom was so worried about me. She didn't know what to do. She had me see a therapist from church. I hated it. I just went through the motions, going because she wanted me to." Spencer reached up with one hand and pushed away the errant hairs from his forehead.

"I was angry for a long time. I got hooked up with the wrong crowd and started drinking and smoking pot. Pot was my vice. It made me forget, feel numb. I was so depressed, and when getting high didn't help anymore..." Spencer hesitated before he spoke again. "My new vice was sex. I was sixteen, knew the girls were attracted to this face, so I used it. I slept around... a lot. But that changed with Lance."

"What happened," I asked, not taking my eyes off him.

"He hooked me up playing with his church band. I went just for the music and loved it. When Lance heard my voice, he wanted me to be the lead singer. It scared the crap out of me." Spencer glanced my way. His lips curled up into a ghost of a smile. "So, you see, I do know how it feels to be nervous, 'cuz I sure was. Anyway, Saturday nights I was sleeping with girls, and Sundays I was singing songs in church. It started to get to me. A few days before my nineteenth birthday, Lance spoke to me about life not being fair, choices, and sin." Spencer stopped talking. His eyes shifted to his lap and then back to me. "It broke me."

I lifted Spencer's left hand and pointed to his tatted ring finger.

"What does this mean?"

"My father was Italian, and my great-great grandparents were from a small village in Italy called Amato."

"Amato?" I blinked up at him.

"It means beloved. Someday, my wife's going to cover this with a ring. It's my reminder to wait for her."

His sad, beautiful confession, combined with the look in his eyes, was getting to me. My stomach fell, and my heart sank when realization set in. The possibility Kara could become that to him was like a dagger to my heart. I turned away from him just as a tear started to fall. "Spencer, I'm so sorry you lost your father and Sierra."

He lifted my chin to make eye contact and brushed away the tear. "Hey, I didn't tell you all this to upset you. I just wanted to answer some of your questions."

He was so close to me I was getting lost in his eyes, and his gentle touch was starting to consume me. In hopes of dismissing my battling thoughts, I backed away and asked him something else. "Is that why you have so much?" I sniffed.

"Yes. Life insurance policy." Spencer wiped away another stray tear from my cheek.

I glanced at his bedside clock. It was just past midnight. "I'd better go."

Spencer got up and moved while I scrambled across his bed. "Okay. Let's go." Spencer reached out to grab my hand, but I shook my head.

"I'm good, thanks." I knew the feel of his touch would be too much. Between my heartbreak from Aidan, my feelings for Spencer, and his relationship with Kara, I knew I had to get out of there. Spencer opened the door and began to walk me out. I placed my hand on his chest and stopped him before he could follow me.

"No, no. It's okay. I drove tonight." I made my way to my car and got inside, leaving Spencer standing in the doorway as I drove away.

Chapter Twenty-Three

It was a sunny Friday, day six post-Aidan. Summer was just a month away. Senioritis was running rampant through our graduating class. Since the weather had warmed up, more kids were cutting school. I wasn't one of them. It just wasn't my thing.

Posters lined the school walls: senior breakfast, grad night, and the one that was like a knife in my heart... prom. I had been so excited when Aidan bought our tickets, but now it was just a painful reminder of what could have been.

I pushed my way out the doors of the C Building, and there he was. My stomach did a few flip-flops while I observed him. He was standing next to a brick bench, near a tree. There was a slight breeze in the air, and I watched as his hair fell perfectly into place.

I had avoided him all week. And here he stood, surrounded by a bunch of girls. Word was out we had broken up, and the vultures were circling. Just like old times. Aidan hadn't seen me, so I took a few minutes to watch him. Kind of like the first day I'd seen him, back in the lunchroom.

He was smiling his movie star smile that had the girls giddy. Even though Aidan had betrayed me, and I'd been the one to end things, it still hurt to witness the old Aidan back in action. When I couldn't take it anymore, I made my way toward the parking lot.

I was just about to unlock my car door when I heard faint footsteps coming my way. Aidan's voice said, "Hey."

We hadn't seen each other since our heart-wrenching goodbye in the park. After several uncomfortable moments I broke the silence.

"How are you?" I knew it was a dumb question, but I didn't know what else to say.

"Honestly? Pretty crappy."

I glanced away from his pained expression. A few girls were pointing and whispering.

"I miss you, Liz."

"Aidan, stop." My heart was beginning to thaw, and I knew I had to get away from him. "Look, I'm gonna take off." I reached for my car door.

"Wait a sec." Aidan stroked my left arm. "I want you back, Liz. I'm so sorry. I just want you back."

Aidan tried to pull me in close, but I held my ground. The sadness in his face broke my heart. His look was so desperate and sincere I felt myself weakening. I wanted to hold him and tell him everything was okay until... the wind picked up. Aidan's button- down shirt began to ripple in the breeze, instantly transporting me back to that night, that horrible night. Vivid images of Nina's body wrapped around Aidan's flashed through my mind. My hand came up to stop him from talking. I shut my eyes tight and shook my head back and forth, trying to shake the seared memory from my brain. I stepped back and unlocked my car door.

"I can't do this." My voice was shaky and came out in a whisper. I got inside and shut the door. Aidan slammed his hand down on the roof of my car before I sped out of the parking lot.

****

Saturday morning, I didn't feel much like running, but I decided it might help pull me out of my funk. Donning my usual garb, I grabbed Maggie's leash, clipped her to it, and headed out the front door. When I jogged past Spencer's house, my mind was consumed with thoughts of him. He had shared so much with me and finally opened up. It pained me to think he would be doing the same with Kara. I hated myself for feeling that way. My only hope was, as time passed, I would eventually get through it and be happy.

Maggie and I rounded the corner and entered the creek bed. It was packed. Summer was in the air, and it seemed like everyone in Dana Point was out enjoying the day. I ran at a quick pace with Maggie at my side. There was an overweight girl up ahead doing her best to maneuver herself through the crowd. Watching her brought back memories of how difficult it had been for me to get the weight off. I still felt fat sometimes. I knew I wasn't, but I wondered if the feeling would ever go away. When I passed her, I wanted to smile and say something encouraging, but I remembered how I felt during my struggle. If anyone had said anything to me, I would have hated it. I just kept running and hoped I would see her on the trail in the future.

At the park I climbed the stairs, and, when I reached the top, I was surprised when I saw Shawn and Simon.

"Lizzie!" Simon shouted. He threw his arms around me while Maggie pranced around us. *What a sweet kid.*

Shawn casually walked over to us, all cool, like, *I'm a teenager.* "Hey." He gave me the customary head nod.

"Hi, guys." I glanced around looking for Spencer, but I didn't see him. Kara was not in sight either. "So, are you guys playing football?" My eyes were still scanning the park.

"Yep! Ya wanna play?" Simon started pulling my arm toward the grassy area.

"No, not today. I have Maggie and some stuff I gotta do." I actually didn't have to do anything. I just was trying to stick to my vow of *me time.* "Where's your brother?"

"Bathroom," Shawn answered. But Simon cut him off. "Yeah, he said he felt like he was gonna barf." Simon's facial expression was all contorted, like *he* might barf. I glanced toward the park bathroom.

"Has he been in there a long time?" I asked.

"I guess." Simon was petting Maggie. I glanced at the bathroom again, and Spencer emerged. His hair was pulled back and he was wearing a white, sleeveless t-shirt and loose, black shorts. From far away he looked perfect. When he saw me, he smiled and walked toward us.

"Hi, Elizabeth." Up close he didn't look so good.

"Are you okay?" I reached out and touched his arm. He felt clammy and warm.

"No, I feel awful." Spencer turned toward the boys. "Hey guys, I thought I was up to playing, but I gotta get home."

Simon let out a whiny "Aww," and Shawn jogged over to pick up the football.

"You look terrible. Do you want me to drive you home? That is, if you don't mind dog hair in your jeep."

"That'd be great."

We all crammed into the jeep, and I adjusted the seat and mirrors. The boys were in the back with Maggie between them. Spencer was in the passenger side with his head tipped back on the headrest and eyes closed.

"Maybe we should go to Urgent Care?" I was starting to get worried about him.

Spencer didn't move. He just weakly said, "No. Home." He never opened his eyes.

When I pulled into his driveway, I got out and scurried to his side of the jeep as he was getting out.

"Do you need help?"

"No, just open the door please."

I ran ahead and had the door open before he got there. Simon had Maggie, and I asked him to put her in the back yard. Spencer went straight into his bedroom. I wasn't sure if I should go back there, so I made myself busy.

The kitchen was a mess. I opened his cupboards in search of canned soup, crackers, anything he might want to have. Nothing. I opened his fridge and grabbed the orange juice. I poured a glass and headed down the hallway. Simon was in the yard playing with Maggie, and Shawn was texting on the couch near the piano.

Spencer's door was open. I was expecting him to be in his bed, but he was in the adjoining bathroom. His bed was a disheveled mess. I placed the orange juice on his bedside table and pulled his covers up, then down on one side, so it looked inviting. I thought he might need some aspirin or something, so I went in the extra bathroom and rooted through the contents of the medicine cabinet. When I found some ibuprofen, I grabbed two and went back to his bedroom. Spencer was in his bed with the covers pulled up around his neck. His eyes were closed. I felt his forehead. *Hot.* He opened his glazed eyes.

"Here, take these." I grabbed the juice and handed him the pills. He sat up a bit and downed the drugs.

"Thank you." He breathed. His head was back on the pillow in seconds. He turned and said, "I just need sleep."

"Do you want me to call somebody? Your mom?" *Kara?*

Spencer turned with his back to me.

"No. My mom's outta town. I'm keeping the boys until tomorrow."

"Don't worry about your brothers. I'll take care of them." I glanced back at him before I walked out his room. "You rest."

He gave me a weak smile and then shifted on his side.

I let the boys know we were going to be hanging out at my house for the rest of the day. It surprised me they both seemed excited about it. Before we left, I decided to clean up Spencer's kitchen. Forty-five minutes later, we were on our way to my house with Maggie leading the way.

When we approached the house, the garage door was open. I heard Mason's electric guitar. I unhooked Maggie's leash, and she bounded inside. I was gearing myself up for seeing Aidan, but when I peered inside, all I saw were Mason and Kyle. Kyle was writing notes in a spiral binder. No Aidan. No Derek.

"Cool!" Simon shouted then he ran into the garage and jumped behind the drums. I was impressed he could keep a beat.

Apparently, so was Mason. He stopped playing his guitar, looked at Simon, and said, "Sweet."

I glanced at Shawn. "Do you play?"

"Guitar and piano." He walked over to the keyboard and asked if he could play.

Kyle shrugged his shoulders and said, "Sure."

Shawn started playing. Mason picked up his guitar and joined them.

Kyle stepped toward me, shoulder to shoulder and asked, "Who are these kids?"

"Remember Spencer? The guy I sang the duet with?" Kyle nodded, while keeping his eyes focused on the trio.

"These are his brothers." I pointed to each of them. "That's Shawn and that's Simon."

"Impressive." He nodded.

"When they finish, I'll take 'em inside. I don't want them bugging you and Mason. Where are the rest of the guys?" I was curious if Aidan was going to be showing up. I wanted to be prepared.

"They're both working. Mason and I just wanted to get together. We're workin' on a song."

Relief washed over me when I realized I wouldn't be seeing Aidan today.

"I'm sorry about you and Aidan, but... I never thought he was good enough for you."

"Thanks, Kyle."

When the mini-jam session ended, Kyle and I applauded. The boys both approached me. Shawn already seemed bored, but Simon looked up at me with bright eyes.

"Now what?" He beamed.

I had a feeling entertaining these two was going to be exhausting. I texted Melissa. Reinforcements were in order.

****

Simon and Shawn were beat. We had spent the day at the beach. Mason had been a lifesaver and had joined up with Melissa and me. He'd spent most of his time in the water with Shawn boogie boarding. Simon had befriended a couple of kids and built an enormous sandcastle. My mom insisted the boys stay for dinner, doting on them like they were her own. The boys seemed pretty content, and I felt satisfied they'd had a good day, considering they'd had to spend it with me.

When we approached Spencer's front door, Simon opened it for me. I had rifled through our pantry and produced a care package of canned soup, crackers, and juice. Shawn went to take a shower. Simon stretched out on the floor of the family room and turned on the TV.

I emptied the contents of the bag on the kitchen island and began opening drawers in search of a can opener. I heated up the soup, arranged a layer of saltines on a plate then grabbed a bowl, napkin, and spoon. When the soup was warm, I filled the bowl, placed it next to the crackers on a tray, and carried it down the hallway to Spencer's room.

His door was still open. I noticed he'd drunk the orange juice. He stirred as I placed the bowl of steaming soup on his bedside table. I grabbed his empty glass and went back to the kitchen to refill it. When I returned, Spencer was sitting up, blinking the sleep from his eyes. I grabbed his extra pillow and helped him place it behind his head. His face was pale, eyes glossy, and he had nasty bedhead. He glanced at the soup.

"Hungry?"

"Yes."

I looked around his room for something I could put his lunch on. When I eyed a laptop desk for the bed, I grabbed it. Spencer sat up straight. I handed him the mini-desk, and, after he'd placed it on his outstretched legs, I set the soup on top of it. He took a spoonful of the broth and slurped it down.

"Thank you."

He continued to eat his soup and crackers. I sat on the edge of his bed near his feet.

"Have you been asleep all day?"

"Pretty much. I was so out of it I forgot you had the boys." "They were great." I told Spencer about our day while he finished his soup. He placed the empty bowl and plate on his bedside table.

"Feeling any better?"

"Pretty good. Do you mind bringing me a few more ibuprofen?"

"Not at all."

The extra bathroom was still steamy from Shawn's recent shower. I grabbed the pill bottle and opened it on my way back to Spencer's room. I gave him two tablets and handed him the remaining juice. He swallowed the pills and drank the rest of his drink. He tossed the mini-desk to the side, slid lower into his bed, and curled his body toward me. His gaze met mine.

"Thank you for today, Elizabeth. You're a lifesaver." "I guess we're even now."

Spencer's eyes crinkled in the corners, and he smiled at me. I stood up and grabbed his dirty plates. "I'll be right back."

I went into the kitchen, cleaned up the mess, filled a glass with water, and went back to his room. Simon was standing over him going into animated detail about his day. Spencer cut him off mid-sentence and told him to go and take a shower.

Simon is cute, but exhausting. I giggled and held up the glass. "Water?"

"I'll drink it later." He closed his eyes, and I placed the water on the bedside table.

"I'm gonna take off, Spencer. Don't worry about tomorrow.

Mason and I can handle it." Spencer's eyes popped open.

"No. I'll be there." I reached over and felt his forehead. Still warm.

"No. You need to get better. Do you want me to come by in the morning and get the boys?"

He rubbed his face with his hands.

"No, my mom will be here in the morning. Are you sure you guys will be okay without me?"

"We'll be fine."

"Alright," he answered, closing his eyes again. "I'll stop by tomorrow and see how you're doing."

I was a step outside his bedroom door when I thought I heard him say, "My angel."

Chapter Twenty-Four

We got through the church service with only a few slip-ups. I'd talked Mason out of having me do my solo. There was no way Spencer would have let me get away with not singing, but I think Mason had been relieved. Me freaking out on stage had been one less thing for him to worry about.

He was quiet after our performance. I knew he was disappointed things hadn't gone as well as he had planned. I collected the music sheets and handed them to him.

"Hey, Mase, don't beat yourself up. You did great."

"I don't know. It seemed like everything was rushed." "It was fine."

"I hate that word... *fine*. I know you mean it as a compliment, but it doesn't sound like one."

"Okay, you were great, fantastic, even better than Spencer!" I glanced over at Mason and smirked.

He raised his arms in the air and yelled out an enthusiastic "Yes!"

That was one thing I loved about my brother. You could easily get him out of a bad mood. I giggled and walked off the stage.

"I'll see you at home. Bye, Mase." "See ya, Liz."

****

I took my foot off the gas when I approached Spencer's house. I was about to pull up to the curb, but

Kara's car was in the driveway. Stopping for a moment, I decided if I should go in or not. My thoughts went to the promise I'd made the night before to stop by. But he didn't need me. He had Kara. She'd take care of him. I knew I'd get used to seeing them together. No sense in having their relationship flaunted in my face. Since I had a choice, I chose to go home.

****

It was after 7:00 p.m. My emotions were all over the place until I finally decided, yes, I was going to go check on Spencer — only because I told him I would, and I wanted to make good on my promise. Kara's car was gone, and the house was dark. I placed my ear to the front door, straining to hear any activity. Nothing. I rang the bell and waited. About the time I was ready to turn around and walk away, the door opened.

"Hey," he said.

Spencer was wearing black pajama pants, no shirt, and his hair was wet. He had a brown towel draped around his neck. The sight of his shirtless body had me in awe. I couldn't help but stare at a few droplets of water falling from his wet strands, dripping down his bare chest.

"I… I… came to check on you," I stammered out.

"Come on in." He motioned. Spencer used the towel around his neck to dry his hair.

"How are you feeling?" I asked.

"Much better." Spencer gestured to the couch. "Have a seat.

I'll be right back."

I sat on the couch and waited for Spencer. A few minutes later he came down the hallway, pulling a white t-shirt over his head. He sat on the loveseat to the side of me. I nibbled my thumbnail as he slicked his damp hair back with his fingers. I knew he was going to ask me about the solo.

"So, how'd today go?"

"Well, we had a few mishaps, but I think it went pretty good."

"How was Mason?"

"I thought he did great, but he didn't think so."

Spencer flashed me a knowing smile. "I knew he'd be hard on himself. It's good for him. How'd you do?"

"Umm, I didn't do it."

"Elizabeth." Spencer shook his head back and forth. "What am I gonna do with you?" He shook his head and smiled. "Come in my room. I want to show you something."

Spencer led me down the hallway to his room and pulled out his computer chair for me. After I sat down, he leaned over me. My skin tingled from being so close to him while the scent of his body-wash enveloped me. He opened his laptop and clicked on an email account.

"Look at this." He lightly tapped on the screen. "I get emails about you daily."

Shocked, my gaze met his.

"As of today, there are one hundred and ninety-six emails begging me to have you sing more often. Go ahead, open a few."

He sat on his bed while I opened email upon email. People I didn't even know had written the kindest things about me. It was overwhelming. I turned the chair so I could look at him.

"See what I'm up against?"

"Ya know, a lot of these emails mention you too." Spencer dismissively waved a hand in front of his face.

"It's you they want, Elizabeth, and it's you they're going to get." Spencer eyed me before he spoke again. "What is it that makes you so nervous? I'm trying to understand."

It took me a few minutes before I could look up and answer him. "I don't know. Maybe because I was picked on as a kid — frizzy hair, being overweight, not measuring up, I guess." I bowed my head and started biting my thumbnail again.

Spencer rose from the bed and kneeled in front of me, forcing me to make eye contact.

"Hey, you're not that girl anymore.

"I'm trying to believe that. It's just still hard," I whispered. "Believe it. You're beautiful, and you don't even see it. And I'm not just talking about your face or your voice. The way you look after people. The way you took care of me, and my brothers. Even now, your being here to check on me. You have a goodness in your heart and a gentleness in your soul."

I didn't feel like my heart was good. I had just ended things with Aidan. Spencer had Kara, and I couldn't focus on anything but being wrapped up in his arms with his perfect lips on mine. It took everything in me to forcefully push the image from my thoughts.

"Thank you for saying that."

Spencer sat back on the edge of the bed, reached for the computer chair, and rolled me between his open knees. He was quiet for a moment, his eyes assessing me.

"I want you to do something for me," he finally said. "I want you to continue to sing your solos at church, but I also want you to sing with Mason's band."

My eyes widened. "What? No, Spencer, I don't want to." "Remember when you said you trusted me?" he questioned. "Yes, but…" I faltered.

"But nothing." Spencer reached out and squeezed my hand. "It will help you. Trust me?"

His reassuring touch had me nodding yes before I knew what was happening.

"Good girl." He smiled. "Wait, wait, wait."

I shook my head back and forth. Spencer silenced me with his long index finger over my lips.

"Too late." He chuckled, pulling his finger away. "Besides, I already talked to Mason about it."

I couldn't hide the shock in my expression.

"And don't worry. I'll be there. Mason and Kyle are working on a duet for us. I'm going to sit in with the band for a while."

"You are?" My mind was reeling.

"Yep, I need to rearrange a few things, and then I'll start." "Okay." Again, I responded without much thought. My brain was too busy spinning into overdrive. I stood up and pushed the computer chair back under the desk. "I should let you get some rest."

Spencer got up and gave my arm a reassuring squeeze. "Don't stress. This is going to be a good thing." He smiled and walked me down the hallway toward the front door. Once the door was open, he leaned forward and caught my gaze.

Feeling the familiar pull, I wondered if he felt it too.

He tucked a stray lock of hair behind my ear. "Stop overthinking and trust me."

I sighed, feeling defeated, and stepped out the door. "Goodnight, Spencer."

"Goodnight, Elizabeth." Soft laughter was the last thing I heard as he closed the door.

****

Mason was in the kitchen eating his usual after dinner snack, a bowl of cereal. I pulled out a chair and sat next to him. He glanced up after taking a large spoonful. My scowling expression and arms folded in front of me let him know I wasn't happy.

"I take it you talked to Spencer?" Mason dipped his spoon back in the bowl.

"Mason, why didn't you talk to me first? Don't you think this is going to be awkward for Aidan and me? I never wanted to sing with you guys. Now I'm stuck." I sat back in the chair feeling defeated and rubbed my face with my hands.

Mason slurped the last of the milk from the bowl and licked his upper lip. "Look, first of all, this was Spencer's thing. I told him you wouldn't like it. So don't get mad at me."

"I know… it's just… ugh… I hate this." I began to nibble on my already too short thumbnail.

"Liz, listen to me." Mason pushed his empty bowl to the side and leaned closer toward me. "A few days after you and Spencer sang, the manager called me. He's been getting inundated with phone calls asking when you two are going to sing again. I haven't even told Spencer about it. I was so sure you'd tell him no, I didn't want to say anything." Mason sat back in his chair. "I think you should do this, Liz."

I felt myself beginning to weaken. "What about Aidan?"

"I'll talk to him. Besides, he might want to dump the band.

He's leaving for school after summer." "What?"

"He got accepted to UC Santa Barbara."

Hearing Aidan's good news made me remember our

first tutoring session in my room when he'd told me he'd applied there. The thought of him leaving tugged at my heart, but I was proud of Aidan, and that made me smile.

"What?" he asked.

"I'm just happy for him."

"Yeah, he said he couldn't wait to get away..." Mason cringed and stopped talking.

"That's okay. I'm sure he's ready to get out of here and away from me." We were silent for a few minutes.

"I'll talk to the guys, and don't worry about Aidan."

Mason picked up his bowl and placed it in the sink. I got up from the chair and headed toward the stairs.

"Liz?"

"Yeah?"

"I'm glad you're doing this. It's gonna be great."

"Hope so." My thoughts turned to Aidan. If he didn't decide to quit the band, this was not going to be good. Not good at all.

Chapter Twenty-Five

My mom came into my room and clasped my hand in hers. Together we stared at the prom dress that hung over my closet door.

"I'm sorry, honey." She hugged me as I held back my tears. "You could go with your cousin, Alex." I backed up and laughed at her attempt to make me feel better.

"Mom, I'm not going with Alex." I stepped toward the edge of the bed and sat down. She sat next to me.

"I just don't want you to miss your prom. Is there anyone else you'd like to go with?"

The image of Spencer dressed in a dark suit holding a corsage entered my thoughts. "No, no one."

Not wanting to look at the dress anymore, I fell back on the bed and stared at the ceiling.

"I know it seems like the end of the world right now, but eventually you'll feel better. About Aidan, the prom… it just takes time."

"I know, Mom." I exhaled.

We were silent for a long time. Eventually, we both got up, and Mom hugged me again. "My baby girl," she whispered. "You're all grown up now. I'm so proud of you, Liz, and I love you so much."

"I love you too," I said. Mom kissed my cheek and then left my room.

I rose from the bed and stared at my dress one last

time before I removed it and placed it deep within my closet.

****

The music drifting up into my bedroom told me the guys were practicing. Mason had let me know Aidan wasn't leaving the band until the end of the summer, so I figured he would be there. In an attempt to get over the awkwardness and make peace with our *situation,* I decided to go downstairs and sit in on a few of their songs, hoping we could get past the anger and hurt and move forward.

My heart was pounding as I stood at the hallway door that led into the garage.

What am I going to do? Just go in there and sit down like everything is normal?

Instead, I pushed through the front door and headed to my car, like I was on a mission. I opened the back door and looked around the back seat like I was desperate to find something. When I felt like enough time had passed, I casually walked from my car up the driveway to the open garage door. I knew it was a cowardly way to approach Aidan, but if it worked, it worked.

It didn't.

The smirk on Aidan's face assured me he'd seen right through my feeble attempt to fake him out. Certain my cheeks were red, I avoided eye contact with him and plopped down on the couch. When the guys finished their set, Mason approached me.

"Wanna sing?" His bright eyes looked hopeful.

I glanced at the guys. Aidan still had that smug look on his face. I responded yes before I'd even thought about it. Aidan's expression went from arrogant to stunned within seconds.

Mason seemed surprised. "Okay, then." He smiled at me and then turned to Kyle. "Grab the lyrics to the new song."

Kyle picked up his spiral binder and approached me. "Here ya go, Liz. Look this over, and then we'll run through it."

My head was beginning to spin. What was I thinking? While glancing over the lyrics, I noticed Mason was on his cell phone.

"Yep, she wants to. I know… okay, great… see ya in a few."

I placed the binder on the couch and met Mason as he picked up his guitar. "Who were you talking to?" My voice was just above a whisper.

Mason answered me in his regular tone — loud — and everyone heard him. Everyone.

"Spencer. He'll be over in a few minutes."

I glanced at Aidan. His eyes were ice cold. He stepped away from the guys while I made my way back to the couch and sat down. Aidan sat next to me as his lips brushed against my ear.

"Well, isn't this going to be fun?" he icily whispered.

My attempt to make things better was backfiring. This was not what I wanted. I placed my hand on Aidan's leg to calm him.

"Aidan, please," I whispered.

He opened his mouth to say something, but the roar of a motorcycle silenced him. He turned his gaze from me toward the rider.

Spencer got off the bike, took off his helmet, and placed it atop the sleek seat. He raked his hand through his hair while he confidently walked into the garage. He gave me a warm smile. His eyes drifted from my face to my hand, still on Aidan's leg. His smile faded, and he turned away from me as Mason approached him.

"You've met Derek and Kyle." Mason motioned to the guys.

Derek gave him a head nod from behind his drums. Kyle was more respectable. He made his way to Spencer and shook his hand.

Then Mason turned toward Aidan. "I don't think you've met Aidan yet."

Aidan stood, eye to eye with Spencer. Mason broke through their alpha moment with an awkward introduction.

"Aidan, Spencer. Spencer, Aidan."

Spencer extended his hand first. Aidan, with an arrogant look on his face, shook it. My brother must have felt the tension between the two. Without missing a beat, he grabbed his guitar and gave it to Spencer.

"Here ya go."

Spencer released Aidan's hand to grab the guitar.

Mason turned to Aidan. "Let's start on 'Feel Again' while they both get up to speed on the new song." Aidan picked up his bass and scowled at Spencer before he started to play.

Mason grabbed the music sheets for the new song and handed them to Spencer.

"Elizabeth." He smiled. "You surprised me, I thought you were going to fight me every step of the way." Spencer sat on the couch and moved in close. "Let me take a look at those lyrics." He reached across my lap to grab the spiral binder. Goose bumps rose on my skin from being so close to him.

I didn't have to look up to know Aidan was

watching us. I could feel his intense gaze burning into me. Spencer glanced over the sheet music and then back to the lyrics. He started to hum the song. My heartbeat began to increase when his humming turned into words. Hearing Spencer sing with the accompaniment of his guitar or the piano was amazing, but hearing him sing a cappella was beyond sexy. I felt myself getting lost in the moment until I heard a loud cough. My eyes shifted from the soft grey gaze of Spencer to a fiery blue that was Aidan.

Spencer stopped singing and handed me back the lyrics. "Now it's your turn." He picked up the guitar and glanced at Aidan. "Let's practice out here." He motioned to the front yard.

I was more than happy to follow him. I wanted to get away from the daggers Aidan was shooting at me.

Spencer sat cross-legged on the grass. I sat down in front of him, mirroring his image. He began strumming the guitar, glancing at the music notes every now and then. He strummed through the song several times while I read over the words. When I glanced inside the garage, Aidan was still focused on us with such disdain it made my insides tremble.

Whenever Spencer's eyes were on the music notes, my eyes were on Spencer. He was so handsome it was hard to look away. His beautiful eye color, long dark lashes, perfect face, and sculpted jaw. My hands ached to reach up and feel the rough stubble. I admired the way his forearm flexed as he played, the way his tattoos moved. I thought back on when I'd run my fingertip over the fine detail, and I had an overwhelming urge to do it again.

In an effort to shut out the desire that filled me, I

closed my eyes and continued to sing. Spencer's soulful voice joined me in the chorus, so seductive and smooth. My thoughts went from the perfection of his voice to his heart. Selfless and sweet, encouraging and kind, tender yet strong. What a good, good man.

A series of images went through my mind. The day we'd met in the music room. The instant attraction I'd felt for him. After the dog attack, when I'd cried on his shoulder, the comfort he'd given me. Football in the park, dinner at Donny's, our many nights together alone, singing and laughing. His kindness and encouraging words that had always soothed me. The dedication he'd willed me to better myself and become more.

The feelings I had buried were now uncovered and raw. I couldn't suppress them any longer. In that moment I realized why I could never say the words that Aidan had longed to hear. My heart had been elsewhere. It had always been with Spencer. I was in love with him. I finally allowed myself to feel the love that I had tried so hard to push away. But, it was too late. Kara was in his life now. He deserved happiness, and I wasn't going to get in the way of that, no matter how much I wanted him.

When I opened my eyes, Spencer's eyes were on mine.

"You okay?" He stopped playing and studied me. The concern on his face made my heart ache.

I realized a tear had fallen from my cheek. I was able to shake it off like it was nothing. I took a deep breath and smiled. "I'm fine."

Spencer glanced toward the garage. "I think your boyfriend might have a problem with me. He hasn't taken his eyes off us since we've been out here."

"He's not... he'll be fine." I was going to confess to

Spencer that Aidan and I weren't together anymore, but I stopped. Somehow, I thought if he still assumed I had a boyfriend, it would make things easier on me.

"I don't know about that. He looks like he wants to kill me." Spencer's eyes shifted from mine to the open garage.

"Don't worry about him. I think I'm ready now."

Spencer gave me a warm smile and reached out a hand to help me up. Without thinking, I leaned over and brushed some grass clippings off his thigh. On our way to the garage, my eyes met Aidan's, and I thought he was going to erupt.

Mason was finishing up one of the band's original songs when we entered the garage.

"Over here, Liz." He gestured to the makeshift stage.

Upon entering the garage, I could feel Aidan's anger radiated toward Spencer.

Spencer stood a few feet in front of me. Mason's eyes met mine. "Ready?"

I nodded in response. Mason lifted a finger for Derek to begin.

Derek started tapping out the song, followed by Kyle on the keyboard. Mason, Spencer, and Aidan all came in at the same time. Then I began. I thought I would be nervous, but Spencer's warm eyes and smile reassured me. I held the spiral binder and belted out the song. Spencer came in on the chorus. Mason held up his hand and stopped playing.

"Hold up. Hold up."

Everyone stopped. I heard a deep, loud sigh come from Aidan.

"Spencer, remember it's a duet." Mason reached out

for the binder, and I handed it to him.

"See?" He pointed to each of the paragraphs on the page. "Alright, I got it."

Mason had me move next to Spencer. Mason motioned to Derek to start again, and everyone else joined in.

While I sang, I made a conscious effort to avoid eye contact with Aidan. I closed my eyes and allowed myself to get lost in the music, the emotions I had stirring inside me, my love for Spencer, and the loss of Aidan. I used how I felt to fuel the powerful voice within me.

When I finished the song and opened my eyes, I glanced at Aidan. His expression was not what I expected. So I held his gaze. I thought I would see his wrath, but instead I saw the smile that used to melt my heart. There was softness in his eyes I hadn't seen in what seemed like forever. In those few moments, I saw the boy I had cared for, laughed with. Who'd made me feel special.

Derek's boisterous voice brought me out of my sweet memory.

"For crying out loud, Lizzie, that was awesome!" He jumped up from behind his drums, picked me up, and gave me a bone- crushing squeeze. "Just awesome!"

"You're hurting me." I squeaked out.

"Oops. Sorry." He gently put me down. "You were just so good. You too, Spencer."

I glanced at Spencer, and he softly laughed.

Mason leaned in and whispered, "Good goin', Liz." He kissed my forehead.

Kyle gave me a warm smile from his keyboard and mouthed *"Good job."*

When I glanced at Spencer again, he winked. My

eyes met Aidan's as he approached me.

"You were amazing." I met his gaze. His expression seemed pained yet proud.

"Thank you, Aidan."

He stepped back and picked up his bass.

Spencer approached me, leaned in close, and whispered, "Be proud... beautiful one."

My heart rate spiked as he brushed past me, and his words trailed off.

Mason turned toward me, raised an eyebrow, and asked, "Again?"

I surprised myself when I laughed a little and said, "Okay."

An hour later, we had sung through the song four times, and it had actually been fun. Kyle grabbed a few water bottles from the garage fridge and tossed them around. Aidan was holding a full bottle but put his hand up for Kyle to toss him another. When he had two bottles in his hand, Aidan walked toward me and handed me one. He glanced at Spencer, who was sitting on the couch engaged in a conversation with Mason.

"I need to take off, but will you walk with me?" Aidan's eyes widened, waiting for my answer.

"Sure."

As we exited the garage together, I opened my bottle and took a sip then screwed the top back on.

When we arrived at his truck, Aidan opened the driver side door and tossed his water bottle on the passenger seat. He stood facing me with his back to the garage, while I began to peel back the paper on my bottle.

"I got accepted to UC Santa Barbara."

I looked up from peeling the paper. His words made me smile.

"I know. Mason told me. I'm so happy for you, Aidan."

"When I found out, I wanted to tell you so bad… but…" "I know." Instinctively, I reached out and rubbed his arm. "If you hadn't helped me figure out calculus…"

"No, Aidan, you did it. Not me."

"Well, for what it's worth, I just wanted to thank you."

Aidan started to move in for a hug. I was tempted to resist him, until I realized this was his attempt at making peace between us. I stepped into his grasp and relished the familiarity of being wrapped in his arms. The feeling was bittersweet. I think in that moment, Aidan realized things were over between us, and there was no going back. I held him close and inhaled deeply. I knew this was the last time I would hold him and smell his fresh scent. I stepped back and looked at his face as the setting sun cast highlights against his soft hair.

"You're welcome, Aidan."

Our moment was interrupted when the sound of Spencer's bike started up. I backed away from Aidan in time to see his unreadable expression before he put on his helmet and rode away.

Chapter Twenty-Six

Mason's voice woke me. "It's almost time for dinner." He walked closer to my bed, but I didn't budge. The bed dipped down where Mason sat. I stretched my arms above my head and yawned. I had been sleeping more than usual. I was mentally drained. Sleep seemed to be the only thing that freed my thoughts.

When my eyes adjusted, I looked at Mason. He seemed to be deep in thought, regarding me speculatively.

"What?"

Mason held something in his hand. "Aidan wanted me to give you this." He handed me an envelope.

I sat up in my bed, glanced at Mason, and ripped open the envelope.

"Do you want some privacy?" he asked.

"No, it's okay." I pulled out a handwritten note on lined notebook paper.

Dear Liz,
This belongs to you.
The choice is yours.
Aidan

Out from the folded paper dropped my prom ticket. "Is he going?" I asked.

Mason shrugged his shoulders. "I don't know. He

only said he wanted you to have it."

My mom's voice beckoned up the stairs and summoned us for dinner.

"You've got twenty-four hours to think about what you want to do."

"I know." I read the ticket one more time before I placed it on my bookcase and went downstairs for dinner.

****

No regrets.

That was the first thing that came to mind as I stared at my prom dress which now lay draped across my bed. The second thing that came to mind was Mrs. Chapman. I walked toward the small white canvas and the unopened pack of watercolors that sat proudly on my bookcase. I reached up and read the inscription on the back of the canvas, allowing my fingers to skim across the shaky black script.

Sweet Elizabeth,
My life is near its end and yours is just beginning.
A blank canvas of life is before you.
Remember my words and use every color.
Love, Barbara

I placed the canvas back and smiled, knowing she would have been proud of me. Good or bad, I had made the decision to go to my prom. I took a deep breath, picked up my dress, and hung it on the doorjamb of my closet. I applied the finishing touches of my make-up.

The shrill of my mom and Melissa squealing downstairs wafted up into my bedroom. They were so similar it was frightening. I was in the process of shimmying the dress on when Melissa burst through my door.

"C'mon, Liz, time for pictures." She beamed. Melissa motioned for me to turn around and then zipped up the back of my dress. "I'm so glad you're going." She hugged me as we walked out of my room to the waiting paparazzi of my parents below.

****

A parade of busses lined the school parking lot. I stood between Melissa and Mason while we slowly moved along, inching our way toward the check-in table. Once we were on the bus, the feeling of humiliation set in. Everyone was paired up. Too bad parking at the prom site was limited. If we could have driven ourselves, I wouldn't feel so exposed. I sat in the first empty seat I came to. Melissa sat in next to me, and Mason squished in beside her.

"You guys, they're not gonna let you sit here," I protested.

Mason gave me a wink. "Don't worry about it, Liz, I'll handle this." He rarely used his good looks and charm to get away with things, but I guess he felt he'd pull out the big guns to help out his pathetic dateless sister.

With clipboard in hand, Ms. Dunbar approached us as she checked off each student in his or her designated seat. She glanced at the three of us, Mason gave her his best smile. He reached out and said something to her. But with the hum of the motor and the chatter that echoed throughout the bus, the only thing I heard was her response to him. "Nice try."

Mason leaned in and whispered. "She never liked me anyway." He smirked.

"Listen, I'm fine. You guys can just sit over there." I pointed to a couple of empty seats a few rows back.

"No, you're not sitting alone, Liz." Melissa started to say something to Mason while she motioned to the seats toward the back of the bus.

"No, Melissa. Please. I'll feel horrible if you both don't sit together. I'm fine. It's just a bus ride. Please. Go." I could sense her unwillingness to leave me. I continued to persuade her until she left my side to go sit next to Mason. I glanced over my seat and smiled at them both before I sat back down and gazed out the window. My mind drifted to what was ahead. If the empty seat next to me was any indication, it was not going to be good.

****

The three of us entered the resort hotel. A grand staircase was the focal point of our prom venue. Several kids had already grouped together, whipping out their cell phones to take pictures. It made me laugh when Melissa and Mason got bombarded. It seemed like each group that took a picture wanted the potential king and queen of the prom to be in their shot. I left them and moved beyond the staircase into the massive ballroom.

A least a dozen large chandeliers cast a soft glow over the luxurious room. A sea of round tables covered in white linen surrounded the already-crowded dance floor. I made my way to one of the empty tables and sat down, taking everything in. I had left my sullen mood on the bus. Since I'd made the decision to be here, I was going to make the best of it. This was my prom, and I was determined to have a good time. Melissa soon joined me.

"Sorry about that, Liz. That was nuts." Melissa

pulled out a chair and sat next to me.

"Where's Mason?"

"Who knows? Over there somewhere." Melissa motioned to a large group of kids still snapping pictures. I just laughed and shook my head.

The music went from slow and romantic to upbeat and loud. Melissa started dancing in her seat, and the next thing I knew she was up gyrating around my chair.

"C'mon, Lizzie." Melissa giggled then pulled me up from my chair onto the dance floor.

Melissa and I danced to several songs without stopping. I started to feel guilty, wondering where my brother was, but Melissa didn't seem to mind. Guys she knew kept bouncing between the two of us. Melissa rolled her eyes and smiled when Mason finally found us. Several single girls who wanted a turn at dancing with my brother followed him. It didn't seem to bother her. They were both so confident I could see why their relationship had survived high school.

The football team joined our dance party, and soon we were all singing in unison to the song that blasted through the speakers. It didn't seem to matter I was alone. Everyone just melded together, and before I knew it, a handful of guys I casually knew had asked me to dance. It was hard to avoid the wandering hands of a few of them but, all in all, I was proud I was able to handle myself.

Melissa and Mason motioned they were headed back to our table. I nodded that I understood, but since I was having such a good time, I stayed. The upbeat song that hummed through the speakers was soon replaced with a romantic one. I had already chastised the handsy guy I was dancing with during the more upbeat songs. I decided it was safer if I excused myself when the slow song came through the speakers.

I was leaving the dance floor when my eyes locked on the profile I knew all too well.

Aidan.

I hadn't seen him all night, so I had assumed he had decided not to come. But here he was, looking perfect in his dark suit. And here I was, a sweaty, hot mess. I picked my hair up from my shoulders in a makeshift ponytail and waved it up and down in an attempt to cool my heated body. To avoid eye contact with him, I made a beeline for our table.

Melissa and Mason returned with their dinner plates just as I sat down.

"You want some?" Melissa asked as she sat between me and Mason. "The buffet line is packed."

I glanced over her plate of chicken, some sort of pasta, and broccoli with cheese sauce. "I'm not hungry yet." I guzzled my water and then whispered to Melissa. "I just saw Aidan."

Melissa had just taken a bite of her pasta. She quickly swallowed.

"He's here?" Her wide eyes darted around the ballroom. "Yes. I saw him, but he didn't see me." Melissa nudged Mason, and I heard her tell him Aidan had showed. He leaned in so he could hear our conversation.

"I didn't think he was coming. Are you okay?" Mason asked with a look of concern in his eyes.

"Yeah, I'm fine." I took another sip of my water. "He has every right to be here. It's his prom too." I shrugged. "Things between us are actually pretty good."

I thought about the other night when we'd stood near

his truck. The moment we'd shared. It felt like we had resolved our differences and were respectfully moving on. At least *I* felt like that. Until I glanced to the dance floor and saw Aidan. It was my eighteenth birthday all over again. There he was with his hands all over some chesty girl in a low-cut dress. Watching them together made my stomach turn.

Melissa leaned in close. "Don't look at him, Liz."

Mason started to get up. "I'm gonna tell him to take it to the other side of the dance floor."

I tore my eyes away from Aidan and looked to Melissa and Mason.

"Mason, sit down. He can dance with whoever he wants." "But…" he started to say.

"But what? We're broken up." My fake smile was in place as I rose from the table. "I'm going to go use the bathroom. I'll be right back."

"I'll go with you," Melissa chimed in. "No, Melissa, sit and eat. I'll be fine."

I got up from the table before Melissa followed me. I wanted to be alone to gather my thoughts. Five minutes ago, I had felt like Aidan had enough respect for me to at least honor what we had. Instead, it seemed like he was shouting to everyone he was a free man, up for grabs. Seeing him act that way made me question if he'd ever been who I thought he was.

I washed my hands and wiped the sweat from the back of my neck with a paper towel. When I felt composed, I made my way out of the bathroom. Some fresh air would be great right now, and I wasn't ready to go back and sit at our table quite yet.

Several of my classmates were milling around the hotel as I made my way through an open door that led to the outside. An empty bench served as my refuge. I removed my shoes and began to massage my aching feet. A few minutes later, a group of kids burst through the doors, putting an end to my time of solace. I grabbed my shoes and slipped back into the hotel before the doors closed.

The hotel was so large it was confusing trying to find my way back to the ballroom. I meandered through a large hallway and pushed past several doors that led me back outside again. From across the courtyard I could see the windows of the ballroom. With my heels in hand, I breathed a sigh of relief and headed across the beautifully manicured grounds. The entrance to the ballroom was in sight. I was a step away from the door when my heart rate accelerated.

Not again.

From what I witnessed, I wasn't even a thought in Aidan's mind. My eyes swept over my ex. He and the girl he had been dancing with were all over each other. His hands were up her dress as hers were wrapped around his hips grinding into him. I saw more of her tanned skin than I cared to.

Apprehension filled me while I reached for the door. For a moment, I thought they might not even notice me. No such luck.

When I nudged the door open, the sounds of the music from the ballroom distracted them from their... activities.

Aidan flicked a glance my way as the girl continued to run her lips the length of his neck. His expression was blank until his brain must have registered it was me. My heart sped up when our eyes met. His eyes widened, and I held his gaze. His jaw clenched for a moment before he pushed away from his… *date*. He opened his mouth and was about to say something, but I slipped through the door before he had the chance.

Determined to hold it together, I made it to our table just as Melissa and Mason were being crowned king and queen of the prom. My mental turmoil was forgotten for a moment while I watched my brother and my best friend glide across the dance floor. Kids began to stand up to get a better look at the perfect couple. I shuffled through the crowd and made my way to the edge of the dance floor. My brother was dressed in a black tux with a blue tie that matched Melissa's dress perfectly. She was all sparkles and glitter. Watching Melissa and Mason sway back and forth made my heart swell with pride.

In that moment, I was happy. I hoped one day I would have the love that was reflected in the eyes of my brother and my best friend. Aidan and I had never shared that, and a part of me wondered if I ever would.

****

The bus ride from the venue to home was quiet. It was late, and most of the kids were exhausted. For me, it was more mental than physical, although my feet still ached. I was thankful the night had come to an end and I hadn't seen Aidan again. I considered telling Mason and Melissa about what had happened, but I didn't want to ruin their night. Besides, what was the point? It was over… truly over.

I glanced a few rows back to look at Mason. His eyes were closed, and his arm was draped around Melissa. She was asleep nestled on his shoulder. Her hair was a mess, her crown was cocked to the side, but she still looked beautiful. Looking at the two of them made me smile. My eyelids grew heavy, and I leaned my head back. The hum of the engine lulled me to sleep.

"Liz, get up." It took me a minute to realize I was still on the bus. I rubbed my eyes and glanced around. Most of the kids were already gone. Mason helped me up, and then the three of us walked to his car. "I'll drop you off and take Melissa home."

"Alright." I yawned.

Mason pulled into the driveway, and I got out of his car. Melissa smiled and waved to me through the passenger side window. I waved back before they drove off. I made my way up the driveway. All I wanted was my bed. When I got to the front door, I gave the handle a shake.

Locked.

Maggie was whimpering.

"It's okay, girl." I tried to soothe her. I went through the side gate to the back door. *Locked.* Slider, *locked.* I even tried the doggie door. *Nope.*

For a minute, I considered waking up my parents. I checked the time on my cell phone: it was almost 2:00 a.m. I knew Mason would be right back, so I went to the front of the house, sat down in a chair on the porch, and waited.

I tapped out a text to Mason.

Hurry.
I'm locked out.

To pass the time, I started playing Words with Friends. I was putting in my final word for an easy win when I heard Spencer's bike. I tried not to imagine where he had been, but thoughts of him and Kara on some fabulous date tormented me.

I tried to camouflage myself behind one of my mom's large potted plants, but no such luck. The porch light above my head was like a beacon in the night. Spencer pulled his bike to the curb, got off it, removed his helmet, and slowly approached me. I got up and met him at the halfway point of the driveway. He looked like a sexy bad boy in his brown leather jacket and dark jeans. Before I knew it, I was smiling at him, dismissing the thoughts of Kara from my mind.

"All dressed up and nowhere to go?" He smiled. His question made me giggle.

He sounded concerned. "What are you doing out here?" "Locked out. Mason dropped me off, but he'll be right back.

Tonight was our prom."

"I figured that." Spencer's eyes ran the length of my body. "You're beautiful." His voice was warm and husky.

The scrutiny of his gaze made me blush. "Thank you." "Ya know, I never went to my prom."

I glanced up at him, surprised.

"Yep." He smiled and took a step closer. "Never got to dance with a pretty girl to some cheesy song." Spencer closed the distance between us while he stretched his hand out for me to take it. He leaned in and began to hum.

A shy smile spread across my face as I placed my hand in his. "I've never slow danced before."

Spencer stopped humming to answer me. "There's nothing to it." He inched forward. "I've got you."

He placed his hand on the small of my back while my free hand grasped his shoulder. Spencer smiled and began to hum again. We swayed back and forth on the driveway. I couldn't help but giggle when Spencer twirled me around and then skillfully dipped me. He brought me back to my feet with grace then whirled me around the driveway. His lips brushed up against my ear. The sensation sent a shiver through my body.

The innocence of our dance shifted as Spencer's pace slowed, our bodies were barely moving, just a slight sway. He moved in close — so close I could feel the warmth of his body as it was perfectly wrapped around mine. I wasn't sure if it was because of the emotional drama of the prom or the comfort I felt in the strength of his arms, but I instinctively laid my head on his shoulder. A feeling of peace overwhelmed me while he continued to softly hum in my ear. In his arms I was safe. He made me feel whole. Being with him felt like home.

Suddenly my head woke from the hypnotic spell it was under. My thoughts began shouting this was wrong. As much as I wanted him, Spencer wasn't mine. I lifted my head from his shoulder, and when my eyes met his, I felt helpless. I couldn't resist him. Every rational thought I had was met with confusion. All I could focus on was I was in love with him. I didn't care about Kara. I didn't care about being the good girl or doing the right thing. All I cared about was him. I wanted nothing more than to feel his lips on mine.

I moved my hand from his shoulder and slipped it around his waist. His breath caught, and he stopped humming. The soft light from the porch was reflected in the heat I saw in the depth of his eyes. My heart was pounding. My lips parted in anticipation for what I knew was coming. Spencer's lips were so close I could feel his warm breath mingled with mine.

We were both so caught up in the moment we didn't hear Mason's car as it sped into the driveway. We broke apart as the headlights passed over us. Spencer pulled me out of the way just before Mason screeched to a halt, inches from hitting me.

Mason was horrified and sprang from the car. "I didn't see you guys. Are you okay, Liz?"

Spencer's arm was protectively wrapped around me, his eyes etched with concern.

My voice trembled while I replied, "I'm okay." I left the warmth of Spencer's arms as Mason reached out and hugged me.

"I'm so sorry," he murmured. He released me and glanced at Spencer. "Wait, what are you doing here?"

"I was on my way home and saw Elizabeth. I wanted to make sure she was okay." Spencer glanced at me. He seemed closed off. "Well, since you're home now." He took a few steps backward and walked toward his bike.

Mason placed his hand on my shoulder, and we walked into the house. "What a night, huh?"

I heard the roar of Spencer's bike as I nodded, and Mason closed the door behind us.

Chapter Twenty-Seven

Mason and I stood side by side, dressed in our cap and gowns while our dad proudly snapped pictures of us. Mason wore blue, and I was in silver... our school colors. I stared down at my neck draped with gold cords and a scholastic medallion for maintaining a 4.0 the entire four years of high school. I felt proud of myself, but a part of me wished Mason was as decorated as I was.

Mom had been tearing up on and off all day. Mason left my side to go and hug her.

"Mom, we're not even going off to school. We'll be right here at college... in town. Home every night for dinner." He chuckled.

"I know. It's just, I can't believe you both are graduating high school. It went by so fast." She sniffed.

I joined Mason, and we wrapped our arms around our emotional mother for a group hug. My dad blinked back a tear and took one last shot before we left for our graduation.

****

"Pomp and Circumstance" echoed through the high school stadium. Mason and I smiled as we walked in unison down the athletic field to our waiting seats in the distance. Since high school had been emotionally difficult for me, I didn't think I would be affected, but I was. While watching the chairs filling up with my classmates, my emotions were bittersweet. However they had treated me, good or bad, this time in my life was over. My mind wandered as the seemingly endless list of names was called.

Mason and I had taken Sunday off from our church activities, so I hadn't seen Spencer in almost a week. But that didn't mean I hadn't thought about him. I'd barely thought of anything else. Our night dancing on the driveway, how he'd sung to me, held me, and the way he'd looked at me. I wondered what it would be like when I saw him again. Would he say anything? Was it just me or did he want to kiss me too? I felt guilt for what had almost happened. Spencer had someone in his life, and there I was, practically throwing myself at him. Maybe I should just ignore everything, act like nothing happened, because, nothing *did* happen.

My thoughts were interrupted when I heard the name Aidan David Mitchell resonate through the speakers. Applause, met with howling from the females in the audience, was almost embarrassing. I rolled my eyes when I heard a group of coeds scream out, "We love you Aidan!" He seemed to take it in stride as he sauntered down the aisle. He scanned the crowd of blue and silver gowns. I hunched down, just in case, it was me he was looking for. When the next name was called, I sat back up in my chair.

Mason fiddled with my gold cord as we stood in procession, waiting to receive our diplomas. "Such a nerd." He teased then nudged me when the line started to move.

My heart pounded as Principal Fick called my name. "Elizabeth Katherine Ryan." I walked toward him, and he glanced at my academic achievements that graced my gown. He gave me a wink and a smile, shook my hand,

and gave me my diploma. I returned his smile and made my way past the podium to the steps below.

Cheers erupted from the graduating class when my brother's name was called. I had to laugh when Mason held up his fist in triumph. Howling continued as he made his way back to his seat, and I could have sworn I heard Melissa yell, "Yeah, baby!"

Mason and I smiled at each other when the principal announced our graduating class. We placed our tassel from the right side to the left as clapping and earsplitting cries surrounded us. We both laughed and tossed our hats in the air. Seconds later, a sea of silver and blue graduation caps rained down upon us. Mason hugged me tight. I glanced over his shoulder and saw that Melissa was fast approaching. She grabbed us both for a group hug.

"We did it!" She squealed. Mason and I both laughed. She hugged me again and then grabbed my brother for a passionate kiss.

I left their side to go and retrieve my hat. I found one. It wasn't mine, but I guessed it didn't matter. I tucked it under my arm and glanced up to the bleachers. A parade of parents and grandparents were making their way to the field. I stood for a minute to take it all in.

A gentle tugging on my gown made me turn around. His blue eyes roamed over my face, gauging my reaction. All I could do was stand there. He picked up my gold cords.

"You always were too smart for me." His smile was guarded, but beautiful just the same. I exhaled and tried to think of what to say to him, but it didn't make any difference. Several girls grabbed for his blue robe, pulling him away from me. He tried to resist, but I just walked away. When I glanced back, he was gone.

I turned when I heard Melissa shout my name. She was standing with my parents and Mason, near the exit of the field. "C'mon," she yelled. "We're outta here!"

****

Maggie was panting when we made our way through the front door. I had run extra hard that morning, and she seemed to be paying the price for it. Knowing I was going to be practicing with the guys later, I'd felt the need to clear my head.

I unhooked her leash, and she bounded toward her water bowl in the kitchen. I was surprised when I heard Mason's voice greet her.

"You're up kinda early. I thought you'd sleep till noon, like you did the last three days." I reached in the cupboard and grabbed a glass so I could fill it with water from the refrigerator door.

"The guys are coming to practice. Did you forget?"

Mason was waiting for his frozen waffles to pop up from the toaster.

"I thought it was tonight."

"Spencer can't make it. Sorry, I thought I told you." Mason grabbed his waffles, put them on a plate with some syrup, and started cutting into them with a fork. "Are you gonna be able to practice with us?"

I tried not to let my mind question why Spencer couldn't make it later. "Umm, what time is everyone coming over?"

Mason swallowed a large bite before he answered me. "Eleven."

I glanced at the microwave oven clock. It was 10:15 a.m. "Yeah, I just need to take a shower." I drank the rest of my water and hurried up the stairs. I almost didn't have time to think about Aidan and Spencer coming over… almost.

****

My heart rate picked up when I peeked out the front window. Spencer's bike. Aidan's truck. I tried to calm my breathing while I stood at the door that led to the garage. Glancing down at my white beach cover-up made me feel a little better. Knowing Melissa would be coming over and we were going to the beach assured me our practice time wouldn't take too long. I only had to run through the song a few times. It wouldn't be so bad, would it?

Mason was chatting with Spencer when I entered the garage. Aidan was tuning his bass. Kyle was scribbling notes on his spiral binder, and Derek was sitting behind his drums. I think he was admiring his newest tattoo. Glancing up, he saw me first.

"Lizzie's here," he bellowed. All eyes focused on me.

"Over here, Liz." Mason placed me next to Spencer. "You've got the words down, right?"

"Yep, I think so." I turned my attention to Spencer. I glanced up at him through downcast eyelashes. "Are you ready?" I shyly asked.

He took a step toward me and raised my chin to meet his gaze. In that moment, I felt like it was just he and I in the room. His eyes were kind and almost apologetic. His touch was soft and gentle.

"I'm ready." He gave me an encouraging smile.

When his hand dropped away, I felt a loss from the physical contact.

Mason gestured to Derek to start. The guys all joined in, and I began. Spencer took a sidestep closer to me and sang his part of the song. His look was so heated and sexy I was having a hard time remembering the words. My thoughts kept spiraling back to our night on the driveway together. When I emerged from my hypnotic state, I tore my gaze from Spencer and looked at Aidan. He was staring down Spencer with so much hate in his eyes it was frightening.

Spencer joined me in the chorus and shifted his body so he was directly in front of me. There it was again, that magnetic pull that seemed to be between us. When Spencer finished out the last line of the song, he reached out and stroked my bare shoulder, causing my skin to tingle. I managed to back away before I lost all control and lunged myself at him.

"One more time," Mason shouted.

Derek tapped out the beat to the song, and we began again. Melissa drove up and waved as she entered the garage.

After she plopped herself on the couch, her eyes ping-ponged from me to Aidan and then to Spencer. Finally her furrowed brow settled on me. I knew that look. Nothing got past her. I could almost see the wheels spinning in her head as she assessed the situation. I tried to keep my distance from Spencer while we finished out the last chorus together, but it was too late. Her raised eyebrow and knowing smile assured me she had figured it out.

When we closed out the song, Melissa stood and glanced at me with *the look* then made her way toward Mason.

He kissed her forehead then stepped back and looked at her short beach cover-up. He strummed his guitar a few times and crooned, *"My baby looks good in blue,"* a few times. Mason's affectionate display distracted her momentarily.

Spencer pulled his cell phone from his pocket and checked the time. He glanced at Mason, who was now sitting on the couch with Melissa on his lap.

"I need to take off, Mason, but I think we're good." Spencer took a step toward me.

"How do you feel, Elizabeth?"

How do I feel? I feel like I want to wrap myself in your arms. I feel like I want to run my hands in your hair and feel your perfect full lips against mine. "I feel good." I looked away from his perfect face and cast my eyes downward.

Spencer crouched down so he could look into my eyes. "I'm glad you feel good." His lips curved into a smile. "I feel good too." He backed away and walked out of the garage. As I watched him leave, my mind was plagued with thoughts of why he had to leave so early, where he was going, and if he had a date with Kara. I flinched when I felt the sensation of warm lips near my ear.

"You used to look at me like that," Aidan angrily whispered.

I whipped my head around to meet his gaze. His eyes were ice cold. "Don't even start with me, Aidan. You're the one that messed us up, not me!" I started to walk away from him, but he grabbed my arm and yanked me back.

"Seriously, Liz?"

"Don't twist this around and make it my fault." I jerked my arm from his grasp just before Melissa approached us.

"Ready to go?" she asked. I was thankful she hadn't

heard my exchange with Aidan.

"Yep, just let me get my bag." I stepped away from Aidan, dismissing the twinge of guilt I felt for the feelings I had for Spencer. I knew I had tried with Aidan, and he had hurt me more times than I cared to count.

****

After we grabbed a couple of beach chairs, Melissa closed her trunk, and we made our way down to the sand. I was expecting her to bombard me with questions about Spencer on the drive, but she was preoccupied talking about how sweet my brother was. I thought I was off the hook, but the minute we set up our chairs, she started in.

"What's going on with you and Mr. Smokin' Hot Music Man?" She was grinning at me like the Cheshire Cat from *Alice in Wonderland.*

I just shook my head. "Actually, nothing."

"It didn't look like nothing. You guys seemed pretty steamy!"

"Melissa!"

"Seriously, Liz, what's going on?"

I contemplated what I should say to Melissa. I had always been more of a, *figure everything out yourself and hold it in* type of girl. After a few minutes, I exhaled and turned my eyes to hers.

"I started to feel something for Spencer when I was with Aidan, but I thought it was just an infatuation. Ya know, 'cuz he's so good looking. I kept thinking I'd get over it." I stopped talking. Everything had been bottled up too long. My feelings began to overwhelm me.

Melissa's grin was gone. Her curiosity spiked, she shifted her chair and moved in closer. "Did anything happen? While you were with Aidan?" She held my gaze with the look of concerned concentration.

When the words started to flow, so did my emotions. I felt like a dam had burst as the truth finally spilled from my lips.

"Nothing ever happened. I mean, he never kissed me or anything." The driveway memory flashed through my mind. "And it wasn't like that... not at the beginning anyway. At first it was just us singing together. He knew I had a boyfriend, so it was easy for us to become friends. But the more I got to know him and watch him, be around him, things started to change. For me anyway."

For once Melissa didn't have anything to say. She was so absorbed in my confession, she was silent. After a few moments of nothing but the sea air flowing between us, she managed to say two words.

"Go on."

I rubbed my hands over my face before I began again. "I felt like we connected, more than I ever had with Aidan." When the words left my lips, tears sprang from my eyes. "I wanted to love Aidan... I cared for him. I still care for him. He was so sweet in the beginning but then got so possessive, and that's not love." I was sobbing now. "I tried with him... over and over I tried."

Melissa reached out and clasped my hand. Her touch sent me over the edge.

I pulled my hand away and cried into them. "He cheated on me."

The warmth of Melissa's arms was instantly around me. The tears continued to fall as my best friend tried to comfort me. I felt her body tense when she whispered, "That jerk."

I backed away, horrified, and realized what I had confessed. "Please don't tell Mason. Please." My tears stopped as I contemplated what my brother would do to

Aidan.

"Why are you protecting him? Liz! He cheated on you!" Melissa's anger was palpable.

"I know, Melissa, but he was good. A part of him was good.

I think he wants to change... he just doesn't know how."

"Oh, Liz." Melissa hugged me again. Her body went from tense to slack. "You're too sweet."

"No, I just think he deserves a chance." I shifted back and wiped my face with the back of my hand.

"Do you want to talk about what happened... when you caught him?"

"Not right now." I was surprised Melissa didn't push for more information. That was so out of her character.

"Okay, then, tell me more about Spencer."

"At first it was just his looks, but his heart... he's so good and kind. He encourages me. Makes me laugh. Makes me feel safe, special. I've never felt the way I feel when I am with him." I wondered if I should confess my true feelings for Spencer, but I didn't have to. Melissa said the words I feared to utter.

"You're in love with him." All I could do was nod.

Melissa couldn't hide her excitement. "Liz, I'm so happy for you."

"He has a girlfriend." My words halted her enthusiasm. "What? Are you sure? But, the way he was looking at You..."

"I'm sure." I interrupted her. "Remember that girl we saw him with in the restaurant?"

Melissa nodded.

"Well, that's her, Kara." I sat back in my chair and rubbed my temples.

Melissa seemed crushed. "Are they serious?"

I shrugged my shoulders. "I have no idea. That's the one thing we don't talk about. In fact, he still thinks I'm with Aidan."

"What? Why?"

"Just makes things easier."

Melissa seemed to ponder my words. "I guess," she finally answered. "But, I think you should tell him, maybe if he knew you didn't have a—"

I cut her off mid-sentence. "No, Melissa, I don't want to get in the way. I hate to admit it, but Kara's sweet. They'd be good together, and even though it hurts, I want him to be happy. He deserves that."

Melissa's eyes glazed over. She sat silent for a few moments, a tear fell from her cheek. "If that isn't love I don't know what is." She sniffed. Seeing my matter-of-fact friend show such unbridled emotion shocked me.

"Melissa." I reached out and hugged her. Together our tears turned to laughter as we sat back in our chairs.

Chapter Twenty-Eight

Melissa held my gaze while I maneuvered through the crowded venue. The band was in full swing, and Mason crooned in the background. The regulars were packed in tight. I was jostled on my way toward our table. I heard a chuckle as I brushed past someone in the crowd. My heart sank — Nina. The sight of her made me ill.

I made my way as fast as I could to the open seat and sat next to Melissa.

"I can't believe she's here." Melissa scowled.

A few days after my beach confession, Melissa had ambushed me in my room. She hadn't been able to wait any longer. She'd wanted details about my break-up with Aidan, so now she knew everything, and, true to her word, she'd kept it from my brother.

I glanced back at Nina. She was as close to Aidan as she could get without actually being on stage with him.

"I can't think about her. I'm gonna be singing soon."

Melissa looked me up and down. "Well, my friend, you look fabulous."

Spencer and I weren't supposed to go on until the second set, which worked out in my favor. I was so nervous I had tried on at least six different outfits before I settled on my black birthday dress. The fact was I liked the dress, and pushing all the memories aside, it was what I wanted to wear.

"Have you seen Spencer?"

Melissa nodded, and her eyes shifted to a table off to the side, near the back. My heart dropped like it was on the decline from the highest point of a rollercoaster. There he was... and there she was. Witnessing the striking couple sitting side by side made my already fragile heart ache even more.

I glanced at Melissa and could see the pain reflected in her eyes. I tried to smile, but I just couldn't and thankfully, I didn't have to fake it anymore, at least not with Melissa.

My eyes darted around at the commotion behind me. Seconds later, I was swallowed up in arms of the young boy I had come to adore.

"Lizzie!"

"Simon! What are you doing here?" I reached around and hugged him tight.

"We came to see you and Spencer sing." I glanced around, but I didn't see anyone else.

Then my eyes caught sight of the people surrounding Spencer's table. Simon was chatting in my ear, but my mind tuned him out when Spencer glanced my way. Seconds later, his family was headed to our table.

Shawn made it to our table first. "Hey, Shawn," I said. "Hey."

"This is my friend, Melissa."

Shawn responded with the teenage head nod. Spencer pulled up a couple of chairs and placed them at our table.

"Do you mind?" he asked.

"Ahh, no... not at all." I stammered as I stood up. "Elizabeth, I'd like you to meet my mother, Sharon."

Spencer backed away while his mother approached me.

"Hi." I reached out to give her my hand, but she wrapped me in her arms instead.

"Oh, Elizabeth, I've heard so much about you. I feel like I know you." She squeezed me tight. "My boys have raved about you, all of them." She pulled back to look me in the eyes. "And the way you took care of Spencer when he was sick, you're just a dear, dear girl."

I was taken aback by the onslaught of affection and a bit surprised by it. I glanced at Kara, who was now seated at our table.

Her reaction was similar to the way Melissa would handle things. So confident, not a shred of jealousy crossed her face as Spencer's mom showered me with affection.

"Thank you," I responded. Melissa raised an eyebrow to me before she lifted her hand to greet Spencer's mother.

Sharon took a seat next to Kara while Simon and Shawn went looking for a few extra chairs.

"You remember Kara?" Spencer questioned. "Yes. Hi, Kara, this is my friend Melissa."

My faithful best friend looked Kara over before she gave a curt "Hello."

The boys soon returned with the chairs, and the awkward introductions were over. Spencer pulled out a chair next to Kara and sat down. Our table was cozy, to say the least.

My cell phone was face down on the table when it vibrated. I picked it up and Melissa's name flashed across the screen. I glanced down at it and almost laughed out loud when I read the words.

You've got to be kidding me!

I closed my cell phone and shot her the look to *be nice.* I stuffed my cell in my purse and focused my attention on our boisterous table. Between Spencer's mom, Simon, Kara, and Melissa, it was a wonder we could still hear Mason singing on stage.

Spencer leaned in close. "Are you okay?"

"I think so." My eyes scanned the packed bar area and dance floor.

Spencer reached his hand to mine. "Don't do that," he demanded.

"Do what?"

"Over think. You're amazing." His thumb swept back and forth over my hand.

Kara was eyeing me. I pulled my hand from his and placed it under the table.

"Hey, hey, hey." Spencer's soft words broke through the haze of my panicked emotions. He stood up, leaned over, and whispered across the table, "Come with me."

Melissa must have seen our intimate exchange because she nudged my leg with hers before I got up to leave.

I rose and followed Spencer. I didn't look back at the table, but it seemed like our absence hadn't fazed them. Everyone was still talking when we left.

Spencer clasped my hand in his and led me through the venue. I glanced over my shoulder before we turned down a small hallway. Aidan's fiery blue eyes were the last thing I saw before I was whisked into Spencer's strong arms. He held me for a moment and pulled back.

He snaked his hands from around my back and rested them on my hips.

I blinked up at him a few times, trying to decipher my frenzied thoughts.

"You were getting that deer in the headlights look about you. I had to get you out of there."

Lost in the intensity of his eyes, I was speechless. "You think you're gonna be okay?"

I realized my hands were holding his muscular arms. To anyone looking at us, it may have seemed like a couple in love trying to steal a few quiet moments. I allowed my hands to fall away then stepped from his grasp. I cleared my throat before I answered him.

"Yes, I'll be fine."

Spencer glanced down the hallway and looked at the exit sign. "Do you want to go outside and practice a bit?"

"Sure." The small confines of the hallway were getting to me, and I could definitely use some air. I walked down the hallway, and he held the door for me.

The change of scenery and fresh air helped clear my head a bit. Spencer glanced around then motioned to the side of the building.

"This will do," he said with a smile.

He began tapping out the beat of the song on his thighs and nodded for me to begin. I fiddled with the hem of my dress and sang the words. When it was time for Spencer to join in, he stopped tapping and grabbed my hand. He gave me a half-smile and shook his head, as if to chastise me for pulling on my dress. His fingers were intertwined with mine while we belted out the song together.

"Now you're ready." He winked. I felt myself blush as we walked toward the exit door. Spencer was just about to open it when he leaned in close to my ear. "After you, beautiful one." His voice was barely above a whisper.

"Thank you." I glanced back at him.

We walked down the hallway and were soon back in the chaos of the crowded venue. My eyes shot to the table, and to my surprise, my parents were there. I glanced at Spencer and mouthed *"My parents."*

His eyes crinkled when he smiled, like he already knew about it.

I approached the table and was immediately greeted with a bear hug from my father, and when I was free from his grasp, my mom kissed my cheek. My confused expression had my mom answering me before I had even asked the question.

"What? Did you think we'd miss your first official public performance?" She hugged me before she sat down and started chatting with Spencer's mom.

"I just hope I don't disappoint you all." My nerves were starting to get to me. I began nibbling my thumbnail. Spencer was still behind me. I felt him brush up close to my ear as he reached around and pulled my hand away from my mouth.

"You won't," he whispered.

Melissa suggestively raised an eyebrow at me. I ignored her and sat down at the only empty seat at the table, next to my dad. Simon and Shawn had moved to a table of their own, and they were both eating burgers.

Spencer stood behind Kara and had his hands resting on the back of her chair. He leaned over and whispered something in her ear. She smiled and nodded.

I was surprised at how much watching their small exchange bothered me.

Mason let the crowd know the band was going to take a fifteen-minute break. My eyes followed Spencer as he made his way to the stage. Mason set up our mics while Spencer tuned his guitar. My eyes shifted from Spencer to Aidan. The look he gave me chilled me to the bone. I could almost feel the animosity radiating from his piercing eyes. It made me wonder if he'd ever truly loved me at all. I turned away from his heated gaze and leaned over toward Melissa.

"Bathroom?" I asked.

Melissa was up in a heartbeat as we made our way back toward the small hallway. Of course, there was a line. We jockeyed for position and leaned against the wall as the line slowly inched forward.

"Finally," she said. "I've been trying to get your attention since you got back to the table. What happened? You both were gone for a while."

"He saw I was starting to freak, so he took me outside, and we ran through the song once."

"Is that all?" She raised an eyebrow.

"Stop it!" I pushed her forward as the line moved a bit. "How was Kara? When we left... did she seem... upset?"

Melissa thought about the question before she answered me. "She watched you guys leave, but she seemed okay. I wasn't watching her though. That's when your mom and dad came in." She shrugged.

Finally we made it into the bathroom. I ran my hands through my hair as Melissa grabbed a tube of lipstick from her purse.

"Here, put this on. You know what your mom always says." In unison we both giggled as we mimicked her words.

"Lipstick is to brunettes as mascara is to blondes."

After I applied a sheer coat of pale red, Melissa looked me in the eye and held the door. "Ready?"

"No, but it's too late now." I smiled.

"True." She smirked and playfully slapped my butt when we walked out the door.

****

Melissa and I sat back at the table, then the band started up again. The dance floor was abuzz as Mason sang his heart out. I kept trying to distract my thoughts, knowing I would be up on the stage soon. I glanced around our table. Melissa was enthralled watching my brother. My parents were still talking to Spencer's mom, occasionally glancing up at Mason. Kara was twirling her long hair around to make a bun, but she ended up twisting it into a knot, and it actually held. Spencer nodded in approval when she finished. His eyes caught me watching them, and I bashfully turned away. Simon was playing with straws at the table behind us, and I had no idea where Shawn was.

Mason sang the last song of the set and spoke into the mic. "Thanks everybody. Before we close for tonight, we have something special planned. Give us a few minutes, and Random Plan will be right back." Mason stepped away from the mic, and the venue broke out in applause.

I knew that was my cue. I got up and heard my dad say, "Good luck, sweetie." Melissa squeezed my arm. I made my way up the steps to the stage. Mason was chatting with Kyle as I approached them. Aidan was nowhere to be seen. I scanned the venue, and from what I could tell, Nina was gone too. Spencer was still seated at the table talking with my parents, so calm and at ease with himself, like he wasn't about to perform in front of a bunch of strangers. He kept glancing up at me and back to my parents. Almost like they were all talking about me.

Kyle gave me a warm smile. "You look great. Are you ready?"

"I think so."

Derek heard my response. "Ya think so? C'mere, Liz." I was a little hesitant as I took a few steps toward him.

He stood and stepped out from behind the drums. His eyes scanned the length of my body. "You've got the voice of an angel wrapped up in a wicked package."

Mason glanced back at us. "Way to give a compliment, Derek."

"Hey, I was sincere." Derek sat back behind his drums. He almost seemed wounded from Mason's words.

"Thanks, Derek." I knew coming from him, it had been a compliment.

"Where's Aidan?" Mason looked around on the verge of frustration. He pulled his cell from his pocket and held it to his ear. When I walked past him, I heard him say, "Get in here."

A few seconds later Aidan was back. He wouldn't even look at me. I wanted to ask him what his problem was and why he was being such a jerk. But, instead I just ignored him. Aidan's mood swings had stopped being my problem when our relationship ended.

I focused my attention on Spencer. He was still at the table, but now he was standing with Simon attached to his hip. He said something to his little brother that made him laugh before he headed up the steps to the stage. He stood on the opposite side near the back and summoned me with his index finger. When I reached him, he gave me one of those dimpled smiles that left me breathless.

"You good?" He gave my hand a squeeze and pulled me close to his side.

I was distracted by Aidan's stoic demeanor. "Yes, don't worry. I'm good."

The crowd started to gather around the stage as Mason reached for the mic. From my position, I could see the table of our families. Each face was beaming with pride. I felt my nerves begin to build, and my breathing increased. Spencer placed his hand in mine.

"Remember, it's just you and me," he whispered. I nodded.

When Mason began to speak, the crowd moved forward, and several people seated at tables in the back stood up.

"Thank you all for comin' out."

A few girls howled which made my brother chuckle.

"We've got a treat for you all. Random Plan wrote a new song." He smiled, causing more shrills from the females in the crowd.

After Mason's announcement, the restaurant and bar area erupted. More people swarmed around the already-packed dance floor. Sensing my anxiety, Spencer gave my hand a squeeze. When the applause died down, Mason spoke again.

"A couple of special people are gonna sing it tonight. I'd like to introduce you to a good friend of mine, Spencer Hayes, and someone dear to my heart, my sister, Elizabeth Ryan."

I felt the adrenaline course through my veins as the

crowd cheered. Spencer's hand was still in mine, and he led me next to my brother. The audience continued to applaud. Spencer released my hand, and I stood in front of the mic. When the splattering of applause died down, Spencer picked up his guitar and gave me one last encouraging smile. Mason kissed the top of my head before he leaned into the mic.

"This song is called 'Love's Hold.'"

Mason glanced at Derek, who started tapping out the intro, and the guys joined in. Spencer's eyes were on mine, and I took a deep breath and began. The words were sentimental and romantic. Spencer nodded and smiled as soon as I got through the first several lines.

When it was his turn to sing, I let my eyes glide over the crowd. Some of the college girls were swaying, most were smiling, but one, in particular, was scowling. I turned away from Nina's hatred toward me and glanced at the table that seated our families. Melissa's smile was so big it almost looked cartoonish. I had to look away before I started laughing.

When I joined Spencer in the chorus, he moved in close. The rasp in his voice, the hunger in his eyes, I couldn't help but feel that magnetic pull between us. My skin began to tingle when he moved in to share my mic. His eyes roamed over my face. I found myself lost in him while we continued to sing of words having to do with love and desire. A few girls squealed as Spencer's lips were inches from mine. Between his heated gaze and the words to the song, it was no wonder I heard someone yell out, "Kiss her."

Spencer's lip curled up on one side, and I blushed, knowing he'd heard the girl too. We continued to sing the romantic duet, inching closer with each poetic lyric.

When the song ended, I was certain everyone within a ten-foot radius could feel the underlying sexual tension radiating between us.

The crowd's reaction broke through the bubble that surrounded us. There was an eruption of applause followed by a burst of whistles and howling. Spencer seemed pained as he tore his gaze from mine. Mason came up alongside and clapped him on the back before he pulled me in for a hug. He grabbed the mic with one arm still draped around me.

"Give it up one more time for my sister, Elizabeth, and Spencer."

The cheers continued. Mason whispered, "That was awesome."

The boys in the band came around to congratulate us. Derek was the first to whisk me up into a bear hug.

"Whoa, Liz, that was hot... you two... smokin' hot." He smirked as he put me down.

Derek's words brought our moment on stage to the forefront of my mind. The passion, the heat, the desire. Embarrassment and shame filled me when I realized my parents had watched our suggestive display. Spencer's mom had witnessed it, and poor Kara, how had that blatant disregard of her relationship with Spencer make her feel? The guilt I felt was halted with Aidan's cold stare.

I turned away and was thankful when Kyle approached me. He had such integrity. I was certain he didn't want to acknowledge what he'd just witnessed, so instead he rubbed my arm and said I sounded amazing.

I heard Aidan mumble something when I brushed past him, but I didn't turn back. I just wanted some air. I left Spencer behind and made my way to the table of my parents. My mom grabbed me first.

"Lizzie, that was beautiful."

Beautiful?

"Ahhh... thanks, Mom." *Had she not seen what everyone else had just seen?*

My dad held me close and said I'd sounded wonderful.

Spencer's mom reached for my hand and gave it a squeeze. "You two were fantastic together."

I tried to shake my rattled thoughts.

What is going on?

Even Kara approached me. No malice. Just a look of sincerity as she leaned in and said how awesome we'd been.

Puzzled, I glanced at Melissa. "Come with me for a minute."

Melissa followed, then I glanced over my shoulder and said, "We'll be right back."

We made our way toward the bathroom, but before we turned down the hall, I saw Spencer approaching the table, grinning, with Simon and Shawn at his side.

I stopped just as we entered the hallway.

"Melissa. What's going on? Didn't everyone notice how we were singing together... the way we looked at each other?"

"Liz, nobody but me knows how you feel about Spencer, so to everyone else it just looked like you were playing a part, ya know, caught up in the song."

"Yeah, but did you hear that girl scream out for us to kiss each other? And Derek, he was practically panting when the song was over."

"I heard that girl. We all heard her." Melissa chuckled. "But, everyone just assumed you two were playing it for the crowd. And Derek?" She raised an eyebrow at me. "Derek always thinks that way."

My thoughts spun into a downward spiral. What if Spencer was just playing it off, caught in the moment?

Am I delusional?

I exhaled and leaned against the wall. Several girls scurried by on their way to the bathroom. One of them shouted to me I sounded awesome.

"Thank you," I murmured, unsure if she even heard me. I glanced up to Melissa.

"I wasn't acting," I whispered.

"I know, Liz." Melissa reached out and hugged me.

"I've got to get over this, Melissa. He's here with his girlfriend. I have to quit reading into what's not real. He doesn't want me, and I must quit thinking he does. I need to get out of here."

Melissa gave me a squeeze before she pulled away. "I'll let Mason know we're leaving and tell your parents you have a headache. We'll be outta here in ten minutes."

"Okay." I closed my eyes and leaned my head back against the wall. I brought my thumb and index finger together while I pinched the bridge of my nose. Melissa wouldn't be lying when she told my parents I had a headache because I felt one coming on strong.

"Hey." I opened my eyes to an intense grey that took my breath away. He leaned in as I removed my hand and placed it at my side. "Headache?" he asked.

"Something like that." Spencer gently placed two warm fingers over each of my temples and began to slowly rub them in a circular motion. The feel of his touch made me groan with pleasure.

"Better?"

"Mmm-hmm." I moaned.

My eyes snapped open. Wide-eyed, I was caught in his gaze again. He was looking at me with the same look that crossed over his face when we were at the park, dancing on the driveway, and ten minutes ago singing on the stage. My conflicting thoughts told me to back away, that whatever I felt was just me. Not him.

It's just me. Not him.

His nearness was consuming me. I was fighting a losing battle. If I didn't back away, I'd regret it. But then the crackle of electricity sparked between us as Spencer was lurched forward with the passing swarm of girls headed toward the bathroom. His hands dropped to my hips as he brought his forehead to mine. The warmth of his breath was upon me. He closed his eyes, and I watched while his tongue darted out and skimmed across his lips. My heart beat faster when I realized I wasn't imaging it. He felt it too. He wanted me, and I couldn't deny it any longer.

I stood on my tiptoes and brought my lips inches from his. Spencer opened his eyes. His breath caught as his heated gaze flicked over my lips. The pain was evident when he exhaled in frustration. He was still for a moment before he chastely kissed my forehead and backed away.

"I'm sorry," he whispered.

My heart and brain struggled to think of something to say. My passion-filled eyes met his. Before I could think of a rational thought, the words impetuously spilled from my lips.

"Don't be."

That was all the encouragement he needed. Within seconds, he pulled me into the warmth of his chest as my body melted into his. I gasped as one hand tightened firmly around my waist while the other snaked behind my neck. Unabashed and desperate, my hands slid up the sides of his back and gripped his t-shirt. His eyes flamed a dangerous shade of grey before he closed them. His lips hovered over mine, the warmth of our breaths mingling as one, until finally, eagerly, he kissed me. My hands glided across his back, and I heard myself moan as he deepened the kiss. My hands clutched his arms while the intensity of his kiss increased. Spencer pulled back. Our eyes met briefly before he softly smiled and brought his lips back to mine. I heard him groan as I let my tongue glide across his lower lip before I hungrily kissed him again.

My back was pressed up against the wall while Spencer's body ran the length of mine, and still it wasn't close enough. I wanted more. His masculine scent, the way he kissed me, so demanding yet gentle, my body was crazed with pleasure from being wrapped in his arms. I was lost in a sea of passion until my mind shifted from desire to reality.

Spencer wasn't mine. As much as I felt in his kisses, they belonged to someone else… Kara.

It pained me when I pulled away from him. The loss of our connection made me feel bereft. I closed my eyes and whispered the words, "I'm sorry, I'm so sorry." I began to back away from him while my senses came flooding back to me. "I shouldn't have kissed you. It was my fault… forgive me… I'm sorry."

The distress on Spencer's face pained me. I knew he'd have to confess to Kara, but at least he could blame me for it. I started to walk down the small hallway toward the exit door, my steps quickened as my guilt overtook me.

My thoughts were a mass of contradictions as I tried to make sense of what had just happened, but Aidan's enraged voice broke through my jumbled thoughts. He grabbed my arm just before I could push through the back door.

"I knew it." He scowled.

"What are you talking about?" I didn't have the emotional strength to deal with Aidan.

"I saw you." The hostility in his tone was menacing. "Kissing him." Aidan clutched my arm a bit tighter. "How long has this been going on?"

I exhaled in frustration. "I was always faithful to you... always! So don't go there with me. In fact, why don't you go back to Nina. I'm sure she'll take good care of you." My eyes glanced down at my arm. "And let go of me."

I tried to pull away, but Aidan gripped me harder. Spencer was coming toward us. There was a purpose in his steps and intensity in his eyes I had never seen before. I knew I had to free myself from Aidan before things got out of control. "Let me go." I said louder with a sense of urgency.

Spencer brought his body protectively close to mine. "You'd better drop that hand or I'll do it for you." His dominate stance conveyed a sense of power and authority.

Aidan turned his gaze from mine to Spencer's. Panic swelled within me as I felt the tension between the two.

"Well...?" Spencer's ridged profile glanced down at my arm and then back to Aidan. Aidan released my arm, but not before shoving me back, causing me to fall to the ground. Spencer immediately pulled me into his arms, but just as quickly his body was yanked from mine.

Aidan grabbed Spencer's forearm and whipped him around. I watched as if in slow motion as Aidan's fist connected with his jaw. Spencer was stunned for a minute, and I witnessed a rage within him I hoped I would never see again. I instinctively took a step back as Spencer's fisted hand swung forward and landed a punch across Aidan's face.

Girls exiting the bathroom began screaming that a fight had broken out. I watched in horror, terrified. I had never seen a real fight before. I was unprepared for the brutality, and the sounds echoing off the small confines of the hallway made my stomach turn. Before their scuffle could escalate further, some men from the bathroom came and pulled them apart. Mason jogged down the small hallway and maneuvered his way between the two. Melissa was behind him, holding my purse with a stunned expression on her face. Mason glanced toward me and then back to Melissa.

"Get her outta here," he shouted.

My insides trembled as Melissa grabbed my hand and pushed us through the back door.

Chapter Twenty-Nine

Melissa led me to my car, pulled the keys from my purse, and unlocked the passenger side door, allowing me to get in. She quickly got in on the driver's side, adjusted the seat back, and started up the car.

"What happened?" She took her eyes off the road to look at me. "Liz?"

It took me a few minutes to emerge from my confused state. "We kissed. Aidan saw us, and the next thing I knew they were fighting."

"Details, Liz, start with the kiss... who kissed whom?"

I could hear the frustration in Melissa's tone, but it still took me several minutes to decipher my muddled thoughts. "He kissed me... but... I'm not sure he wanted too."

"What? Melissa's tone went from frustration to confused. "I'm such an idiot, Melissa. It was more me than him. He tried to back away but I told him not to. I can't believe I did that. I'm sure he wouldn't have kissed me had I not thrown myself at him." My eyes started to water. "It was so different than kissing Aidan. With Aidan, I always felt like we should stop, ya know? But, with Spencer, I didn't want to." I placed my head back against the seat and deeply exhaled. "I feel so guilty. I told him I was sorry and backed away. I was headed toward the back door when Aidan caught me by the arm.

288

He was so angry." Now the tears started to fall. "He thinks I cheated on him, but I never did. I tried with Aidan. I tried so hard with him." I sobbed.

"I know, Liz." Melissa reached over and rubbed my arm. "Aidan had me by the arm and wouldn't let go. Spencer came up to us and told Aidan to back off. Aidan pushed me, and I fell to the ground. The next thing I knew, they were fighting. It was so scary." I wiped away my tears with the back of my hand, but they kept falling. Melissa pulled up to my house and parked the car. She opened my glove-box and rooted around for a tissue, paper towel, anything. She grabbed a napkin from under some old CDs and handed it to me. I blew my nose and wiped my tears then we exited the car.

"C'mon, I'll stay with you until everyone gets home.

The thought of everyone coming home made me ill. I was going to have to tell all of this to my parents. Melissa opened the door, and Maggie came bounding toward us. I barely greeted her as we walked upstairs to my room. I kicked off my shoes and went in my closet and slipped out of my black dress. I pulled my purple sweatshirt over my head and slipped on some pajama bottoms before I curled up under my pink blanket. Melissa sat on my bed, pushed the blanket aside, and leaned back against a pillow.

"It's gonna be okay, Liz"

"What do you think is happening?" "I have no idea." She sighed.

We both were silent. I think I might have even dozed off for a few minutes until Maggie's bark alerted us everyone was home. I glanced at the clock. It was close to 1:00 a.m. Melissa gave me an encouraging smile before she got up, and we went downstairs. When we entered the kitchen, everyone was standing around the island, but all eyes shot toward me. My mother was the first to approach me. She hugged me tight for a minute and then backed away. I pulled up a seat at the kitchen table, and everyone else did the same.

"So, what happened after we left?" I asked and glanced at Mason.

My parents were both quiet, which was unusual… especially for my mother.

"I helped the two guys from the bathroom pull them apart. Aidan started accusing Spencer and you about having a thing for each other."

I glanced at my parents and started to feel uncomfortable. I focused my attention back on Mason.

"What did Spencer say?" Melissa eyed me and looked back to Mason.

"Spencer said he wasn't sorry he kissed you. He was only sorry you were mixed up with someone like Aidan. Aidan lunged at him again. I pushed him back and told Spencer to just go, that I'd deal with Aidan. He walked out the back door."

My mom started to question me about what had happened before the fight, and all I could focus on was Spencer wasn't sorry he'd kissed me.

I was as brief as possible and then ended the conversation. "I'm tired."

My parents seemed satisfied with my compressed version of the night's events, and I was thankful. They said goodnight and went upstairs. Melissa and I headed toward the front door.

"He isn't sorry he kissed you," she whispered.

"I know, Melissa, but we're forgetting about Kara."

"Well, maybe he's forgotten about her too." She

smirked.

Mason was soon behind us with keys in hand, ready to take Melissa home. I glanced up at my hopeful friend.

"I doubt that. I'll talk to you tomorrow."

When I closed the door behind them, Spencer entered my thoughts. My stomach turned, knowing I was going to have to face him. He may have said he wasn't sorry he'd kissed me, but he'd been caught up in the moment. I'm sure the minute he'd looked in Kara's eyes, he'd felt guilty. He didn't deserve that. It was my fault, and as much as it was going to destroy me, tomorrow, I would make things right.

The memory of Spencer's lips on mine echoed in my head before I fell into a dreamless sleep.

****

I was hoping after the night's events I would have been able to sleep until noon. No such luck. My body was so accustomed to waking up early it didn't matter what time I went to bed. A part of me considered not running today, but only for a second. I knew running was exactly what I needed. I pulled my hair up in a ponytail, grabbed my white tank-top, sports bra, and black yoga shorts and got dressed.

Maggie and I bounded out the front door and headed toward our usual route. I didn't even stretch. Once I was outside with my music blasting, breathing in the fresh air, I just wanted to run. We quickly passed by Spencer's house. I knew I was going to make seeing him my top priority today, but now was not the time. Maggie and I picked up speed, maneuvering our way up the creek bed toward the ocean. With each thrust of my arms, I felt a dull ache on one side. I stopped for a minute and twisted my arm so I could inspect where the pain was coming from. My left arm was bruised in three places. I knew the minute I got home I'd have to put on a different shirt. If Mason or my dad saw my arm, they'd kill Aidan.

I continued my run, and when my feet hit the sand, I stopped in the same spot where Aidan and I'd had our fight where he'd first gotten physical with me. I remember being scared, but since he'd never hit me, it hadn't seemed like a big deal. When I glanced down at my bruised arm, I realized how wrong I'd been.

My mind kept replaying last night in my head. He was so angry. What had happened to him? Where was the guy I'd once cared for? Was he still in there? There was good in him, I knew there was. I sunk my knees in the sand and began to think about the troubled boy lost inside of him. Pushing my fears aside, I had an overwhelming urge see him. If the Aidan I once cared for was still in there, I was going to find out.

****

When I opened the front door, I unhooked Maggie's leash, and she immediately laid down on the cool tile floor with her legs sprawled out behind her. After I hung her leash in the hall closet, I jogged up the stairs to my room. Mason's door was shut, and I knew he was still sleeping. I grabbed my car keys, grey hoodie, and wallet and was back outside within five minutes and on my way to Aidan's.

His truck was parked in the usual spot, and a part of me was relieved when I saw Natalie's car in the driveway. I didn't think Aidan would hurt me, but the pain radiating from my arm told me differently. He already had. I glanced at the clock on the dashboard, 9:47 a.m. It was early, but not too early. I knocked on the front door, and when Natalie opened it, her eyes widened with surprise.

"Liz, how are you? It's been so long." Natalie had a new haircut and her short sassy layers had been replaced with an even shorter cut that made her brown eyes pop.

"I'm fine. Umm... may I see Aidan please?"

Natalie opened the door for me to enter. I took a step inside as her cell phone rang.

"You know the way," she said. "I think he's still asleep, but go ahead and wake him." She winked. "He'll just love that." Natalie focused her attention on her cell phone while I walked down the hallway to Aidan's room.

Walking down the hallway, I felt confident in what I wanted to say to him but anxious just the same. I had never acted so impulsively, and when I approached his bedroom door, a large part of me wished I had called. Aidan was a heavy sleeper so when I lightly knocked, I knew he didn't hear me. I clasped my hand around the doorknob, and a second later I was in his room. I took a step inside and closed the door behind me.

The sun was streaming through his slatted blinds, so I took a few minutes to survey his room before I woke him. Everything seemed the same: clothes scattered on the floor, his bass guitar in the corner, and his laptop on the bedside table. He was asleep on his side facing me. Even with the nasty bruise on his cheek, he still looked beautiful, angelic even, a far cry from the anger that had covered his face last night. His lower body was under his green blanket, and he was wearing a blue t-shirt and, I hoped, pajama pants. I sat on the edge of the bed and gently placed my hand on his arm.

"Aidan," I whispered. "Aidan." The second time I said it a little louder.

Aidan groaned and slowly opened his eyes. He

blinked up at me, stunned, almost like his brain couldn't process me sitting there.

"What are you doing here?" he finally asked. "After last night, I felt like we needed to talk." "And you couldn't have called first?"

I could sense he was feeling ambushed, which, technically, I guess he was. "Do you want me to leave?"

"No, it's fine."

He sat up, and I quickly moved as he swung his legs to the floor and got up from the bed. No pajama pants, but at least he was wearing boxers. Aidan grabbed a pair of jeans from his drawer and glanced at me over his shoulder.

"I'll be right back."

A few minutes later, he entered his room dressed in his jeans and same blue t-shirt, but now his hair was slicked back. I had pulled the blanket up on his bed and was sitting on top of it. Aidan's body language seemed tense as he sat next to me on the bed. His stoic expression and the coolness in eyes let me know his emotional walls were up.

"I came here to show you something." I shifted my body so I was facing him. I twisted my arm so he could see the bruises.

His expression went from cool and distant to shock and disbelief. His eyes scanned the length of my arm, and his eyes met mine.

"I can't... believe I did that." His voice was barely above a whisper. "I... I didn't know I had your arm so tight. Liz. I'm so sorry." His eyes softened while he ran a hand through his damp hair.

The anguish on his face made me almost whisper the words *It's okay*, but it wasn't. He had to hear everything.

"You pushed me too... do you remember doing that?"

Aidan's eyes were in a glossy haze of guilt and regret. He shook his head no. I didn't say anything else. As difficult as it was for me to sit and observe his internal struggle, I knew that was the reason why I was here. I couldn't let the goodness I'd seen in Aidan become lost. There was still hope. But the choice was his.

"I was so angry. When I saw you two... together... I lost it. I saw everything. The way you looked at each other, the way he kissed you." Aidan's eyes met mine. "The way you kissed him back. I thought we had that, and to see you and him... I just couldn't take it." Aidan's eyes never left mine. "When you told me to go back to Nina, it set me off. Nina was just a convenient distraction. She doesn't mean anything to me. You're who I want — you're who I love."

I stared into the depths of his eyes and shook my head.

"No, Aidan, that's not love. Love is respect and trust. Not control and jealousy." I reached out my hand and placed it on his arm.

"Did you ever care about me at all?" he asked. His words sounded small and sad.

"Of course I did — I still do. That's why I'm here. You made me feel special, beautiful, you made me laugh, you opened up to me, and for the most part, you made me happy. That's why I made excuses for you. For your... anger."

I glanced up at Aidan to hopefully get a feel for his reaction.

He was listening, so I continued.

"Over and over again, you would get so jealous, and I allowed it, hoping you would change. I should have ended things with us sooner, but I always saw the good in you. I still do."

I watched as a few tears spilled down his face. I reached out and held him.

With his head nestled into my neck, I whispered in his ear. "Aidan, I want you to talk to someone. You have a lot of pain inside of you, but you have so much to give. I know you do."

My words were his undoing, and his silent tears became sobbing.

"Please promise me you will. Please."

He continued to sob, and I held him for what seemed like hours, until finally, he spoke.

"I will. I promise."

His tears subsided while we continued to embrace each other.

"I'm so sorry, Liz, for everything." "I know you are."

When we broke apart, Aidan glanced at my tear-stained tank top.

"I'm sorry about that."

"That's alright. Tears cleanse the soul."

As soon as the words left my mouth, I thought of Spencer. I glanced at Aidan's bedside clock. It was almost noon. "I should probably get going."

I rose from the bed and Aidan walked me to the front door. When I turned to leave, I reached out and hugged him one last time. Aidan held me tight and kissed the top of my head, before he said goodbye.

****

My stomach growled from lack of food. I knew I should eat, but the thought of having anything heavy didn't sit well with me. I drove through a smoothie place and ordered a raspberry protein drink. Not quite ready to go home yet, I pulled into the parking lot of Lantern Bay Park and walked over to the stone bench I loved so much. I sipped my shake and thought about Aidan. Seeing the bruises on my arm may have been the turning point for him. I hoped so. With all my heart, I hoped so.

The sun was warm and felt good against my face. The ocean water was glimmering in the distance, and the slight breeze cooled the warmth of my skin. I drank the last of my shake before I placed the cup next to me on the bench and pulled my hair band out. I ran my fingers through my hair. The Park was quiet. Only a few joggers were running the stairs. I took comfort in the peace I felt and I leaned back and closed my eyes. The night's events and this morning with Aidan had left me feeling spent. I began to drift off until something shadowed the brightness behind my eyelids. Assuming it was a passing cloud, I kept my eyes closed.

"Elizabeth." My heart leapt as I opened my eyes, and my breathing stopped for a second. My eyes roamed over his handsome face. His jaw was slightly swollen and bruised, but other than that, his face was untouched. His grey eyes were unusually light from the angle where I sat, and his dark hair was tousled in a way that made me ache to run my fingers through it.

"May I?" He motioned to the bench next to me.

I was still surprised to see him, so I just nodded.

Spencer sat and shifted his body so it was facing mine. "I've been looking all over for you. Didn't you get my calls?"

In my rush to see Aidan, I had left my cell phone at home, so I shook my head no.

Spencer gave me a ghost of a smile and softly

chuckled. "Are you gonna talk to me or just nod your head?"

"I'm sorry. I'm just shocked to see you." I shifted my body so it was facing his.

"After last night, I wanted to make sure you were okay." His soft gaze traveled from my face to the length of my body. When he saw the bruises, his jaw clenched before he frustratingly blew out a breath of air. He gently lifted my arm to examine it further. I could sense he was trying to rein in his anger. "Did he hurt you anywhere else?"

Spencer reached to place a stray lock of my hair behind my ear.

My eyes didn't leave his. I whispered, "No."

"Why, Elizabeth? Why would you be with someone who treats you so badly?" His eyes softened, and his words sounded pained.

"He wasn't always like that. He's a good guy."

A concerned expression covered his face. "Don't." He commanded. "Don't make excuses for him. No man has a right to put his hands on you. I don't care how good you think he is."

His grey eyes bore into mine. I had to temporarily look away.

I blinked back up at him. "He said he'd talk to someone to work through his… issues."

Spencer exhaled in relief. "Alright, but if he ever touches you again… ever. You must promise me you'll leave him. Do you understand?"

"But…"

"No Elizabeth, promise me." Spencer's lips were pressed in a thin firm line, waiting for me to respond.

"Aidan and I aren't together. We've been broken up

for a while. He just overreacted because he saw us last night."

Spencer's facial expression went from concerned to confused.

"What? You're not with him? But, I thought."

"I just let you think that way because you were with Kara, and…" I couldn't finish my sentence until I looked away from him. With my head bowed and eyes downcast, I continued. "I knew I had feelings for you… I wanted you to be happy, and I thought…" My words cracked with emotion while my eyes welled with tears. "I thought if you assumed I was still with Aidan, it would be easier for me, but it wasn't… it wasn't easier… and then last night… I'm so sorry about last night. It's my fault. It was all my fault. I know you would never cheat on Kara, but… I threw myself at you. I'm sorry." I shut my eyes in anguish as the tears began to fall.

"Hey… hey… hey." Spencer lifted my chin to meet his gaze. "I'm not with Kara," he whispered.

"What?" I sniffled.

"Why would you think that?" He cupped my face with his hands and wiped my tears away with the pad of his thumbs.

"Because… I… just thought — she's at your house a lot." It was hard for me to speak in between my tears and chaotic thoughts.

Spencer shook his head back and forth while he continued to brush away my tears. "No, Elizabeth, she's a friend, like a sister to me. Kara was Sierra's best friend."

"All this time… I thought…" I tried to blink the tears from my eyes.

"Shh… don't cry anymore." His words were soft

and soothing as he brought his lips to mine.

Spencer kept whispering "Don't cry… don't cry…" in between tender kisses laced with the salt of my tears. It was almost like he was trying to kiss away the past, the pain, and the heartache of not being together.

My heart swelled with so much love for him it overwhelmed me. He removed his hands from my face while my arms slid up his back and held him. He tightened a hand behind my neck and pulled me in close as our tender kisses deepened into more. Reveling in his touch, I shifted my body forward and desperately kissed him again. Spencer abruptly backed away. He just as quickly brought his face back to mine, nose to nose, and whispered, "Ouch."

I bit my bottom lip as I backed away from him and said, "I'm sorry."

I lifted my hand and slid it over his bruised jaw then softly kissed it. Spencer sat back against the bench, and I nestled into his neck. He tenderly stroked my hair while we sat in silence for a few minutes.

"I can't believe this." Spencer continued to run his hands through my hair. "All this time." He kissed my forehead before he shifted back so he could look me in the eyes. "Do you know how much I've wanted you?"

I looked at him as a shy smile crossed my face. "Yes." I whispered. "As much as I've wanted you." And with that said, he smiled a dimpled smile and kissed me again.

Chapter Thirty

Five Months Later
"Let's go, darlin'. We're up."

Hearing Spencer refer to me using my pet name still made my skin tingle. Remembering the moment when the sweet word was silenced from his lips was a bitter memory, so hearing it, no matter how often, was never taken for granted. I clasped my hand in his and we made our way to the stage. Mason stood behind the mic and introduced us to the familiar crowd.

After Aidan left for school, Spencer had joined the band. It had only taken one passionate kiss from my sexy music man to have my head spinning in a haze of *"Yes, I'll join too."*

Spencer and I finished out the set with our signature song, "Love's Hold". We always ended the song with a kiss that had our female fans howling for more. We took our final bow, and as Spencer was gathering up the gear with Mason and the guys, I hurried to our usual table where Melissa stood hopping up and down on her heels. When I reached her, we hugged with a combination of tears and laughter.

"I'm so happy you're home!" "Me too." She squealed.

I pulled back and looked at the tear-stained face of my beautiful friend. "How long is winter break?"

Melissa sat down and she waved a hand in front of

me.

"Oh, I don't know, sometime in January. I don't even want to think about going back!"

"At least you're only at San Diego State. I don't think Mason could handle it if you were any farther."

"Me neither." She beamed. "He's been so awesome. I love that he comes to see me all the time. Hey, speaking of coming to see me." Melissa raised an eyebrow. "You and Spencer need to ride that mean machine out again."

"We will." I grinned, remembering what a fun time we had when we'd ridden out to see her in early fall. "We definitely will."

Melissa kept looking up at the stage at Mason. I rolled my eyes and said, "You can go."

She had already spent the day with Mason, but from experience, I now knew exactly what it felt like to be apart from the one I loved. Time together was never enough.

Melissa scurried up the stage to Mason's waiting arms as Spencer was making his way toward me. I was admiring his gorgeous face and smile until it faded. Spencer's eyes shifted from mine to just over my head. I glanced over my shoulder to see what had caused the sudden change.

I hadn't seen his blue eyes since we'd said our final goodbye, when he'd left for school. His hair was longer, and it made my heart swell a little when he swept his soft bangs to the side. Spencer and Aidan reached the table at the same time. I stood up and glanced at Spencer before I greeted Aidan. Spencer gave me a warm dimpled smile before he reached out his hand to Aidan and confidently shook it.

"I'm sure you're here to talk to Elizabeth. I'll give

you guys some privacy."

I turned my gaze to Spencer, and, in that moment, I didn't think I could love him anymore. He winked at me before he turned around and went back to the stage.

I hugged Aidan and squeezed him a little tighter as his fresh scent enveloped me. When we broke apart, our eyes locked.

"It's so good to see you. How are you?" he said then we both sat. "You look beautiful." His blue eyes crinkled, and a soft smile slid over his face.

"Thank you, Aidan, I'm good. How are you? The last text you sent me said you were kickin' butt in your classes. I'm so proud of you." I beamed.

"Yeah, well, the grades aren't in yet, but I think I did pretty well."

"How's everything… else?" Aidan had also let me know he was making good on his promise to seek counseling, so I didn't feel bad asking him. He knew what I meant.

"A struggle." He breathed. "Especially being in a frat… alcohol, girls, partiers." He chuckled.

"Maybe joining a fraternity wasn't the best idea."

"It'll be alright. There's a lot of good that goes with it too."

There was a change in Aidan's smile, almost like he was hiding something from me. But I knew him too well to let it slip by. "What?" I leaned in close. "What aren't you telling me, Aidan Mitchell?"

"I met someone." His blue eyes seemed to warm at the thought of his mystery girl.

"What's she like?"

"Well, she not you." He smiled. "But she's special." His shy smile told me it was serious.

"I'm so happy for you." And I was. I truly was.

"I have something I want to give you." He nervously bit his lower lip.

"Oh?"

"Close your eyes and open your hand."

I gave him a smirk, closed my eyes, and extended an open hand. The silver chain felt cool against the warmth of my palm, and I knew it was the tanzanite necklace. When I opened my eyes to his, they were soft and full of sorrow.

"I want you to keep this. You don't have to wear it, but I just wanted you to have it. To remember the good times."

It broke my heart to hear the pain and regret in his words.

"Of course, Aidan, thank you."

I smiled and placed the chain in the zipper compartment of my purse then glanced back at Spencer. He, Mason, and the guys were in an intense conversation with some good-looking guy in a suit. Melissa's mouth was gaping, and she seemed to be hanging on every word. Spencer caught my eye and motioned for me to come over.

Aidan noticed. "I guess I should let you go. Let's get together over break and catch up."

"I'd love that." I smiled.

We both stood, and as Aidan reached down and hugged me, he whispered, "Thanks for believing in me, Liz…"

I touched a few strands of his soft hair before I pulled back and looked into his bright blue eyes one more time. He turned and I watched as Aiden walked out the door.

When I made my way up to the stage, Mason was near the exit door with the guy in the suit. Spencer snaked his arm around my waist, and he had something in his hand. Melissa seemed to be trying to contain her frenzied emotions. Derek, for once, was stunned to silence, and Kyle was shaking his head in disbelief. Mason returned and stood next to Melissa.

"What?" I questioned.

Spencer's facial expression was unreadable as he held a small business card in the light so I could read it.

Christopher David, C.D.C. Records.

My eyes widened and I glanced to each of them. When I looked at Melissa I thought she might burst as she screamed. "They want to sign the band!"

"What?" My mind was spinning. I heard Spencer softly laugh while my legs started to give out from under me. Melissa turned to Mason, and they both hugged each other. Melissa's excitement was contagious. My brother, Derek, and Kyle began to jump up and down and join her in a happy dance. Derek yelled out a string of expletives while he bounced around the stage.

"C'mere, Elizabeth. You're gettin' that deer-in-the-headlights look about you." Spencer walked me to a private corner of the stage and cupped my face in his hands. "You alright?"

I nodded yes.

"You know all this doesn't matter to me, right?" I nodded.

Spencer glanced over his shoulder to everyone who was now skipping around. "It matters to them." He chuckled. "Not me. You're all that matters to me." Spencer moved in close and whispered, "I love you, Elizabeth."

His gentle eyes slid over my face and gave me the assurance that whatever was ahead in our future, he would be there to support me, encourage me, comfort me, and love me. I reached up and clasped my arms around his neck as he held my gaze.

Then I whispered, "I love you too," as he brought his lips to mine.

A word about the author...

Mary Cope is a freelance writer of romance. Her book, Beautiful One, is the first in a planned series. Mary enjoys spending time with her family, socializing with friends and not taking life too seriously.

Mary is currently writing the sequel, Beautiful Mess.

Thank you for purchasing
this publication of The Wild Rose Press, Inc.

For questions or more information
contact us at
info@thewildrosepress.com.

The Wild Rose Press, Inc.
www.thewildrosepress.com